THE BLOCKCHAIN AFFAIR

THE SEARCH FOR SATOSHI NAKAMOTO

JONATHAN W. CLARK

ARK MEDIA LLC

To my wife Kara, whose constant love and encouragement has pushed this book toward the finish line from day one.

I would also like to thank my mother, Janet, for the many years of feedback on all of my writing and speaking.

And special thanks to the beta readers—Carlos, Erik, Greg, Jack, Jacquie, Jane, Janet, Julian, Lauren, and Norm—for the comments and suggestions on the early drafts.

PROLOGUE

St. Petersburg, Russia, November 5, 2013

He was alone but regularly glanced over his shoulder to make sure. His soft-soled shoes preserved the silence of the early morning as he cautiously moved away from any street that could be found by a tourist. His warm breath rose from his upturned coat like a gentle fog.

Staying close to the walls of the buildings, he was careful to pause in the darkness of doorways in a systematic but seemingly random fashion. With a precision that came from years of repetition, he passed deeper into older alleys, unnoticed.

He ducked into an alcove and stared into the sky as he waited for the clouds to cover the waxing moon. After pulling up a coat sleeve and removing his glove, he gently pressed a button on his watch, revealing a soft indigo light. Moments later, in a window across the street, a curtain parted in the darkness, answering the silent inquiry from below.

He placed the glove back on his hand and waited exactly thirty seconds before swiftly crossing the street. The door opened as he approached then closed softly as he slid through. He took narrow stairs up two at a time, careful to stay close enough to the stucco walls to feel the stiffness against his gloved hands.

Upon reaching the third floor, he stood silently against the wall until a door clicked open and stopped with the chain. After a quick whisper, the door closed and reopened. Stepping inside, he clenched his fists until a small glimmering lamp was clicked on.

He did not remove his coat as he took the only remaining empty chair near a laptop computer. He gave a small nod to the three other figures in the room and took control of the keyboard. The glow from the LCD screen reflected a slight glare off the lenses of his glasses.

He stood up only sixty seconds after sitting down, his transaction complete. He nodded at the others and turned toward the door to place his hand on the doorknob but waited thirty seconds before opening the door—protocol. He glanced back and, upon seeing the three men busy at the computer, turned the knob, eased the door open, and peered into the hall.

The first bullet stopped him, striking the middle of the forehead just above the eyebrows as it came from the hallway. The hollow thud of the second round hung in the air as his body crumpled to the ground just inside the threshold. The sound of six additional bullets leaving the chamber quickly ended the commotion within the room, with the noise of chairs falling to the cement floor.

Two figures methodically entered the room. One dragged their first target from the doorway and toward the computer, while the other one stayed near the door, leaving it open just enough to hear anything in the hallway.

One of the figures searched the dead man's pockets and removed his mobile phone. She removed the dead man's glove from his right hand and placed his lifeless thumb against the fingerprint reader on the device. She quickly opened the desired application from the unlocked device and knelt by the computer. Moving between the device and the computer, she needed only three minutes to initiate a series of twenty-five transactions.

She removed a small bag of cocaine from his pocket and opened it. She slowly placed each man's dead hands into the bag and moved them around just enough for the substance to touch the majority of their fingers. After taking a few grains between her gloved fingers, she flicked them on the floor near the table. Then she closed the bag, returned it to his coat, and looked at her watch.

The two intruders stood silent and motionless for twenty minutes until they heard the vibration of their phones. After removing the phone from her pocket, she read the text from an unknown number: "Complete."

She returned her mobile phone to her own pocket and went back to the dead man at the threshold to return his mobile phone to his jacket pocket. Then she fired one quick round through the phone and into the man's chest, shot from a slight distance and made to appear as accidental damage. "Nine," she whispered out loud.

She lifted one of the other dead men from the floor and sat him in the metal chair, slouching over the computer. She moved back toward the doorway and aimed at the lifeless body. Three more quick shots passed through the neck and into the table. The computer let off a quick spark of light as the bullets entered the plastic case before the screen went black.

"Ten, eleven, twelve..."

She collected exactly twelve shell casings—no fingerprints, no DNA, no evidence they had ever been in that room.

She took a slow visual inventory of the entire room, making sure everything was in order, then joined her partner at the door. The door was left open as the two figures left and faded into the darkness.

1

____

David Turner had graduated from MIT with both an undergraduate and a graduate degree in computer science. His transcript indicated that he was an average student, but his style was to underachieve in every educational facility where he was enrolled.

During his last year of undergraduate studies, David had risen above mediocrity to impress his professors for the first time. His senior design proposal, to create a new way of encrypting information sent over the internet, was assigned to one of the many tenured professors at MIT. Students had to select their own proposals, but the dean preferred projects that might bring a revenue stream into the university's growing endowments.

In 2006, the internet was hitting a new stride after recovering from the dot-com bubble of the late nineties. The smart money was on the possibilities of social media as companies like Twitter were launched publicly. Facebook was challenging Myspace as the largest social network, and the investment world was growing enamored with financial derivatives called mortgage-backed securities.

David didn't dislike social networks but just did not trust how companies were using the data. All these internet users were assuming their data was safe because it was encrypted, but David wondered what would happen if they were wrong. The possibility plagued him. The entire internet was predicated on the fact that the data transferred across thousands of unknown servers was only visible to the sender and receiver.

Teams of computer scientists had created a process of changing the real data in a message into a series of random letters and numbers. This process, or algorithm, for turning data into secret codes was called encryption. The source code for doing the encrypting was released publicly to prove that it had no vulnerabilities. The internet was booming, and everyone trusted that it was secure.

But David was not convinced, and he voiced this to one of the faculty at MIT.

"If the internet encryption algorithm is not random," explained David, "it can be vulnerable to exploitation."

"This is interesting," responded Dr. Babbidge, "and a little scary, to be honest. This has deep implications, which must be treated with an abundance of caution."

"The encryption they are using has predictable patterns. That is really bad. We need to get the word out as quickly as possible."

David continued to raise eyebrows with other faculty, but the staff agreed they needed to tread lightly. He gained approval for his project, but only under the administration's condition that it not be published outside the university.

Others in the cryptography field were also raising alarm bells, and by the time David graduated with his master's degree in 2007, the *New York Times* reported that the NSA had secretly and intentionally introduced a vulnerability into the encryption standard, allowing the US government to read all encrypted information passing over the internet.

David's project was eventually published in obscurity since the moment for notoriety had long since been claimed by others. Nonetheless, he was able to secure a good job at a local tech firm in Boston, where he managed to survive but grow very bored.

David stayed in Boston rather than returning to his childhood home near Washington, DC. He hated politics, and Boston's history of rebellion from tyrannical government control suited him. His Libertarian ideals were only solidified when the news of the NSA sabotaging the encryption standards confirmed his many conspiracy theories. So in addition to being bored, he became more and more cynical about the government. His cynicism provided him the passion to become a pioneer in the field of cryptography and decentralized computer systems.

A computer nerd since age nine, he was nevertheless convinced, like most nine-year-old boys, that he would eventually become a Major League Baseball player. But after leading his team in strikeouts, he realized his life might need a new direction.

In the summer after third grade, his parents signed him up for a summer programming course at the local community college to help him overcome the painful lessons of Little League. Even though he was the youngest camper, he quickly outshone the rest of the class. He still enjoyed sports, but a new passion was born in his heart.

Recognizing David's talent with the computer, his parents financed his inevitable plunge into the world of programming. His father was a public school teacher and was able to bring home a computer for David to use on weekends. When the school upgraded its computers, his parents purchased one of them for him.

He spent long hours on the computer and learned to create many different computer programs. David's ambition for tinkering with the computer's hardware fueled a desire to purchase additional parts, but since his parents' income could not keep up with David's ambition, he started a lawn-care business to support his habit.

"If I can get twenty customers per week, then I can earn enough by the time school starts in September to buy a Gateway PC with a Pentium processor. Windows NT will be out by then," David told his parents.

"Have you factored in the price of a mower and all the gas?" asked his father.

"Yes, and I will sell the mower at the end of the summer to get some of those costs back," replied David.

By the time David reached middle school, he was far beyond the other students in his computer prowess and entrepreneurial drive. His parents encouraged him not to be limited by the classroom. By the end of middle school, he had already built and sold several computers.

David tested out of most of the computer courses at his high school because he'd already mastered the course content. The one or two courses he was able to benefit from were completed by the end of his freshman year. He continued to learn on his own outside of school, but his lack of scholastic enthusiasm caused his grades to stay too close to average to attract any interest from college scholarships.

In his senior year of high school, he entered a programming contest at the local university, called a code-a-thon. The twenty-four-hour event called for creating a working solution that addressed a systemic social issue. David's team won the contest overwhelmingly, and when it was learned that David had done all the coding, he started to receive letters from some of the leading universities.

"David! You have another letter," his mother called up the stairs one day.

"Who is this one from?" asked his father.

"The University of Michigan, and yesterday, it was UCLA."

After taking the letter from his mother, David looked at the envelope and handed it back without opening it. "I'm holding out for a better offer," he said with a smirk.

The code-a-thon fame, coupled with his perfect score on the mathematics portion of the SAT, was enough to overcome his average grades and waitlist at MIT. David received his acceptance letter in early August, just in time to pack his bags and move to Boston.

Mediocrity in his studies persisted in his early years at MIT. The discipline of the rigid curriculum did not satiate his natural curiosity, and David pursued the social scene for the first time in his life. During his sophomore year, he met two people who would prove very important in his life.

He met Thomas Randall during a one-credit tennis class, each of them having come independently to the conclusion that learning to play tennis might be a good way to attract athletic women. When it became clear they both had the same strategy, they decided to join forces rather than compete. Teaming up on the tennis court would foreshadow a long business relationship between the two men.

The tennis dating strategy proved somewhat successful, and David dated several different girls during his early years at MIT but never had any serious relationships until he met Mia Nelson. His friends thought it was her slender five-foot-seven frame or her shoulder-length red hair that caught David's eye, but the truth was that she was the first girl who could keep up with David's intellect.

Mia was an accounting major at Boston University and at the top of her class. She had a fire in her brain that matched her hair, along with a passion for life. She was not afraid to challenge David's views on politics, and she was the only person he didn't mind losing to in a debate.

David and Mia dated throughout their undergraduate years and moved in together right after graduation. Mia worked at a top accounting firm in Boston while David pursued his graduate degree. Soon after they married, their son Owen was born, and the three of them lived in a tiny Back Bay apartment in the heart of Boston. Life was simple in those days, and they often took their son on long strolls through Boston Common. Mia was able to continue working as the two young parents tag teamed in the raising of Owen.

"The software industry is changing; it's all about the money," he said one day.

"Isn't everything about the money?" replied Mia.

"I don't mind the developers making a living, but the companies are sacrificing quality and security to rush products to market. They are stunting true innovation."

So when buzz started on the internet about groups of strangers collaborating to create software that was free to everyone, David's passion for life was rekindled.

This free software would be called "open source" because anyone could see the computer code or even contribute to its creation. The final product would be owned not by a single person or organization but by society in general. David worked late into the night on a couple different projects and became a vocal proponent of the open-source world.

As their son Owen grew, David and Mia discussed giving him a private-school education. Out of love for his son, David abandoned the world of free software and accepted a role with more responsibilities at a tech firm. The pay was better, which allowed them to move into a larger apartment, but David no longer had free time to work on open-source software.

David was a great father, even finding time to coach his son's baseball team, but he was growing increasingly depressed with his vocational life. On one particular late-spring night, he came to a crisis point. He was coaching his son's baseball game, and Owen was the tying run on third base. The pitcher made a wild throw, and the ball got past the catcher, so David sent Owen running toward home plate. Owen ran hard and slid, but the umpire called him out, and their team lost the game.

David felt terrible over his coaching decision and tried to console his son, but Owen seemed unfazed by the ending of the game.

"Dad, I'm glad you sent me home on that play," he said. "If you didn't, we'd always wonder what might have happened. At least now we know."

The wisdom of Owen's words haunted David the rest of the night. *How would I ever know what would happen unless I tried?*

That night, David and Mia stayed up late as David spilled his heart.

"I feel like I'm dying in the lonely cubicles of corporate America!"

"Then quit. We'll figure it out. I've been offered some extra assignments at work. We can make it work," offered Mia.

"I used to have ambition and drive," said David with

tears in his eyes, "but now, I just feel like I'm watching my life pass, like a spectator in the bleachers."

Mia just listened and let him vent, and they agreed to sleep on it. In the morning, she repeated her admonition for David to quit his job.

"I'm your biggest fan, David. It's time for you to go for your dreams and pursue your destiny."

He gave her a long hug and left the house to ponder his future.

On September 15, 2008, David took the elevator to the floor that contained his six-by-six cubicle. He would often recall that day with perfect clarity, as his parents used to talk about the day John F. Kennedy was assassinated. The office was already in a panic when he arrived, and people were busy reading the breaking news on the internet. Lehman Brothers, one of the largest financial institutions in the world, was suddenly bankrupt, sending a wave of panic around the globe.

In the weeks that followed, David went from being ready to quit his job to being grateful he even had one. The realities of paying rent and supporting a child became critical as Mia worried about losing her job too. As David watched the government's reaction to the financial crisis, he grew angry and disillusioned at the world banking system.

On one particular evening, just before Christmas 2008, David invited his best friend, Thomas Randall, over for dinner. After the expected college reminiscing and perhaps one too many drinks, David eventually switched the conversation to the economic troubles.

"The financial world is collapsing, and our lovely government cannot bail it out," said David. "The greed of the bankers has created a perfect storm. They created the storm. They ignored the signs of trouble. They covered up the symptoms of the collapse to protect their money at our expense, and now they can't bail us out because they're the problem."

He got up and walked over to his desk, retrieved some computer printouts, and placed a copy into Thomas and Mia's hands. "I want you both to read this. I've been doing some research on what's really going on."

Thomas silently read the title then asked David, "Who is Satoshi Nakamoto, and what is Bitcoin?"

"Just read it, and then we'll talk," replied David.

David went to the kitchen to make some coffee and gave them thirty minutes to digest what he'd handed them. When he returned, he spent the rest of the evening giving them their first introduction into what would come to be known as "cryptocurrency."

"Since the dawn of civilization, people have been looking for ways to store value. In the beginning, everyone worked the fields and harvested crops, and they had to store their produce so they'd have enough food for the winter. But it was more than stored food—it was stored value. Everyone had to grow whatever they needed to survive. Then they figured out that it's much easier to grow a single crop instead of all the crops they needed. So they focused on one crop and traded with someone else who had the other things they needed. They made deals to swap corn for wheat or vice versa. They didn't realize it, but they were exchanging value with each other. Today, we call that an economy.

"Over time, people figured out it was too hard to literally swap bags of produce, so they created coins. Basically, these coins were just tokens, things that represented a certain amount of value. As long as everyone agreed that these coins were valuable, the system worked. So they created coins made out of precious metals to make sure people valued them, like gold and silver or even bronze. And boom, we get the concept of currency. Are you following?" David's eyes were large and his body language pronounced. "Stored value. Barter systems. Currency. Stay with me."

Mia and Thomas exchanged glances and let him continue.

"But we all know that those in control do whatever is necessary to stay in control. And the ones in control were the governments because they were the ones creating all the currency and thus controlling the economy. When coins made of precious metals became cost prohibitive or inconvenient, they created tokens for the coins. Do you see how ridiculous it's getting?" David exclaimed to the two puzzled faces in front of him. When they remained silent, he continued.

"The coins made of precious metals were tokens already, and now they created tokens that represented tokens—paper money that represented a certain amount of precious metal that in turn represented a certain amount of value produced by someone. Our modern-day investment bankers were not the first ones to create a system of derivatives, a world where you make more money from money rather than actually doing something useful.

"And if that wasn't messed up enough, over time, the paper money didn't actually represent anything at all! Did you know that the US dollar has not been based on gold since 1971? It's no wonder the whole thing has crashed like a house of cards. The system is messed up... to the very core. We have tokens that represent tokens that are no longer based on anything real, and everyone in America still places their blind faith in the US dollar! And then all of a sudden, the house comes crashing down.

"We don't need a bank bailout. We need to fix the system itself. That's where this thing called cryptocurrency comes in," said David, pointing at the printout he'd given them. "Why should the government be the one issuing and controlling the currency? It's not the proper role of government to dictate what I place value in or where I store that value. We have become slaves to the government because we need their precious tokens to do everything in our lives, and we don't even know we're being manipulated.

"This idea is for something called cryptocurrency. A new place to store and exchange value. No more banks to hold all the money. No more banks to take a cut of every financial transaction we make. It's called Bitcoin, and I think it is a revolutionary idea," concluded David.

The room was silent as Thomas and Mia digested David's monologue.

"You don't have time for open-source software right now," said Mia. "You promised you'd stay focused on your job. We can't afford to lose any income right now."

"This is different. This guy, Satoshi Nakamoto, is onto something, and I want to help."

Mia didn't share David's antigovernment views, but she knew that ship had sailed. David might hold onto his job for a little while, but he was a man on a mission. In the months and years to come, David would get only a few hours of sleep per night as he became a leading cryptocurrency developer. Many things would happen in the next nine years that would guide David toward his destiny.

2

———

Boston, Massachusetts, present day

David Turner pressed the unlock button on his key fob, and his Toyota Highlander chirped in response, the noise echoing through the empty parking garage. He slid into the driver's seat and let his body relax into the cool leather upholstery. He paused, staring at the digital dashboard clock. It read 9:13 p.m. His mind drifted back to the events of that fateful night almost a year before.

"Now batting, number eight, Owen Turner," said the Little League announcer.

"Protect the plate, eight! Make him pitch to you!" yelled David toward the center of the field in an attempt to distract the other team.

With a crack of the bat, Owen exploded toward first base as the ball sailed over the center fielder's head. David grew more animated as his son rounded second.

"Get down! Get down!" yelled David as Owen slid into third base.

David glanced into the stands as Owen wiped the dust off his pants.

"Where's Mom? She should have been here by now."

Mia was never known to miss a single inning, let alone an entire game. David grew more concerned as the game played on.

After the game, he tried calling her mobile phone, and each time, it went directly to voice mail. He tried to hide his concern from Owen on the way home, but he was a perceptive young man.

David received a call at exactly 9:13 p.m., according to the clock above the kitchen counter.

"David Turner?"

"Yes, who is this?"

"My name is Sergeant Davis, Boston PD. We need you to come down to the station. It's about your wife, Mia."

It took David and Owen about twelve minutes to reach the police department, where they were debriefed.

"The car lost control, based on the tire marks and other evidence at the scene," the sergeant said. "There are no eyewitnesses, but a passing motorist noticed the flames and called it in. The fire department and some of our boys responded, but the car was already badly burned when we arrived. There was not much left but some twisted metal and loose glass on the hillside."

The sergeant's voice grew more solemn. "There was a single body inside, but it had been burned too severely to make a positive identification. But we were able to salvage the partial license plate. The car was registered to Mia Turner."

While David shook his head in disbelief, Owen protested, "Mom would not just lose control of her car. There must be some mistake."

"The car went off the road and over an embankment, rolling as it made its way down the small hillside. It's not clear when the car caught fire or if the victim inside died on impact... or before the flames destroyed the vehicle."

The clock on the dashboard of David's SUV changed to 9:14 p.m., jolting him from his memories. He started the vehicle and proceeded quickly around the maze of pavement toward the garage exit. He placed his badge against the card reader and watched the boom barrier rise in front of him. After making a quick right-hand turn onto Massachusetts Avenue, he tried to forget his day and focus on his family.

He preferred using public transportation when possible, but after working long days, getting home to his family was easier when driving his own car. This also had the side effect of making him feel more in control of where he was going, both literally and metaphorically.

Despite the time that had passed since the accident, David had trouble avoiding the constant replay of events in his mind, second-guessing himself on things he could have done differently that day. For months, he had tormented himself by thinking about words unsaid and dreams that would never come true. Both David and Owen had seen a counselor for several months, trying to process the loss. David was determined that Mia's death would not lead to any more damage, so as he drove home from work, he considered his relationship with Owen.

As he pulled into the driveway and toward the open garage, he noticed Owen's room was dark. He parked and removed his things from the backseat, making his way into the kitchen. Owen was by the microwave, watching a frozen dinner complete its cooking.

"Hey, buddy, what are you making?" David asked in a cheerful tone as he put his things on the table.

"Food."

"I thought maybe we could order Chinese or pizza. I'm starving."

"Yeah, me too, about two hours ago," said Owen under his breath.

"Yeah, I know. I'm sorry. I get lost in the computer code, and I lose track of time. You know how it is, right?"

Owen had aged a lot in the past year. He was nearly five foot nine, and his slender frame did not seem to reflect his constant intake of food. The largest part of his body might have been his shaggy head of hair, with a tinge of red that he owed to his mother.

Owen didn't answer, and David's mood dampened. *Owen is just a typical teenage boy*, David kept reminding himself. But deep inside, he was very concerned about what happens to a little boy who loses his mother so early in life.

David was under a lot of pressure. He was suddenly a single parent and trying to be a father, chef, and tutor, along with a whole host of other stresses. On top of all of that, he was the CEO of a small but rapidly growing company that was starting to attract investor attention.

David and Mia had always agreed that raising Owen was more important than any other goal or pursuit in life. Therefore, on nights like this, David felt guilty and wished he had Mia by his side for balance.

"How was school today? And don't say 'fine'!" added David with a smile on his face.

"Good," said Owen, a subtle smirk betraying an approaching end to the silent treatment.

David laughed in response, and the mood in the kitchen

lightened. David got another frozen dinner out of the freezer as Owen sat down to eat his. They talked about sports and the favorite teams they shared. Professional baseball had just begun, and the Red Sox were coming off one of their best spring-training sessions. The New England Patriots had just finished up another Super Bowl title, but they decided to skip basketball since the Boston Celtics made that topic too painful.

After dinner and halfway through their tradition of an evening bowl of ice cream, Owen mumbled, "I miss Mom."

David took another spoonful of ice cream before responding, "Me too, buddy."

David and Owen had grown very close since Mia's death, but they were processing the loss differently. The topic of Mia was never far from both their minds, and it frequently came up in conversation.

"Dad, what if that car—" Owen managed to say before David interrupted him.

"Owen, you know what the counselors said to us. We need to face the reality of what happened and not try and hide from it. Mom is gone. And despite what either of us wishes were true, we need to face the facts."

Owen hung his head silently and swirled his spoon in the ice cream bowl.

"A single driver in your mom's car wearing all Mom's jewelry at the exact time and location where your mother drove home from work each day? I would love that to be true. I wish it weren't your mother in that car that day and that she were sitting here with us right now. But we both know it was her. She will always be with us in spirit, but we need to let go, or we are going to get stuck. Stuck in one moment in time, forever grieving. She was an amazing person, the love of my life, and an amazing mother. But she's gone now, and it's just you and me."

"Yeah, I know. It's just different, Dad. You're working late all the time, and the house is empty. It's just me and Lucie, and she only barks and wags her tail," replied Owen, stroking the dog's head.

"Maybe we can spend more time together, then. We can do a project. I miss the days of coaching your teams."

"Dad, if you want me to mow the grass, just ask. You don't have to make it sound like a project."

"You know... I used to mow lawns in my neighborhood for extra money—"

"And you saved up and built your own computer. I know the story, Dad. You have told me a million times."

"Hey, that's it! Let's build a computer. I won't even make you mow the grass to do it."

"I already have a computer."

"Not like the one we will build. This one will be crazy fast."

"Can we use it to mine bitcoin?" said Owen with a chuckle. He knew his father well and knew he hated all things relating to bitcoin. He held up a hand, pleading with his father to not start a monologue. "Dad, I was kidding."

David would not be deterred. He went on for five minutes about the inadequacies of bitcoin and the bubble it had become. How the world needed a new digital currency but had been failed by bitcoin speculation. "If I had a thousand bitcoin right now, I would delete them all."

"If I had a thousand bitcoin," countered Owen, "I would retire."

They spent the rest of the night talking about their computer project before their drooping eyes forced them to stop. Owen left his light on and got into bed, glancing through the latest edition of *Sports Illustrated*. He was fifteen, but he still enjoyed the nightly routine of his father saying good night to him and turning out his light.

David appeared at the bedroom door and leaned into the room, pausing by the light switch, waiting for Owen to put away his magazine. When Owen took longer than usual, his father asked him if anything was wrong.

"Dad, are we really going to build that computer?"

"Of course, buddy. If I say we are going to do it, then we'll do it."

"It's just... Well, I know you are busy with work," said Owen, keeping his head down and not wanting to make eye contact.

David left the light on, slowly crossed the room, and took a seat on his son's bed. "I'm sorry I have been distracted from home lately. I just feel like we are so close at work, almost ready for a breakthrough. I don't want to lose that momentum."

"Is that really why you work late?" asked Owen in a quiet tone. After a couple moments, he looked up at his father. "Dad, I think you're working long hours to take your mind off Mom."

David averted his eyes. His son was perceptive, and his words pierced David's heart. Suddenly, a tapestry of memories flashed before his eyes, catching his emotions off guard. Tears clouded his vision and dropped onto the bedspread. Owen slid over and gave his father a side hug.

David hugged his son back, twice as hard as normal—once for himself and once for Mia. As Owen slid back under the covers, David's tears gave way to a proud fatherly smile. Staring at the face of his son was the closest thing he had left to seeing Mia. He crossed the room and flicked off the lights. "Good night, Son... We are going to build that computer. I promise."

As he closed the bedroom door, he heard Owen singing a soft tune that he knew all too well. David lingered by the closed door and silently mouthed the last line of the song with Owen.

And if the road is too hard to pass,
We'll fly like ponies in the sky,
Like ponies in the sky

3

———

David had decided to drive Owen to school that morning, so he arrived at the office a little later than normal. He made his way through the lobby and proceeded to the elevator and up to the seventh floor. The NuKoin offices occupied only about 2,500 square feet, a very small footprint for a technology startup company, but David was a CEO that focused more on delivering a working solution than marketing and appearances.

David had started NuKoin in the late-night hours at the kitchen table after his family was asleep. But he knew that for his vision to reach fruition, he needed help.

It was after a dinner party late one summer evening back in 2014 that David had consumed enough wine to share his business dilemma. Although many people were in attendance, it was his best friend and college roommate, Thomas Randall, who challenged him in a quiet corner to finally follow through and quit his day job to pursue his dreams.

"That's easy for you to say. You're not the one giving up your paycheck!" David complained.

"Okay, then if you quit, I'll quit," Thomas Randall famously challenged him.

According to company legend, David and Thomas spent the next week charting the course of NuKoin over a steady diet of pizza and carbonated beverages. Mia had become more supportive, delighting in the massive change in her husband's disposition and energy level. Even though she valued a steady income, she realized her husband's dreams needed support.

In 2014, Bitcoin had suffered a major setback when a theft of five hundred million dollars' worth of bitcoin was discovered at a Japanese company named Mt. Gox. Hundreds of thousands of people across the world had counted on Mt. Gox to handle their bitcoin transactions, only to suddenly lose their investments in the massive breach. The price of bitcoin plummeted, and David had grown disillusioned with the bitcoin project. The time had come for him to start a new project, and Thomas was willing to help him.

Thomas played the part of consummate businessman well, leveraging his sales skills to get an audience with several venture capital firms in Boston. David was the technology spokesman, and his enthusiasm and passion won them a series-A funding of two million dollars from Delphi Capital and a chance to achieve a dream. This initial investment round got them off the ground and would enable them to hire more developers.

There was one catch. They needed a chief financial officer to round out their executive team. This was where the 2,500-square-foot office space came in handy, conveniently located in the same building as an after-school program. The convenience of the childcare was how David and Thomas ambushed Mia into quitting her job and becoming the third employee of NuKoin. Mia had always questioned that version of events, but most of the ten employees at NuKoin retold Thomas and David's version of the story.

Even though David was officially the chief executive officer, he acted more like a chief technology officer, focusing on the tech behind the company. Thomas was officially the chief operating officer, but he also handled all things marketing and sales.

When Mia passed away, the board at Delphi Capital took the lead in searching for a new CFO. They took a twenty-five percent stake in NuKoin after their series-A investment and held the right to approve all new board members at NuKoin. They presented David and Thomas with four candidates, and eventually, everyone agreed on Nicole Mancini.

Nicole had a long resume with senior positions at various banks, along with some connections to government contracting that everyone agreed might be useful someday. She also had a strong knowledge of information technology and understood the emerging world of cryptocurrency. But perhaps most importantly to David, she was not a Democrat or a Republican. David did not demand that his employees share his Libertarian political beliefs, but he did feel that the executive team needed to have certain core values regarding the role and size of government control.

Nicole was not married and had few other demands on her time outside of work. Many in the office thought it a tragedy that someone as pretty as Nicole should be alone, but the prevailing opinion of the office gossip was that she was married to her work. At five foot ten, her figure was even more striking. She had deep green eyes and shoulder-length blond hair that disarmed many of the visitors to

NuKoin. She knew the line between modesty and flirtation, and many in the office thought she deliberately kept everyone guessing.

People speculated about Nicole preferring women and about David and Nicole getting together, but all that was misplaced. Nicole was simply focused on her goals, and no one was going to get in her way. David could appreciate her beauty and often did so when he was sure no one was watching, but he was still in love with his late wife and mourning her loss. He didn't mind the rumors but dismissed them as misplaced assumptions over Nicole taking Mia's role as NuKoin CFO. But David and Nicole had a solid business relationship that bordered on friendship.

As David walked into the office that morning, Nicole was the one he bumped into first.

"There you are, David. We need to talk about that ICO notion of yours. I'm going down to grab some coffee, and I'll meet you in your office in five minutes, okay?"

"Sure. I'm in a good mood this morning," said David, still thinking about his time with Owen the previous night.

"I left some documents on your desk. Take a quick look before I get back," Nicole called over her shoulder as she opened the front door of the office.

He walked into his office and hung his coat on the back of the door. He watched Nicole through the closing office door, focusing on her knee-length black skirt. After she was gone, he sat down in his chair and turned on his laptop. He took a couple of long pulls on his coffee as he stared out the window. The sun was shining and warming his office, so he closed his eyes and allowed himself to enjoy the moment of quiet before his day officially began.

David had managed to keep his lean body shape, which had been such an asset on the tennis court back in college.

His brown hair was cut short, but that was more for utility. Since Mia had passed away, he no longer felt the urgency to shave and fully embraced the scruff. At six foot, he was slightly taller than Nicole but subconsciously straightened his posture whenever she was around.

Nicole returned in less than five minutes. Her deliberate stride toward his office alerted him she was coming early enough for David to take a working position at his computer.

"Did you look over those documents I left you?"

"No, not yet. Just taking in some caffeine," replied David. "So talk to me. What's on your mind?"

"I don't think we are ready for an ICO," Nicole declared. "It will distract us, and our immediate need is developers to get this code out the door."

ICO was the abbreviation for initial coin offering. It was just like a traditional initial public offering, or IPO, except that it was faster at raising funds and avoided government regulations. ICOs had become very popular among startups touting solutions in the cryptocurrency space, and David considered it a rite of passage for NuKoin.

"Nicole, you were the one that told me we were almost out of cash. How are we supposed to get code out the door if we cannot run payroll?"

"We get more venture capital money. Delphi might be interested in a series-B funding round if we can get another partner."

"I have a hunch that you already have a partner in mind," said David in a suspicious tone.

"You know me well," retorted Nicole with a smirk. "Shenling Capital has been following our blogs and reached out to me last week. They flew someone here to Boston and would love to meet with us."

"Flew in from where?" asked David flatly as he picked up Nicole's documents and started thumbing through the pages.

"China."

"China? You know how I feel about VC money from state actors! That's the problem with bitcoin. The Russian and Chinese computers will soon be the majority on the bitcoin network. Cryptocurrency was supposed to free us from government intervention, not enable it."

"Would you stop with the spy-novel conspiracy crap? Seriously. Money is green, not Caucasian."

"Actually, the one-yuan note is like a mustard yellow," said David with a smirk of his own. "I have no issue with any person, but governments are a different story. And the Chinese government has an agenda."

"This is a VC firm, not the Chinese government."

"Don't go parochial on me. Money always has a trail. Not all investments are wise."

Nicole decided to let David's diatribe go unanswered, switching the topic slightly. "We need to move up our timeline. Our competition grows every day."

"You know this code is complex. Qualified developers that will work for the wages we pay are not exactly lining up at the door. That's why we need an ICO, so we can lure them in with the incentive of getting a piece of it."

"Shenling Capital has agreed to give us senior developers as part of their capital investment," said Nicole. "At least two developers on site, with a team offshore on an as-needed basis."

David let out a loud groan. "Senior developers? Will I get the right to interview and approve them?"

"You cannot write all the code yourself and run this company at the same time. You need to see the big picture here. We don't have the capital to hire more labor. The alpha launch is delayed, and beta is nowhere in sight. And you want to sell cryptocoins?"

"Is Thomas on board with this idea of yours?" asked David with a little too much disdain.

As if on cue, Thomas Randall eased into the office and closed the door. "You guys are getting a little heated. I could hear you from down the hall. I should have worn my black-and-white referee jersey," said Thomas with a laugh designed to lighten the atmosphere.

"Did Nicole tell you about her plan to outsource our code and get in bed with the Chinese?"

"Okay, buddy. Calm down," said Thomas, raising a hand toward David. "She did run it by me, and I think we need to consider all options. Why not hear them out? Get to know a couple of their tech guys and see if they have the stones—sorry, Nicole—see if they can code in the world of cryptography."

"Okay. I might actually enjoy that," said David.

"You need an open mind," replied Thomas. "It's Nicole's job to watch the finances, and she is telling us we are in trouble. She is coming to us with solutions. The least we can do is honestly consider those ideas."

"What about the ICO?" asked David.

"What about it? You know as well as I do the regulators at the SEC are going after ICOs anyway. Do we really need any more government scrutiny? Our product is a more anonymous version of bitcoin to them, and they already think bitcoin is too anonymous."

David said, "These VC firms give you a little money, and it's like you sold your soul. Series A is one thing, but a series B is going to bring a whole bunch of oversight hand-cuffs. What about our dream? I don't want any VC executives making decisions for us because they want a quicker return on their investment."

"If we don't get more cash soon, there won't be any company to make decisions for," said Nicole.

The three remained silent for what seemed like minutes. Thomas and Nicole were standing but leaning against the walls of the office. David remained sitting, swiveling slightly in his office chair and staring out the window.

"I'm going to personally review every line of code they write," said David to the silent room.

"I wouldn't have it any other way," responded Thomas.

"I will make sure we vet them well," promised Nicole. "I am not going to let us sign away the farm."

"How much equity do they want?" David probed.

"Let's not get ahead of ourselves. Let's get them in here and hear their full presentation," said Nicole calmly.

"Is William DeFrost on board with this?" asked David. "He's the lead guy at Delphi, and they get a veto."

"I haven't told him yet. I would never do that to you. It's up to the three of us to band together and make a recommendation to Delphi Capital. Our board meeting with Delphi is tomorrow, so I thought we should be in agreement before that meeting. I have a feeling he has some ideas of his own."

The three partners spent the rest of the morning discussing strategy and direction. After lunch, David locked his door and retreated into his cone of silence. Writing computer code was his first love, and he was alone with his code then.

Writing complex code required complete focus free from all distractions. Software engineers build mental models in their minds. They see a vision for where the code is headed and write various blocks of code to achieve that vision. Even a simple interruption can cause them to lose sight of the mental model, requiring them to rebuild it.

This was why David locked his office door and placed a Do Not Disturb sign on the doorknob. He turned off his office phone, and his mobile phone was configured to make no noise or vibration except if Owen was trying to reach him.

Very soon, David was lost in the code, oblivious to everything going on around him. The sun sank low on the horizon, but he did not notice.

He was in the coding zone when a knock at his office door startled him from his trance. Annoyed at the interruption, he looked at his clock and realized he was late for his wrap-up meeting with Thomas and Nicole. He rose from his desk and opened the door. They were both standing there, smiling at what had become routine in the office—David losing track of time.

"Sorry, guys. Come in. I got lost in the code again. Give me a second to check it in."

```
bool CCoinsViewCache::SpendCoin(const COutPoint &outpoint,
Coin* moveout) {
    CCoinsMap::iterator it = FetchCoin(outpoint);
    if (it == cacheCoins.end()) return false;
    cachedCoinsUsage -=
        it->second.coin.DynamicMemoryUsage();
    if (moveout) {
        *moveout = std::move(it->second.coin);
    }
    if (it->second.flags & CCoinsCacheEntry::FRESH) {
        cacheCoins.erase(it);
    } else {
        it->second.flags |= CCoinsCacheEntry::DIRTY;
        it->second.coin.Clear();
    }
    return true;
}
```

He saved all his work then saved his code changes to the GIT repository, a software tool for managing multiple people making changes to the same source code. All the changes were logged into a master database so that everyone working on the code could see it and collaborate on making changes. Every change was tracked and logged, creating a permanent record when anyone made changes to the code. Part of David's job was to review all the changes before they were accepted into the master database.

"So are we on the same page for tomorrow?" asked Thomas.

"Yes. We are pushing for an ICO, right?" said David with a grin.

"Come on, bro, it's getting late," Thomas said with a sigh.

4

———

After a long day, all three NuKoin executives were ready to call it quits. Their fatigue was mental but exhausting nonetheless. Nicole and Thomas left David's office to gather their things, but David remained sitting at his desk, almost too tired to go home. He cast an empty, distant gaze out the window and onto the streets below.

Thomas was back outside David's office soon, hurriedly putting on his coat while juggling his briefcase. Nicole walked up beside him moments later and asked David if he was planning on leaving.

"I think I will putter around for a little bit and unwind," explained David.

"I thought you wanted to get home to spend time with Owen," said Nicole.

"He's sleeping over at a friend's house tonight, so there's no rush to get home."

Thomas shrugged and said, "Okay, I'm headed out. There's pot roast in the slow cooker, and I want to make sure they save me some. Nicole, want me to walk you out?"

Nicole paused. "No, I'll be okay." She motioned silently to Thomas that she was going to stay a moment and see if David needed an ear.

Thomas left while Nicole put her coat down on the table and took a seat across from David at his desk.

"Want to talk about it?" she offered.

"Talk about what?"

"What's bothering you. We haven't known each other for a long time, but I think I know you well enough to see that you might need to talk something out."

David kept his gaze out the window and let a few moments pass quietly. "Today was great. We got a ton done and worked as a team. But..."

"But what?"

"It comes and goes. Some days, I can focus so deeply on my work that I forget she's not around. Then all of a sudden, it hits me out of nowhere," said David sadly.

"She must have been an amazing woman. I wish I could have known her."

"She was amazing. When she joined the team at NuKoin, it was like a boost to our marriage. Working side by side, sharing the same dream... Now it's like my dream is always half dead."

"Dreams are a funny thing. They motivate us, but they should never define us," said Nicole. "Success is not whether we attain the dream we originally set out for. Success is whether you are happy with the steps in life you end up taking."

"Wow, that was deep," said David. "Have you ever considered being a therapist? Because that was better than most of what I pay a hundred fifty dollars per hour to get downtown."

"Coaching is part of leadership. It's not just kids who

need coaches on a sports field. We need partners in life, people who cheer us on to do amazing things."

"Yeah, tell me about it," David mumbled.

"David, I am not just talking about a spouse, although that can be the case. It could be a pastor or a professor from your college days or maybe a business mentor from another industry."

"How about you? Who is your life coach?" asked David.

"I have a couple ladies I connect with once a month—women who have the same drive and share the same goal, for women to survive in a man's world," said Nicole matter-of-factly.

"How about any men?"

"As in 'men' or one man?"

David's heartbeat quickened ever so slightly, and he wondered if his face was betraying him.

"Either. I'm just curious if Wonder Woman has a Batman in her life."

"Normally, I'd be offended by such a comment, but I'll let it go this time," said Nicole. "But to answer your question: no, I've never met Batman."

"How about Robin? Ever met him?" David laughed.

"I'm not really into men who wear masks to shield their insecurities."

"I need to meet your coach. You're tough," said David with a twinkle in his eyes.

Nicole softened a little bit and seemed more relaxed. She crossed her legs and straightened her skirt while keeping her eyes on David. "I'm not really sure what you're asking me."

Thinking quickly, David deflected. "I miss being able to debrief with someone at the end of the day. The idea of a life coach sounds intriguing."

"When is the last time you went out or had something in your day other than work and home?"

"A long time."

"Okay. Then tonight, I will be your coach. You look like you could use a drink."

David's heart skipped a beat. A long time had passed since he felt the excitement of flirting. The fact that he couldn't tell if Nicole was flirting back made it even more exciting.

"Okay, that sounds like a good idea," David said with a smile. "Coach's choice."

The two stood and left the office together.

They walked two blocks before David asked, "So where are you taking me? I feel like we passed a few spots that looked good."

"Those are all sports bars, designed to keep single men single and to convince married men to join them. Ladies prefer to actually talk to the people they are out with. Here's one of my favorite spots."

They entered a dimly lit lounge and found a seat near the back. Eighties music was playing loud enough to prevent conversations from being overheard but soft enough that people didn't have to yell.

"Good choice in music," said David.

"I find that it keeps the millennials away. That way, I don't feel old," said Nicole with a smile.

He had never really noticed her smile before. He was used to seeing her in business mode, always on top of her game.

When they were a couple drinks into their conversation, Nicole excused herself to the ladies' room, leaving David to his thoughts.

He had not been on a date in many years. His wife,

Mia, had been captivating, never having given him reason to even notice other women. Even though Mia had passed away, being in a bar with Nicole still felt wrong, so he reassured himself that this was not a date.

He looked up and saw Nicole coming back to the table. She had let down her hair and applied some lipstick. Her slender figure seemed to have more curves than he remembered. Her eyes seemed locked on his gaze, daring him to look deeper. He noticed her blouse was unbuttoned a little lower, but he couldn't decide if it was one button or two. He noticed a couple of men behind her at the bar were admiring her backside out of the corners of their eyes. They turned away when they saw David looking at them.

Nicole took her seat and gave David a smile, tilting her head slightly to one side. She pushed one side of her hair back behind an ear and looked at David.

"Did you scare those guys from staring?" asked Nicole.

Surprised, David squinted.

"David, do all men really think we don't know when they stare behind our backs?"

He was suddenly very nervous, wondering if Nicole was really referring to him or the men at the bar.

"Tell me about Mia," said Nicole.

Her question disarmed him. Visions of Mia suddenly came back into his mind, displacing the fantasies about Nicole that had been building. Momentarily confused, he stared at the table like he had been caught in some mental infidelity.

"She was my college girlfriend. She was a feisty redhead, full of energy and ambition. She stole my mind before she took my heart. She was the kind of woman that you knew you wanted to marry when you first met her."

"Wow, that's a great description. I wish more men thought like that."

"Her best quality, though, was that she valued the valuable things in life. She had her priorities right. She valued people, and she made sure they knew it."

"Was it hard to work together at NuKoin?"

"Not at all. I loved being with her. Having her by my side as we pursued NuKoin was amazing. By her example, the bar was set really high for everyone we hired."

"Well, that explains some things," replied Nicole.

"What do you mean by that?"

"Over the last several months, it has been an uphill climb on this mountain of expectations we call NuKoin. I am starting to understand why."

"Mia wasn't just the CFO—she was like a den mother. She was the glue that bound the office together. She would push people in their careers, but she also seemed to sense when things were going poorly in their personal lives. Everyone loved her in the office. Her passing was really hard on a lot of people."

"Is that why you took so long to fill the CFO position?"

"Everyone we interviewed just didn't measure up. Mia had grown into roles beyond finances," said David. "But that was my fault. My therapist helped me understand that I was treating the CFO search like an effort to replace Mia."

"And you weren't ready for that?"

David looked at Nicole and couldn't tell if she was making a statement or asking a question. Of course no one could replace Mia—that was impossible. *Why did I agree to have drinks with Nicole?* thought David. He took in her beauty, and the thought of being with her in a romantic way teased him. Just as suddenly, his thoughts shifted to Mia and the memory of her embrace.

"No, I'm not sure if I will ever be ready to replace Mia," David said, picking up his glass for a long drink.

Nicole looked into the distance, seeming disappointed at his words or even saddened.

"Owen seems to be doing better," said Nicole.

"Yeah, he's a great kid."

"Did he take the accident hard?"

"Very hard. He has always been a great kid, but now he is a bit cynical."

"He has a right to be. If his mom was half as great as you've described, it must have been devastating."

"It's important not to get stuck," admitted David. "Grieving is a process, and we move through it, but we can't get stuck in it."

"Sounds like you have been seeing a good therapist after all," said Nicole with a slight smile.

"I guess I have learned a few things through this whole mess." Changing the subject, he asked, "So how did you learn about the position at NuKoin?"

Nicole sat back a little in her seat, ruffled her hair a little with her hand, and took a quick drink from her glass. "I had a contact that knew William DeFrost. She had done business with him at Delphi Capital and heard that DeFrost was trying—albeit unsuccessfully—to find a CFO. She made the connection, and DeFrost brought me in to see you guys for an interview."

"DeFrost has lots of shady contacts." David laughed. "Your friend was not one of those, I hope."

Nicole turned a little coy, perhaps playful. She did the duck-lips expression and said, "I cannot confirm nor deny."

David laughed and looked at the table.

Nicole let out a small grunt of a laugh and said, "I think

I've had enough to drink. I'd better be going before tomorrow's meeting becomes a struggle."

David pulled out a couple of bills from his wallet and put them on the table. Nicole objected and tried to put down some money of her own. David put his hand on hers in an effort to convince her to put her money away. When their hands touched, she stopped and seemed to recoil a bit. He pulled back his hand, perhaps too abruptly, when he realized how she had taken it. She seemed to grow suddenly distant, almost as if she had been offended by his sudden withdrawal.

Nicole quickly said, "Thank you for the drinks. I'll see you in the morning for the big meeting. Make sure you get some good rest. You deserve it."

Nicole turned to go and sauntered toward the door of the lounge. David wondered if she was deliberately walking slowly and imagined himself running after her and asking to walk her home. He imagined kissing her softly and wondered how it would feel.

David turned back toward the lounge as the door closed behind her. He sat alone at the table, reflecting on his night and wondering if he even wanted to be with another woman again. He thought about how his life had taken unanticipated twists and turns. He even spent a few minutes thinking about the meeting with the board of Delphi Capital in the morning.

He finished the last few sips of his drink and grabbed his coat before returning to the office to get his car for the short ride home to his empty house.

5

———

The next day, David arrived early, before everyone else in the office. He wanted to be able to relax with some coffee and collect his thoughts. Anticipating a battle with the board of directors, he wanted to focus.

He locked the office door behind himself since it was only 6:15 a.m. and he didn't want to deal with any visitors prior to the office officially opening. After putting his things down on his desk, he went to make some coffee.

About ten minutes later, the office door unlocked as Nicole made her entrance. He could almost hear the resolve in her footsteps as she entered the office.

"Oh, David, I saw the lights on and thought it might be you," said Nicole as she turned the corner to the kitchenette.

"I like the quiet stillness of the morning," replied David. "I made plenty of coffee, if you want some."

"Thank you, but I stopped at Starbucks on my way."

David couldn't understand America's obsession with high-priced coffee. He could understand those who went there for the ambiance and for a meeting location, but to grab an overpriced coffee to go seemed to defeat the purpose.

He returned to his office and closed the door before pulling up the presentation that he would make to the board later that morning, and he practiced his oral delivery. Over the years, he had found that the best way to feel comfortable with a speech was to practice it out loud. Only then would he know if his points flowed naturally.

At about half past eight, Thomas knocked on David's door and let himself in. "Hey, David, are you ready for this meeting?"

"We aren't in college anymore. You can't just knock and immediately walk in."

Thomas sat down in the chair opposite David's desk, turning his hips slightly to get the seventy pounds he had put on since college into the seat.

Thomas ignored David's comment and asked, "So what are you going to say to them?"

"The typical stuff: status from the developers, current risks and projections..."

"And..."

"And what?" asked David.

"The elephant in the room." Thomas laughed. "We are behind schedule, and we need more capital."

"It's Mia's job to handle the finances," replied David.

"You mean Nicole?"

"Right, Nicole. She is the CFO, so finances are her responsibility."

"Are you all right?" asked Thomas.

"I'm fine. Why, do I look sick or something?" David asked with irritation in his voice.

"You just said Mia instead of Nicole."

"Okay, I'm getting old. Parents do that—swap names when they are distracted. Give me a break."

"She's cute, David. I wouldn't blame you. No one would blame you. Half the office is hoping you two get together."

"It's barely been a year, Thomas. Show some respect."

"I didn't say you were going to marry her, just that it would be understandable for you to have feelings toward another woman. Did you notice she was cute?" Thomas chuckled.

"I think we should refrain from talking about a fellow executive of this company in those terms."

"Okay, okay. I'm just making sure you still know how to play tennis—that's all."

"I'm more than fine. I'm ready to challenge the board. This is our company. I'm not going to let some VC executive detour our vision in the name of a balance sheet."

"Ah, now there he is. I knew your passive-aggressive side would come out to play this morning. Just be careful and remember that we wouldn't have a company if that VC guy didn't have us on his balance sheet," said Thomas as he rose and left the office.

David turned toward the window and shook his head at the dilemma. He needed the very financial system that he had grown to loathe, the system that NuKoin would someday tear down. The irony was not lost on him.

At precisely 10:01 a.m., deliberately one minute late, David made his way down the hallway to the large conference room. Nicole and Thomas were already there, joined by William DeFrost, the vice president of emerging technology at Delphi Capital. David did not recognize the other person in the room.

"William, good to see you," said David as he strode

toward DeFrost, holding out his hand.

William DeFrost was in his mid-fifties but had started losing his hair many years before. He was confident, even cocky. He relished his position of power over young entrepreneurs and made sure they knew it. He really didn't need the glasses he wore on his large forehead, but he thought they projected a sense of intelligence.

"David," replied DeFrost, "I'd like you to meet Srinivas Patel, head of US operations at Danzi Consulting."

Srinivas rose and shook David's hand, smiling as if he'd known David for years.

"Where is the rest of the board?" asked David.

"They couldn't make it today, but I can fill them in on the status report later," DeFrost said as he motioned for everyone to take their seats.

Thomas decided to start the meeting off, partly because he was convinced he was the only neutral party in the room and partly because he was pretty sure those would be the last words he could squeeze in during the meeting.

"Let's do a quick review of our meeting last month and then have David and Nicole jump into the status reports," began Thomas before David interrupted him.

"Thomas, let's pause for a minute. William, can you tell us why Srinivas is joining us this morning?"

"Sure, David," replied DeFrost. "Danzi Consulting has access to some crypto developers that can help us accelerate our timeline and get the project back on track."

"Have they signed a nondisclosure agreement?" asked David.

"Yes, they have. And they are here, quite frankly, because of your growing hostility toward the progress of the development team. Srinivas has a reputation for getting the resources needed to rescue struggling delivery teams."

Thomas sat back in his chair with a slightly audible groan. Nicole looked measured, waiting for her moment of entry into the conversation. David's face grew flushed as he sat forward in his chair.

"Struggling? Interesting choice of words," David shot back. "Maybe we should first present the development status, and then we can decide if 'struggling' is the appropriate adjective."

"Actually, I'd like Nicole to go first and give us the state of the union from the financial lens," said DeFrost, glancing over at Nicole.

David mumbled under his breath and sat back in his chair. Nicole quickly fluttered her eyelids, displeased at David's tone.

"From a high level, we have spent about two hundred thousand dollars this past month: seventy-five percent in staffing costs, fifteen percent in facilities, and about ten percent in software and professional dues. That is consistent with the previous month and about a thirty-five percent increase year over year. At the current burn rate, we will need capital infusion within four months or be forced to reduce staff. By my projections, we have four to six months of solvency."

Nicole continued, "It is my recommendation that we should seek a series-B funding round for a capital infusion. We have a few offers out there, and Shenling Capital would make an enticing partner. They would bring financial stability, and they have access to development talent."

Companies like NuKoin needed money to pay their staff. Sometimes, founders could find seed money to get going, but they had to be willing to give up significant ownership rights if they wanted access to large amounts of capital. That next step was called the Series A since it was usually the first time outside investors entered the scene. If the company wasn't able to generate significant amounts of profit to get traction in their industry, further rounds of funding would be necessary. But giving away new company shares would increase the total amount of stock outstanding, causing existing shareholders to own a lower percentage of the company. This dilution required lawyers and contracts to get the original founders to go along.

DeFrost cut Nicole off. "Nicole, we've talked about this in the past. The senior partners at Delphi feel that a series B would dilute the Delphi interests. Is there something new that has happened that gives you the impression that Delphi has changed their opinion?"

Nicole's face changed from measured to irritated, making it abundantly clear that she was exercising great restraint. Deference was not in her nature, but the fact that she was new to NuKoin forced her to hesitate to share her thoughts fully.

DeFrost turned away from Nicole and toward David. "Okay, that seems to paint a pretty clear financial picture. David, can you give us the development-status summary? And maybe offer a solution that won't piss me off."

David looked at Nicole, trying to quickly gauge whether she would support him if he thought quickly on his feet. Nicole had a good poker face, but David knew she was very angry.

"Development has made excellent progress this past month. We have fixed two hundred fifty software defects and completed just under one hundred programming tasks. We remain on track to release our alpha version within forty-five days."

In software development, computer code needs to be rigorously tested to make sure no hidden flaws exist. If hackers can find even one loophole, they can exploit it to produce havoc in unforeseen ways. Alpha testing, named after the first letter of the Greek alphabet, is done without releasing the code to external users. Beta is the second letter, and it refers to testing with small numbers of external users.

DeFrost looked up from his notes with a pained look on his face. "Last month you said you were sixty days from alpha, and that was thirty days ago. Help me understand how sixty minus thirty equals forty-five."

"This is complex software, William. Accuracy is more important than releasing code. One major defect exploited could bring about the end of the company. As you are supposed to know, we are following the agile delivery model. Timelines are estimates—you know that. We prioritize the work every two weeks and re-estimate accordingly."

"And in the agile delivery model, the business customer —which seems to be me, since no one else is paying the bills —decides when to release. Am I correct?" argued DeFrost.

"There are several people who are the stakeholders that agree on the release dates," countered David.

"So are we going to vote on a code-release date, then?"

David closed his eyes and shook his head back and forth ever so slightly in disgust.

"David, releasing code is how we make money. Not releasing code is how we run out of money. You might not remember, but Delphi Capital exists with the fundamental goal of making money," DeFrost said in a condescending tone.

David was about to escalate the discussion, but a glance from Thomas and Nicole made him hesitate long enough that DeFrost continued.

"Mr. Patel is here at my request so we can discuss

bringing on additional development talent to deliver a product to market in fifteen days."

"Fifteen days? Did Mr. Patel provide that estimate, or did you give it to him?" asked David in an irritated tone.

"Mr. Patel has the experience and resources necessary to do whatever we ask him to do," said DeFrost, motioning for his consultant to begin his sales pitch.

"Danzi Consulting has a proven track record of providing high-quality development resources that will work round the clock—" said Srinivas Patel before David cut him off.

"Well, that's a relief. I thought you were offering teenagers from Bangladesh that would be working one-hour shifts."

"Let's keep racism to ourselves," said DeFrost.

"It's not racism at all. I don't care where any bad developer comes from—I will treat them with equal disdain. Tell me, Mr. Patel, what experience in blockchain do these developers have?" said David, speaking of the technology that allowed cryptocurrency networks to remain secure and private.

"We have a vast global network of blockchain developers, some of whom are active developers on the bitcoin core and ethereum opensource projects," said Srinivas, referring to two major blockchain development efforts and attempting to impress David.

"Did DeFrost tell you that NuKoin was a custom build and that we did not use any existing core product like bitcoin or ethereum?"

"Yes, but I did not need him to tell me, because I've seen your code," answered Srinivas.

"You showed him our code?" yelled David.

Nicole and Thomas rose and moved their chairs closer

to David in an effort to calm him down.

"We signed a nondisclosure agreement, David. There is no cause for concern," said Srinivas.

"DeFrost already said that. NDAs don't matter when you are stealing someone's ideas," retorted David. "This was not your code to share, William."

"I beg to differ. I bought your code when I invested in your company. You conveniently forget about that fact. And unless you shut your mouth and open your ears, selling that code might be our only source of revenue left."

David was fuming. NuKoin was his company, his baby. He had personally written most of the code, but he didn't mind other developers contributing, just as long as they were qualified. He had come across many developers who lacked the skills to write complex software like blockchain. But like most good software developers, he took his code personally. He wasn't about to let any random developer help write it.

Thomas took the opportunity afforded by the silence in the room to try to defuse the situation.

"David, let's hear Mr. Patel out. If he can provide quality resumes and William is willing to pay for the extra staff, what's the harm in trying to get back on our original schedule? Today is about options, coming together as a team to address some challenges."

"You know the resume game as well as I do," said David. "Anyone can overinflate themselves on a resume."

"Then how about we get a chance to interview all potential candidates? But we can't continue to burn through our cash and expect the investors to hold back on their ideas for solutions," said Thomas.

"I can guarantee they won't let me interview the candidates," responded David.

"You are free to interview any of our candidates, just as long as you have an open mind," offered Srinivas. "I think you will be pleasantly surprised."

"I'm pretty sure your developers will never forget being interviewed by me," said David smugly.

Nicole spoke again. "I agree that we need more development staff to bring the product to market quickly, but as CFO, I need to see new cash into the equation, not just someone paying for staff with a different income stream. This does not change our cash flow, so I fail to see how it is a solution. I still recommend additional outside funding."

David rose from the table and went to the back of the room to pour himself some water. He stood staring at the wall with his back to the group then took a long drink, consuming half the glass. After a ten-second pause, he finished the water in three short drinks. He thought about the plan they'd had prior to the meeting and decided the time had come to call an audible. He returned to his seat at the table and opened his folder.

"William, I'd like to present something to you that I have been working on," said David in a calm tone. "I'd like you to have that same open mind that I was asked to employ a few moments ago. I'd also like to ask Mr. Patel to leave the room for a little bit while we discuss an internal matter."

DeFrost motioned to Srinivas to step outside the room. Once the door closed, David began. He passed out a printed PowerPoint presentation to each person in the room.

"Gentlemen," David started with an accidental snub to Nicole, "NuKoin is a cryptocurrency that is ready for an initial coin offering. We are unique. We are timely. We are ready for the publicity."

David paused to take in the initial reactions and read his audience. "The ICO is the proven path for a blockchain company to raise capital. I am proposing we issue one hundred million coins. We retain half for future use and release fifty million coins for the ICO. Of that fifty million, ten million goes to Delphi Capital as recognition of their series-A investment and to give them an immediate return on that investment. Two million coins go to Thomas, two million to me, and one million to Nicole. We use five million coins to distribute to the rest of the current employees, commensurate with their years of service and job titles at NuKoin. We still have plenty of coins for future staff incentives, and that leaves thirty million coins for a public ICO.

"We set the initial price at five dollars per coin times thirty million coins, with a target raise being one hundred fifty million dollars. That will give the company plenty of cash. But we lock up the funds in a smooth monthly release of five million dollars per quarter over seven and a half years. This gives us a steady income and prevents the distractions of fundraising. This will free us up to develop the industry-standard product."

David paused again to let all the numbers soak in. DeFrost looked intoxicated with Delphi's fifty-million-dollar take, and David wondered what DeFrost would personally make from the deal.

Nicole looked like a deer in the headlights, caught off guard by a financial proposal she'd been assured by David he would not present. Thomas just shook his head at David slowly like a principal scolding a schoolboy. David was clearly the risk taker of the group.

"David, this is a complex proposal that you probably should have shown me ahead of time," said Nicole diplomatically. "Then I could have offered a perspective as the CFO."

DeFrost did not seem to notice the internal office strife as he flipped through the two-dozen pages of the proposal. "Interesting idea. Can't say I hate it. I'd like to bring this back to our boys and see what they think," said DeFrost. "In the meantime, it looks like you need some extra help after all. You still need to get to market soon, regardless of the funding source."

David moaned. Nicole let the corners of her mouth reveal a slight smile of amusement.

Thomas let out a little laugh and said, "He got you there, David."

"So we have three proposals," Thomas said. "William proposed using Danzi to help with development off the NuKoin books. Nicole proposed a series B with Shenling Capital, who would also contribute development resources. David proposed an ICO and giving the development team the time they need to go to market."

"Proposal four is we do the ICO and use the money to hire Danzi," DeFrost shot back.

"All three of you need to treat this project with respect. We cannot hire some commodity programmers and expect them to produce quality work," said David loudly.

"David, you are crossing the line and are in danger of losing your seat at this table," said DeFrost in an escalating tone and volume. "You better dial it down in a hurry, or you will find yourself forcibly removed from this room."

"Is that a threat?" asked David.

DeFrost pressed the intercom button, which summoned a security guard to the room in just a few seconds. "David, I am going to need you to take a day off. We can touch base in a couple of days when you've calmed down and have realized the wisdom of what has been said today."

"I don't need a day off," answered David.

DeFrost motioned to the security guard, who inched closer to David. Taking his cue, David went silent and exited the room. He got his things from his office, including his laptop, and left for the day. Instead of going home, he drove near Fenway Park and walked to the Charles River, where he spent several hours staring at the water and reflecting on his life and the future of NuKoin.

David might not have been an accounting major, but he knew a thing or two about finances. His mind wandered as he thought of Mia and some of the various financial conversations they used to have.

"We both agreed that it was a good idea for me to get a job. Why the sudden change of heart?" Mia had asked one time.

"I don't object to you working. You just seem different now," replied David.

"If by 'different' you mean confident and feeling productive, then maybe change is good."

"Mia, that's not fair. You know that I have always supported you. I've even helped watch Owen when you've gone out of town on business trips. I just mean that sometimes you seem aloof and unable to leave your work when you get home."

"We agreed that when Owen got older, I would get back into the workforce, and we knew that would mean adjustments for all of us."

"You're right, but maybe this particular job isn't the best choice. You seem physically and mentally drained."

As David returned from his daydream, he regretted that these conversations with Mia had devolved into arguments on too many occasions. What he wouldn't have given for another chance to speak with her, just one last time...

6

David had decided to sleep in, so he did not set his alarm clock. But Lucie didn't get the memo and jumped up into his bed promptly at seven. When David did not stir, she let out a little muffled bark to tell him she was there. David knew the tricolor beagle would start howling if he did not acknowledge her.

"Lucie, your brother Owen is in the room right down the hall. I think he might want to take you out this morning," mumbled David. But he knew his quest for sleep was over.

David got out of bed and threw on some sweatpants. He wandered down the hallway toward the kitchen with Lucie faithfully wagging her tail and following near his feet. David opened the kitchen door to the backyard and let her outside. Despite his current attempt to miss the sunrise, David actually enjoyed the quiet of the early morning.

He turned on the Keurig to make himself some coffee then went to the freezer to get a bagel. He was surprised to hear noises from the living room.

"Owen, what are you doing awake already?" asked David, puzzled.

"This is just like old times, Dad. I get you to myself for the whole day. I wanted to capitalize on it just in case something happened at your work and they called you back in after all."

"I'm pretty sure they won't do that," chuckled David. "I think they will be happy to not have me around for a couple of days."

"Did you throw any punches?" Owen laughed.

"No, I didn't throw any punches. I just got a little energetic—that's all."

"Was it like that time at my soccer game when you fought the parent from the other team?"

"I did not get into a fight with another parent. He was the one arguing with the referee. I just reminded him that he should direct his passion toward cheering for his team and not to direct his energy toward our side of the crowd."

"AJ's mom said you told the guy if he had something to say to you that he should come over and say it to your face like a man." Owen laughed.

"I don't think I said it exactly that way," murmured David. "Besides, I helped him. People think they can say and do whatever they want, no matter how it affects someone else. I was just giving him a life lesson."

Owen laughed and sat down at the breakfast table. David made a second bagel for Owen, and they chatted about sports. In moments like these, David wondered why he didn't do this more often.

When they finished their meal, they shifted topics to the computer project. They made a list of some of the specifications for what they would need to build the computer. Then they went their separate ways to shower and get ready to go shopping. David was intent on making good on his promise to build a computer with his son.

As Owen climbed into the passenger seat, David started the car and backed out of the driveway. They headed west on Storrow Drive, along the banks of the Charles River. The sun was at their backs, and the world seemed to glow in the morning sunlight.

David loved Boston—so much history and tradition, a proud town that had overcome many challenges. He made a couple of turns and headed down Commonwealth Avenue as his thoughts turned to 2013 and the Boston Marathon bombing. Mia had been running that year and was stopped with the other runners just outside the downtown area. As he drove past the finish line, he saw the place where he'd been waiting for Mia when the two explosions went off. Like thousands of other spectators, he fled into the mall at the base of the Prudential Center. Two terrifying hours had gone by before he was sure she was okay.

David slowed the car as they approached Fenway Park, the home of the Boston Red Sox. Owen had been only five years old when David and Mia took him to his first Major League Baseball game. They had grandstand seats for the Red Sox and the Kansas City Royals, but they decided to try sitting in some empty seats near the field, hoping no one came and kicked them out. They had to move a couple times but ended up sitting in the ninth row behind the third-base dugout. At Fenway Park, the visiting team sits behind third base, unlike most baseball fields, so they could see straight into the Red Sox bench across the field. Between innings, some of the young kids would run down the aisles past them to try to get a player to give them a baseball as a souvenir as they left the field of play.

Finally in the seventh inning, Owen was the first one

down the aisle as he waited for the Royals' outfielder to come in from the field. A nearby fan lifted him up onto the dugout and told him to wave his arms. Owen, dressed in all red clothing and a bright red ball cap, did jumping jacks on top of the dugout, begging for the ball. The ball was tossed to him, and the entire section stood and cheered. Owen had returned to the seats, smiling ear to ear.

David smiled thoughtfully as he remembered that moment and many others at Fenway Park over the years. The poignant feeling evoked both the happiness of memories with his son and also sadness, as the image of Mia appeared in each scene.

They turned left down Brookline Avenue and headed out of town toward the computer-parts store. David looked over at his son, who seemed lost in his own thoughts. *Where have the years gone? Wasn't it only yesterday that Owen was just a little boy?*

David eased the vehicle to a stop and turned into a strip mall before parking in front of the Brookline branch of Computer Warehouse. He met Owen by the back of the car and put an arm around his son. "Ready to build the mother of all computers?"

"Let's do it," replied Owen.

They entered the store and paused just inside the door to take in the sales configuration. Owen used a quick nod to direct his father toward the back of the store, where they found rows of parts in aisles clearly marked at the end caps.

"Ok, Son. First step is to find the motherboard," announced David. "Everything else is determined by that one decision."

After they had been looking silently at the stacks for a few minutes, a salesperson came over. "May I help you with anything?"

"Sure. My son and I are building a computer, and we want it to be really powerful. Do you have any suggestions?"

"Sure, we have all sorts of custom bundles. May I ask what you will be using the computer for?"

"Gaming and some advanced programming," replied David.

"We'd like to mine bitcoin," Owen chimed in with a smirk.

Both David and the salesperson rolled their eyes.

"Well, I would suggest you look at our gaming bundle, then," said the salesperson, directing them to a display in the middle of the store. "The modern computer games require a very fast graphics card and the internals that complement that kind of graphics manipulation. And it just so happens that the video cards are really good at mining bitcoin."

David and Owen read the brochures and display information, soaking in all the various options and price points.

"The advantage of selecting one of our bundles is not only a package discount, but we've also made sure that the parts are compatible with one another," explained the salesperson.

"Where's the fun in that?" David laughed. "When I was a kid, we had to do all that research on our own!"

"I suspect it will be much more fun for your son when you finish the project and it actually works," the salesperson said in a sarcastic tone.

David stood for a moment, contemplating whether he needed to teach the young salesperson a life lesson, but a vision of the soccer-field incident came flooding back. He looked at Owen and winked while saying to the salesperson, "Thank you, sir. I think we'll look on our own for a bit."

The salesperson took his cue and returned to the front of the store, where he helped another customer.

"Dad, I like this one, but is it too expensive?"

"Let me worry about the cost. This is a memory-building moment."

David went to get a shopping cart, while Owen started making a pile of boxed computer parts. When David returned, they gently placed all the small boxes inside the cart and proceeded to the front of the store to pay. The clerk at the checkout register started ringing up the parts: motherboard, memory, hard drive, power supply, CPU, and a bunch of other things that pushed the grand total to just under nineteen hundred dollars, including tax.

David pulled out his wallet and produced nineteen one-hundred-dollar bills. The clerk looked confused and asked, "You're paying with cash?"

"That is how you pay for things," replied David.

"Most people use a credit or debit card, sir."

"I prefer good old-fashioned dollar bills, which is still the legal currency in the USA, last time I checked."

"I am going to have to check with my manager," said the clerk as he pressed a switch that caused the giant number two above their heads to start blinking.

David read aloud from one of the bills in his hand, "This note is legal tender for all debts, public and private." He was speaking to the clerk but was being ignored.

The manager came over, and the clerk filled him in on the situation. Turning to David, he asked, "Sir, where did you get all that money?"

"Well, I have this pretty cool job, and each week, they pay me for all my work from the previous week. Then I go to the bank and cash my check, and they give me these," said David, holding up the one-hundred-dollar bills.

"Sir, we don't take cash for purchases this large," explained the manager.

"And why is that?" asked David.

"We have to protect ourselves against counterfeit money and people involved in illegal activities," said the manager.

"Okay, I don't want to get upset or cause a scene here, but I am positive that there are no laws or requirements or restrictions on cash transactions under ten thousand dollars. And I am also positive that the one-hundred-dollar bill is less susceptible to counterfeiting than the twenty-dollar bill, which I'm guessing you do take. I know these things because my lawyer has helped me in situations similar to these in the past. He's a really nice guy, but I don't think you want to meet him," said David with a smile.

The manager did not respond but only grabbed a detector pen from beside the cash register. He took the nineteen bills from David and took his time, marking each bill with ink that would reveal whether the money was counterfeit. After five minutes of silence, he turned to his clerk and said, "It's fine. Finish the transaction."

David said, "Thank you, sir."

The manager and the clerk said nothing in response.

Relishing his passive-aggressive victory, he said in a cheerful tone, "Have a great day, guys. Thanks for your help today."

As they were driving away from the store, Owen asked his father, "Did you really have to do that? Would it have killed you to use a credit card?"

"I don't have a credit card, Owen. I am off the grid!" said David in a triumphant tone.

"You get points toward airline flights or even cash back.

It's the latest rage," said Owen with his own dose of sarcasm.

"If you only knew. Everything you do online, everything you buy, everywhere you go. All of it is stored and sold on the internet. Companies buy all this data and use it to track you and market to you. And the government uses it to spy on your every move. It's out of control. And besides, the government is the one that issued the cash, so why is everyone so afraid of using it?"

Owen said nothing for a few minutes before he chuckled aloud. "That was pretty funny, I have to admit. Would you really have called your lawyer?"

"No, I don't even have a lawyer," said David with a laugh. "Having a lawyer would put me right back on that grid."

"So why use a computer at all if you want to stay off the grid?" asked Owen.

"You just have to know how to set the computer up— that's all. We can install software that will make you anonymous and make it impossible for anyone to know who you really are," bragged David. "You could create a secret code name... Maybe we could call you DragonLord... Have you heard of cookies?"

"Yeah, of course. Websites use cookies to remember information about their customers. They are tiny little files on your computer that are created by websites so that the next time you visit, they know your preferences. But what's the big deal if only the website that created the cookie can read the information inside of it?"

"That's a great question, DragonLord... The websites sell that cookie data to companies called data aggregators. Then the data aggregators sell marketing information to other companies. Since they get all sorts of information from lots of websites, they have a complete profile on just about everyone that uses the internet. They know what you buy and the articles you read. They know if you are liberal or conservative, Democrat or Republican. They link to your social-media sites and know who you are friends with and what opinions you have on all sorts of topics. Since you tag your friends' faces on social media, they even know what you look like, and they get your voice profile from your videos. Then they use the GPS data to know where you travel, where you work, and where you live. It's not that any one company is necessarily doing bad things by using cookies, but the data aggregators have collected it all in one place."

"But how can they sell your data without you giving consent?" protested Owen.

"You gave consent," responded David. "Remember all those terms of service and privacy links? Did you ever read one of those?"

"One or two. They all seem the same and super long."

"That's their goal—hundreds of pages of boring and confusing legal speak. But buried deep within the document, you are signing away the rights to all of your information," explained David. "Even the pictures you post to your social media sites are owned by them. You can delete them if you want, but they still keep them. And if you read the terms of service, they can do whatever they want with your pictures and the information you shared."

Owen was shaking his head silently, so David continued, "Take a second to think about all the information that could be gleaned from your social-media posts. Remember those questions websites ask you if you forget your password and you want to reset it? Well, hackers have written programs that can search all your social-media posts and determine the most likely answers to common security questions. And since most people use simple passwords, they have programs that can guess those too."

"Dad, that can't be legal," Owen protested.

"Well, the hacker part isn't legal. But do you think for a moment that the government isn't watching your every post? Thousands of computers are running algorithms twenty-four hours a day, trying to predict the next terrorist or tax evader."

"But if that's what they have to do to keep us safe, it doesn't seem so bad," reasoned Owen. "Besides, most people are honest, and it shouldn't affect them."

"I actually agree with you if the information is only used for public safety, but it never stops there. Throughout history, people have used whatever they can to exploit other people. All this data will be used to exploit people, and someone is going to get rich doing it."

David pulled into the driveway and parked. They took turns bringing in loads of computer parts and placing them in the middle of the living-room floor. After David got a few bags of potato chips and a couple sodas, they set to work, building the computer.

David showed his son how to use small computer tools and how to make sure he was grounded from electricity before touching the sensitive parts. Occasionally, they would watch a YouTube video if David wasn't sure about one of the more modern installation techniques.

After about four hours, they had nearly completed the machine and sat back to admire their accomplishment.

"Dad, why is there so much extra space inside the computer tower?"

"They give you space for expandability. Extra memory or hard drives, whatever you want," said David. "Hey, I have an idea. Where is that old desktop computer your mother had before she got her laptop?"

"I think it is still in the basement closet."

"Go get it and bring it upstairs. We can try taking some parts out of it and putting them into this new computer. We can even use an extra hard drive for a backup," said David.

While Owen went downstairs, David's phone rang. He looked at the caller ID and decided to take the call. Owen came upstairs, talking to his father, unaware he wasn't listening. Owen's face fell as he realized his father was talking business, but he decided to use the opportunity to try the installation himself.

Owen felt he had learned enough during the day to find the hard drive in his mother's old computer and remove it. He found the slot in the new machine for the second hard drive and screwed it into place.

His father finished his call and came over just in time to witness Owen turning on the machine for the first time. They both let out a cheer when the monitor displayed various installation information across the screen.

"We did it, Dad!"

For the rest of the afternoon, the two installed various software programs on the computer. David made good on his promise to make the machine appear anonymous on the internet by installing various free computer programs with which he was familiar. He showed Owen each software tool and explained how it worked as they used pizza to fuel themselves late into the evening.

"Dad, what about the old hard drive I installed while you were on the phone? Can we check that out? I want to see if I installed it correctly."

David finished a few bites of a pepperoni slice and opened the file-management program. He navigated around and finally announced, "Yup, it looks great. It's not that large, but we can use it as a backup drive for pictures or something. It doesn't have much free space left, so it is probably better if we just reformat the drive and start over."

"We can't just delete all Mom's old files. What about all the pictures and other valuable stuff?" protested Owen.

"Buddy, if we haven't needed it up until now, we probably don't need it at all. That old computer hasn't been turned on for a long time."

Owen scanned through folders and files, reading names aloud to prove that something valuable could be on the computer. They spent the next couple of hours reading old word-processing projects from Owen's childhood and looking at various photo downloads from an old Nikon point-and-shoot camera.

"What are DAT files?" asked Owen.

"It's a generic file extension that just means it contains data. It could be a text file or some other file that only the software that created it can understand," explained David. "Why do you ask?"

"What's this wallet.dat file? It's kind of small, but it sounds important for something," said Owen. "Wallet for what, though?"

"Let me see that," snapped David as he took control of the mouse.

David opened the file, but it contained all sorts of random characters and symbols. "It's in binary format. It's not a text file. If I didn't know where this hard drive came from, I would have told you it might be a..."

"Might be a what?"

"Might be a bitcoin wallet," David answered with a blank stare.

"Mom had a bitcoin wallet?" asked Owen with a laugh. "That's awesome."

"Don't get carried away. Let's see if I can download a bitcoin wallet application and try to import it. At least then we will know if it really is legit."

"What's a wallet application?"

"Every cryptocurrency has the concept of a wallet where users store their encryption keys. We're going to use the wallet application to simply verify whether it is indeed a bitcoin wallet."

David tapped on the keyboard in silence and started up the software. He went to the menu and selected Import Wallet Address. He pointed the software at the wallet.dat file, and a message appeared: Validating... After a few moments, another message appeared: Enter Passphrase.

"Oh my God," said David as he tried to enter the passphrase. Several times, an error message appeared, telling him the passphrase was invalid. He tried "David"... "Owen"... "Mia"... "NuKoin"... "Lucie"... He tried birthdays and anniversaries. He tried nicknames, old addresses, and even phone numbers. After about ten minutes, he sat back from the keyboard and let out a sigh.

"It appears to be a real bitcoin wallet, but we need the passphrase to open it," said David. "And unless we somehow guess what it is, this file is useless to us."

"How much bitcoin is in there?" asked Owen.

"The easiest way to get that information is to open the wallet, but the timestamp on the file is from early 2012." David gasped. "Which means..."

"Which means what?" asked Owen nervously.

"Which means it might be a lot of bitcoin," replied David. "Bitcoin was pretty obscure back then. No one really paid serious attention to it. Some people tried to just hack around and collected thousands of bitcoin, which they forgot about. Then they find the old files, and boom, they're millionaires."

"Millionaires?" asked Owen. "Seriously?"

"Yeah. Back then, one bitcoin was worth less than a penny. If you had a thousand bitcoin, it would be worth less than a hundred dollars. And that's only if someone would actually give you a hundred dollars for it," explained David. "It was quite common for people to just forget about it. Kind of like old baseball cards that turn out to be valuable."

"Bitcoin is worth almost ten thousand dollars each. That same one thousand bitcoin would be worth ten million dollars today!" said Owen with excitement in his voice.

David was silent for a few moments before he responded. "Your mother never told me she had bitcoin, so I suspect it was not a lot. But like I said, we're never going to find out because we don't have the passphrase."

"Why do you keep saying 'passphrase' instead of 'password'?" asked Owen.

"When people think passwords, they usually think small words. You'd be surprised at how many online banking passwords are things like 'password1' or 'bank123'. Don't even get me started on people using the same password for multiple websites," said David with an eye roll. "Passphrases are much longer, like sentences. They are much harder for hackers to guess because they are so long but easy for people to remember because they are sentences."

"You're telling me that we're never going to guess the passphrase because it's too long?" Owen asked in a dejected tone.

"Yes and no. Since we knew your mom really well, it's possible we could guess the phrase unless she used some clever substitutions—for instance, changing all the letter *E*'s to threes, or using an eight instead of the letter *B*."

"Okay, then we could figure this out. We could unlock this bitcoin wallet," said Owen hopefully.

David was not convinced. He had lectured his wife many times on the topic, causing her to be more cautious with her online activities. Mia would not have made the passphrase easy to guess. On the other hand, that was back in 2012, and she might not have been taking bitcoin seriously back then. She might have used a simple passphrase.

As he looked at Owen's face, he realized that Owen needed to try. He needed this reconnection with his mother. But he was also concerned that giving Owen false hope might reopen an emotional wound.

"Owen, this is a long shot—a really long shot. I don't want you to be disappointed," said David.

"Dad, I'm fine... I just want to give it a try for a little while. This is just like one of those riddles Mom used to tell me. It's almost like she sent me one last riddle to figure out."

David nodded his head and gave his son a pat on the back. "I'm headed to bed, buddy. How about you?"

"Yeah, that sounds good. Thanks for spending time with me today, Dad. It was really fun."

David walked back to his son and gave him a hug. "Me too, buddy. I love you."

"I love you too, Dad."

David walked to the stairs, smiling. He got halfway up before he realized Owen wasn't following him. He could hear Owen in the kitchen tapping on the keys, talking quietly under his breath.

"Lights out in fifteen minutes, okay, buddy?" David called down the stairs.

"Okay, Dad."

7

Tina Wood woke a little late the next morning, so she pulled her long brown hair into a single pony-tail as she headed to her meeting with her boss, Jack Dougan. Her commute to the office was usually about nine minutes, five of which took place waiting in line at Starbucks. As she sipped her morning chai tea latte, she considered when she would get the courage to give Jack notice of her departure.

When she got to the office, Tina opened the door and greeted Maggie, the receptionist. Maggie liked to dress comfortably, which sometimes left those visiting the office a little uncomfortable. Tina was unfazed, and after a few moments of pleasantries, she proceeded around the corner and into Jack's open office door with a quiet knock.

"Good morning, Tina. Have a seat," said Jack in his booming baritone. "I wanted to talk to you about a new assignment."

The *Boston Mirror* was a small liberal news agency based in a fifteen-hundred-square-foot converted house near the sprawling Cambridge campus of Harvard University. The Mirror was privately owned and employed a graphic designer, a web developer, two editors that doubled as data-entry staff, a receptionist, and a general manager.

Of the many freelance journalists that provided content for the 250,000 online paid subscribers, Tina Wood was the writer with the best understanding of technology topics. That was a bit of a curse for Tina, and she was beginning to feel trapped in a stereotype that would relegate her to a beat writer. She had told Jack Dougan, the Mirror's general manager, that she wanted assignments with Pulitzer potential, but she was ignored. She had already begun searching for new opportunities, so she had low expectations of her meeting that morning with Jack.

Tina was twenty-seven years old and believed she was far away from that crossroads in life of choosing between a family and a career. She lived in a small six-hundred-foot apartment above one of the many small shops in Cambridge, but she rarely spent any waking hours there. She was a healthy five foot five and 135 pounds but didn't have time to visit bars or perform the flirting necessary to get many dates. She was able to blend into a crowd to avoid raising attention, but she also knew how to accentuate her figure, style her hair, or apply the required makeup when the situation required it.

She had briefly dated several men since her graduation from Emerson's School of Journalism, but her focus on a career relegated men to the role of convenient entertainment—a distraction here and a free meal there. Tina was happily single.

Tina had very few clothes and preferred the casual look of jeans and a sweater. She didn't own a car, and her most valuable possession was her laptop, which she used to create articles for the *Boston Mirror* while seated in the park or at a local coffee shop.

Jack Dougan was in his early seventies but was showing no interest in retirement. He liked to tell people that working turned his hair gray but also kept it on his head. He was no taller than five foot eight, but he knew how to command a room.

"Jack, before you talk about new assignments, I've been wanting to talk to you too."

"There will be plenty of time for that, Tina, but first, I have a story that needs to be told, and you are the perfect person to tell it."

"Jack, I need to branch out a little bit, cover some social issues that genuinely impact people's lives—right the wrongs in this world and help the little guys," said Tina with a twinge of passion in her voice.

"You don't think your stories are making a difference?" asked Jack, a bit surprised.

"Sure, if you're a hedge fund manager and need some insights into the fundamentals of the latest tech startup," said Tina.

"What about that piece you did exposing the biotech firm that was producing the defective heart valves? Or that Ponzi scheme that was preying on seniors living on Cape Cod?"

"I mean something that is more of a direct social issue, not with the technology angle," said Tina.

"Everything is technology. The whole world has got their smartphones in their faces, surfing the internet and posting the life-changing details of what they had for lunch."

"I'm serious, Jack. I didn't become a journalist to be a glorified technology waitress."

"Okay, fine. How about a missing-person story?" asked Jack.

"I'm listening," said Tina with a quiet sigh.

"A visionary with a promising future and a mind full of ideas to supplant the entire world banking system. Big money comes his way, and big money feels threatened. Then one day, he's gone."

"Interesting. Is he American or a foreign national?" asked Tina.

"No one knows," replied Jack with a dramatic and mysterious tone.

"Okay, is he short or tall?"

"Again, no one knows for sure," answered Jack.

"So if no one has ever seen him, how do they know he is missing?" asked Tina, beginning to lose interest.

"His name is Satoshi Nakamoto."

"Sounds Japanese to me," said Tina. "Yeah, I've heard the name but never paid much attention."

"It is a Japanese name, but lots of people believe it's just a pseudonym."

"You make it sound like he's some ghost or something."

"Technically, he is one of the richest people in the world," said Jack with a smile.

"Technically? He either is or he isn't," countered Tina. "Is he an arms dealer or drug trafficker or something?"

"In 2008, Satoshi Nakamoto published a paper talking about a new world currency."

"Fantastic. That street preacher over by Fenway Park was right about the end of the world, then?"

"In 2009, he launched the Bitcoin network while everyone was watching their retirement funds disappear."

"Bitcoin? You want me to write a story about Bitcoin?" Tina asked as she stood up from her chair.

"Tina, this is more than just a tech startup story with a missing founder," Jack replied. "This is global economics, money laundering, and cloak-and-dagger–type stuff."

Tina paused at the back of her chair, reflecting on his words. She shifted her weight slightly and put her coat on the back of the chair.

"And where is the Pulitzer opportunity here? A good journalist needs talent and opportunity, and I am running short on patience."

"Tina, this is big. You find out who this guy is, and this will be the story of the year, maybe even the decade," said Jack in a hushed tone. "But you'll need to be very careful, because this will involve some very powerful people."

"What kind of budget are we talking about?" asked Tina.

"Boston, New York, Washington. The usual deal. And motels are more inspirational than the Ritz."

"Last of the big spenders," mumbled Tina. "You said 'global economics,' so any chance I'm headed overseas?"

"Let's take it one step at a time. Do some research and keep checking in. But if this guy is overseas and we think we can find him, then yes, you are headed overseas," Jack promised.

Tina Wood had never really traveled abroad and only owned a passport thanks to a spring break trip to Cancun. She wasn't sure she believed Jack regarding the Pulitzer Prize potential, but the possibility of traveling on the paper's dime was a bonus. She didn't have any other jobs lined up anyway, so she decided to play along for a while and see if the story got hot.

"Okay, I'll do it."

"Great. I'll give you your first lead. The boys in Washington are really starting to crack down on bitcoin, and there is talk of new legislation being introduced. My guess is that there is a lot more motivation behind the legislation than recouping some tax revenue."

"Thanks, Jack, but I think I know how to write a story," snapped Tina as she picked up her coat and moved toward his office door. "I will check in every couple days via email as usual."

"No email this time, Tina. Let's do it verbally," said Jack, the hushed tone returning. "And in person."

"Oh right, and you should give me a burner phone so they won't be able to track me? And maybe one of those poison pills in case I get captured," replied Tina with sarcasm and a smirk.

"Tina, I'm serious about this. Watch your back. Bitcoin involves a whole lot of money," said Jack.

Tina nodded and left the office, slipping into the busy streets of Cambridge, Massachusetts. She walked a few blocks to an internet cafe and sat down to start her research into bitcoin.

8

———

David's alarm went off at precisely 7:01 a.m., triggering his normal morning routine. He was anxious to get back into the office after his involuntary three-day weekend. Lucie was stretching out in her open crate at the foot of the bed, and David waited to hear the flapping of her ears, her signal that she was ready to go outside.

He got out of bed and met Lucie at the door, giving her a rub behind the ears. They made their way downstairs and found Owen eating cereal in the pale morning sunrise.

"Good morning, buddy. You're up early today," said David.

"I wanted to make sure I had plenty of time with you this morning before you go to work."

"Sounds good to me," replied David. "How about I drive you to school so we have some extra time?"

He smiled as he let Lucie out the back door. Although he'd once hoped to have several children, now he couldn't fathom loving anyone else as much as he loved his only son.

David got a cereal bowl and joined his son for breakfast.

The two spent twenty minutes flitting from topic to topic but mostly just enjoying each other's company before getting ready to leave.

Owen climbed into the passenger seat of their Highlander, and David opened the garage door and backed out onto the street. He drove the two miles to Owen's school and gave him a goodbye fist bump.

David watched Owen enter the school before driving away, as was his habit since Owen had been in kindergarten. As David pulled away, he focused on his day at work. He had been away for only one business day, but he felt disconnected. This was his company, but he was starting to feel like he was losing control of it. This was his dream, and he felt truly great dreams deserved to be fought for.

David parked his car and made his way into the office, slightly disappointed not to be greeted by any fanfare. Everyone was busy with their tasks, and he slipped into his office largely unnoticed.

He was so anxious to check on the development team that he skipped his morning coffee. He logged into GIT, the computer source control system, where he could see all the changes in the NuKoin code. He could see the names of each developer and the specific changes they had made, and he was even able to see the velocity at which each developer was making their changes. That enabled David to keep an eye on the source code and determine who were the best developers. To change any of the critical and complicated parts of the system would require earning David's trust.

As he scanned through the system, he noticed two new usernames. He clicked into their history and saw they had made a couple of small changes to the code over the weekend. He fired off a quick message to his lead developer.

"WTH! Who are rpatel and sgungi?" David typed.

After a few minutes, a reply came back: "New guys from Danzi. Started Friday morning."

"Who gave them access?"

"Thomas."

He stewed for a couple of minutes. "How green are they?" he typed.

"Like leprechauns."

When David was about to write an angry message to his co-founder, he heard a knock at his door.

"Welcome back! How was your vacation?" asked Thomas.

"Bittersweet," said David. "Bro, why did you give access to Tweedledee and Tweedledum?"

"Did you enjoy some extra time with Owen?" replied Thomas.

"Yeah, it was great. Please don't sidestep my questions."

"The idea was that you would take a short break and relax a little bit, but you seem just as wound up as the day you left."

"Actually, I was calm as a cucumber right up until I checked the code this morning," explained David. "Not only did we let a couple new guys near the code, we actually let them submit a change request?"

"These are the guys that DeFrost was talking about, from Danzi Consulting," Thomas reminded David. "We do need the help, and they seem eager. They even worked the entire weekend, getting up to speed."

"Yeah, I can see that. I was just about to baptize them with their first code review from yours truly."

"Maybe you should have a second cup of coffee before getting yourself more forced vacation days," said Thomas with a chuckle.

"I haven't had my first cup yet," said David as he leaned back in his chair and gave a laugh of his own.

Hearing the commotion, Nicole strode through the doorway of David's office. "That's what I like to hear! The boss takes a long weekend and comes back jovial."

"It was more of a maniacal expression as I prepare to reprimand a couple of new developers," said David and let out an evil laugh.

Nicole and Thomas shook their heads.

David shrugged and said, "What? Par for the course."

Thomas and Nicole left the office as David returned to his computer, studying the coding changes from the two suspects in question. He was determined to find something to throw in DeFrost's face and get these intruders off his development team.

Even though the changes were small, David pored over the lines of code with an ultracritical eye. Very soon, he was mumbling insults at an ever-increasing volume. David submitted his many comments online then got up to find his victims.

As he made his way over to the handful of cubes occupied by the developers, several eyes looked up in curiosity. The office was not large, so he found the two newcomers easily.

"Are you the two new high-school interns?" asked David loudly.

"Hello, sir. My name is Ramesh, and this is Satish. We started on Friday and have been studying the code."

"Yes, I saw your code changes and rejected them. Did you have any experience writing code prior to coming here?" asked David in a condescending tone.

The two developers looked confused and struggled to respond.

"You must be Mr. Turner," said Satish. "Mr. DeFrost told us you would be returning to the office today. We are very glad to meet you, sir."

"You can skip the 'sir' and 'mister' stuff," replied David. "Respect is earned, not given, and I am not excited by what I see so far."

"I was just looking at your comments online for our code you rejected," said Satish. "Let me explain. We created a simple method of calculating a user's total balance from their username."

"We don't expose the username to anyone. We keep it encrypted," retorted David. "NuKoin is a totally anonymous service. The username is an internal testing feature that we do not release to the production version of the code."

"Very sorry, sir," said Ramesh. "We were just creating another testing method. This was not going to be submitted for the publicly released version."

David felt himself calming down slightly. "Then add comments indicating they are internal testing methods. And I asked you to stop calling me 'sir.'"

Faces and eyes were peering at him from cubicle walls, like gophers on the thirteenth fairway. He glared at them, and they disappeared from sight. He turned to leave and saw Nicole in her office doorway, motioning for him to come over.

"Close the door, David," said Nicole.

He came in and took a seat after closing the door with a soft click.

"You can't go around yelling at people, no matter how incompetent they may seem to you," said Nicole softly.

"Think of it like fraternity initiation," said David.

"It's more like hazing, which is cause for prosecution these days."

"Are you on DeFrost's side now? Just like you didn't have my back at the meeting last Thursday?"

"That's odd, because the story I saw unfold was you going back on everything the three of us discussed prior to that meeting," replied Nicole. "We all agreed on a strategy, and suddenly, you announced specific ICO plans."

"I had to call an audible once DeFrost threatened to bring in some development clowns," said David.

"You didn't just bring up the ICO on a whim. You obviously had been running hard numbers," Nicole shot back. "Am I not the CFO? Don't you think you should run financials by me before presenting them to the board of directors?"

"Fair point," said David. "But you should know that startups require thinking on your feet. I had to try to distract DeFrost from bringing his new team in."

"Clearly, that plan backfired," Nicole said with slight mockery.

David was silent for a few moments, watching Nicole's body language. She seemed on edge, shifting a little in her seat.

"Nicole, what's really on your mind?" asked David.

Nicole blushed a little and shot a quick glance out the window of her office door to see if anyone in the office was paying any attention to their closed-door meeting.

"David, you're sending me mixed signals," said Nicole as she focused on his eyes. "One day, we're like partners—the next day, you act like an adversary. You seemed to let your guard down with me the other night at the bar after work, but then the next day, that appeared to be a ploy to get me to lower my guard before the board meeting. Are we on the same page here?"

A lump grew in his throat as the awkwardness of her direct questions clouded his mind. Nicole was a confusing persona, causing a mix of emotions to well up within him.

"It's been a hard year. I told you that," explained David.

"Cut the crap. Seriously," snapped Nicole. "You keep flip-flopping between the hurt widower and the cutthroat businessman. Who are you? Do you even know?"

David sank back in his chair, undecided on how to react to her challenge. Part of him wanted to storm out of the room, but another part wanted to start yelling back. And the more he looked at her, the more attracted to her he became.

"Do you think you are the only one taking risks here?" asked Nicole. "I took risks coming to NuKoin. I have a career on the line here, too, you know. Do you think it was easy for me to have DeFrost come in and treat me like a child, offering up stupid solutions that distract us from the real problems?"

David was caught short. He had never considered what it must have been like for Nicole to work at NuKoin, to work with people like him. He looked at her face differently and saw some signs of strain. He saw a few wrinkles and touches of gray in the roots of her hair.

"You never once asked me how I was doing," said Nicole.

"Wait a minute. I thought the other night was you trying to cheer me up," said David.

"I'm not talking about the other night. I am talking about the entire three months that I have been working at NuKoin. Yet almost that entire time, I have been both peer and confidant to you, willing to discuss Mia, Owen, work, or whatever you needed. But at the board meeting, I realized I am nothing more than scenery along your road to success."

"Nicole, I—" David began.

"David, I don't need your apology. I need you to be consistent in what you want our relationship to be."

David was more confused than ever. Was Nicole talking about their work relationship, or was she implying she wanted more?

"I need to know we are on the same team," she said.

"Nicole, I am getting confused here. What exactly are we talking about?"

"Okay, fine. Can we agree to be candid with each other?"

David's heart rate increased, and he realized he was fidgeting.

"Let's start with these new developers. I think if we let them, they will bury themselves. Then we can use that as ammunition against DeFrost," she said, to David's surprise.

Had Nicole been talking about NuKoin business the whole time? David thought. He was thoroughly convinced he would never understand women.

"You want to help sabotage DeFrost's plan of bringing in Danzi?" David asked with a furrowed brow.

"Off the record, yes I do," said Nicole. "But you and I need to work together on this. If you keep getting in their faces and rejecting all their code, DeFrost is going to be on his guard. On the other hand, if you start playing along..."

"Tell me more."

"Then we build a case for Danzi to be removed from the project."

David was silent, soaking in Nicole's words. He'd known she was smart and tough, but ruthless was a new role for her.

"And when they are gone, what's the plan then?" asked David.

"Then we sit down with Thomas, and all three of us look at whether we get new VC funding or look at the ICO," said Nicole.

"I like it," said David, rising.

Without thinking, he approached her for an embrace, but Nicole preemptively shook his hand. Neither spoke, and he opened the door and left the office. She returned to her desk and grew busy behind her laptop. David wandered back over to his desk and looked out the window for a long period of time before firing off another instant message.

Less than a minute later, Ramesh and Satish appeared at David's door.

"Yes, sir. You asked us to come to your office?" said Ramesh.

"Guys, I want to apologize for my words earlier," said David. "I'd like you to make a few changes and resubmit your code to me. This time, I promise to work with you to make sure the changes are accepted."

"Thank you, sir," said Satish. "You will be happy, sir."

Ramesh and Satish gave each other a smile and started to leave .

David stopped them. "But, guys, you have to stop calling me sir. It makes me feel old."

9

———

Tina Wood found a seat toward the back of an internet cafe, away from the front door, where she could see every other seat in the room. She told herself that had nothing to do with Jack's admonition of caution—she just didn't like other people glancing at anything she did on the computer.

She entered "bitcoin history" into her browser search box and glanced over the first page of results. She started by reading Wikipedia, glad no one could see her screen. She would never quote it as a source, but it was useful to get the basic 101 on any subject.

She jumped from article to article in a journey back over a decade of commentary since the launch of bitcoin. She followed the bitcoin ups and downs, scribbling various names and companies in her notebook. Tina was old school, preferring to keep the time-honored journalist notes on an actual pad of paper.

After a few hours, she was distracted by a conversation across the room, where two young men were huddled together and talking quietly. The room was otherwise silent, so when Tina heard the word "bitcoin," her ears perked up. She kept her head down but focused her full attention to eavesdrop on the strangers' conversation.

They seemed to be logged into some sort of financial website and were considering making transactions.

"It's closing above the two-hundred-day moving average, indicating the bulls are in control," one of the strangers told the other.

"Do you want to do a market sell order or just add a trailing stop loss?" said the other stranger.

"Do the trailing stop in batches of ten so we don't spook the market."

"Done," came the reply after a series of short keystrokes.

One of the strangers got up and left the café, while the other lingered. Tina took her cue by ruffling her hair just a bit, applying some fresh lipstick, and unbuttoning an extra button for effect. She picked up her laptop and crossed the room.

Putting on her best Southern accent, she said to the young man, "Excuse me, do you know a lot about technology?"

The young man looked startled, a bit distracted, and at a loss for words. He wasn't used to talking to women—any females, for that matter—and glanced back and forth between his laptop and Tina.

"What do you need help with?" asked the young man.

"I'm trying to clear my browsing history," said Tina. "I don't trust that someone isn't going to hack into my computer and spy on me."

Tina put her laptop on the table and rotated it so that the young man could see her screen. The Google Chrome browser was open, and the main tab was showing the results of a bitcoin search.

"Bitcoin, huh?" the young man asked.

"Oh, that? Well, I have heard so much about it. I was thinking of getting into it myself," replied Tina.

"Cryptocurrency is not for the faint of heart," said the young man. "There is a lot of risk."

"You sound like you know a little bit about it. Are you invested in bitcoin?"

"Who are you again?" asked the young man. "I didn't catch your name."

"I'm Tina Wood, a reporter for the *Boston Mirror*, and I'm researching bitcoin and cryptocurrency."

The young man closed his laptop without saying a word and got up. He put his hoodie over his head and left the cafe. Tina watched in silence, reflecting on the interaction and wondering why the young man was so quick to avoid the discussion.

Being a journalist required her to be a student of people. Stories were all around, but one had to know which buttons to push. She had obviously pushed the wrong buttons with that young man, so she jotted down some notes in her notebook.

Tina returned to her seat across the room and researched how to buy bitcoin. She learned about the need to open an account on a cryptocurrency exchange, which was just like one of the many online stock-trading websites.

Everyone seemed to recommend creating an account on Coinabee.com, one of only a few exchanges based in the USA that allowed one to transfer US dollars from a bank account or a US-based credit card. In order to buy bitcoin, she first had to get US dollars into her exchange account, just like someone might deposit cash into their stock market trading account.

She learned that adding money by bank transfer would

take up to four business days, so she opted for the credit card route. She created a user ID and password for Coinabee, making sure not to use anything that would be connected to her journalist identity. She entered some false personal-identity information, thus beginning her own little attempt at cloak-and-dagger tactics.

She decided to pass on submitting a photo of her driver's license, which restricted her to transactions under one thousand dollars. This was acceptable to her since she really had no desire to invest more than a few dollars anyway. She finished creating her account and used her credit card to transfer two hundred dollars into her new exchange account.

"Thank you for the donation, Jack Dougan," she said with a laugh, knowing she could expense it as research costs.

After she was logged into Coinabee.com and had money in her account, she poked around the website. She read various how-to articles and navigated her way to the pages of the website where she could see the current price of bitcoin.

The Coinabee exchange allowed the owners of bitcoin to post the amount of the cryptocurrency they were willing to sell, along with a specific price. Likewise, Coinabee also allowed people that wanted to buy bitcoin to post how much bitcoin they wanted to buy and the price they were willing to pay for it. If a potential buyer and a potential seller set identical sale and purchase prices, the Coinabee exchange would initiate a transfer of bitcoin from one user to another. The buyer would then own the bitcoin, and the seller would receive a certain amount in US dollars into their account. It was pure supply-and-demand economics.

The interesting part was when a buyer wanted more

bitcoin than the seller was willing to sell or when a seller was selling more bitcoin than a buyer was willing to buy. In such cases, transactions might involve multiple buyers and sellers, with no party knowing the true identity of another.

The price of a single bitcoin was currently $11,500, so Tina knew she couldn't afford one full bitcoin with only a two-hundred-dollar investment, but she learned bitcoin could be purchased in small fragments. So she typed in an order to buy as much bitcoin as she could for two hundred dollars. She set the price she was willing to pay to $11,500 and sat back and watched her screen for a while. She saw the price of bitcoin go slightly up and then back down. After about ten minutes, she heard a ringing bell noise from her laptop, indicating that she was now the proud owner of 0.015 bitcoin. She logged off of Coinabee and returned to her research.

She decided to focus on how the government was reacting to bitcoin. Similar to other nascent technologies, very little legislative guidance on cryptocurrency existed. In bitcoin's early days, the government appeared to have taken no notice. Only when bitcoin's dramatic price increase created bitcoin millionaires did the IRS take notice.

Now dozens of politicians were posturing to form the correct opinion on bitcoin and debating whether the government should regulate or outright ban cryptocurrency trading. Some politicians were even calling for criminal investigations into Ponzi schemes and connections to organized crime.

Tina spent the rest of the day developing a list of politicians and trying to line up appointments for an interview. She couldn't seem to get past the initial phone screen, and no one seemed interested in discussing the topic with her. She couldn't tell if they were avoiding the discussion or were just unimpressed by her media credentials.

By the time her stomach grew loud enough to remind her to go home, she had only managed to obtain a single interview. She pondered whether that was worth a trip to Washington, DC, but finally decided she needed to get some traction.

Tina logged on to a discount travel website and booked a round-trip ticket from Boston to DC for the next day. The ticket was more of her budget than she wanted to spend, so she booked a room at a one-star dive to save some money. She exited the internet cafe and funneled into the busy evening rush of the streets of central Cambridge.

As she walked back toward her apartment, her mind was occupied by the mysterious man she was looking for, Satoshi Nakamoto, the creator of bitcoin. She thought about the massive amount of money surrounding bitcoin and all the financial analysts urging caution. The hype around bitcoin had even reached Capitol Hill. Maybe Jack was right and she needed to be more cautious.

Tina grew more paranoid and ducked into an alcove next to a nail salon. She pressed up against the wall and peered back toward the internet cafe. Masses of people were making their way down the street, none of which looked more suspicious than another—nameless faces, anonymous and unaware.

Tina shook her head and laughed at herself. She left the alcove and returned to the street.

Fifty yards behind her, a man dressed in a black leather coat and a baseball cap did the same thing.

10

Tina spent most of her flight from Logan Airport researching Senator Michael Cornwall, the only politician that would agree to meet with her. He was a second-term Democrat in the House of Representatives, hailing from the great state of Illinois. He was fifty-seven years old and did not have the physical charisma common to many of the power brokers in Washington.

He was married with two adult children and the son of a prominent Chicago banker. He had worked for his father for a little over a decade before moving to the suburbs and running for office. He had served a single term as a state senator before launching a well-funded campaign for the US House of Representatives.

Cornwall voted the party line on all social topics but was more of a moderate on financial issues. His negative view on cryptocurrency seemed to be a perfect marriage between conservative banking and social activism.

Cornwall was outspoken on the topic of cryptocurrency, making a name for himself as the leading contrary voice. Others in Congress showed some level of support but were cautious and measured in their approach. That made Cornwall appear to be an expert even though it was unclear if he was just among the vocal minority.

Tina pored over dozens of photos from press conferences on the courthouse steps and op-eds in the newspapers. Cornwall was the sponsor of seven different pieces of pending legislation relating to cryptocurrency and seemed to be sponsoring no other bills.

As she read, Tina became more confident that her decision to fly to Washington for a single interview was a good move. If nothing else, she could obtain additional contacts and angles for her research. In order to find Satoshi Nakamoto, she had to first understand cryptocurrency, and more importantly, she had to understand the full gravity of what was at stake to discover the players and their motivations.

Tina closed her laptop when the stewardess made the announcement of their descent into Reagan National Airport, and she looked out the window at the approaching city in the late-afternoon light. She saw the spire of the Washington Monument and the Capitol Building before gazing toward the Lincoln and Jefferson Memorials. The city was a living juxtaposition of history and progress, a magnet for those that wished to control the trajectory of American life.

The aircraft landed smoothly and taxied to the jetway. Tina and the other passengers filed out in an orderly fashion and through a series of passageways. Positioned around the corner of one corridor were uniformed men with dogs, motionless as the passengers filed past. When Tina approached the men, one of the dogs started barking. The passengers all stopped abruptly as one of the men approached Tina.

"Ma'am, would you please come with me?" asked the police officer.

"Of course. Have I done something wrong, sir?" replied Tina.

"Ma'am, just come with me, please," said the officer.

Tina followed the man through a door and into a small waiting area. Several passengers were in the room, along with a few security guards.

"Ma'am, please wait here, and someone will be with you shortly," said the officer as he left the room to return to the hallway.

Tina was eventually brought into an adjoining room, where someone was waiting to ask her some questions.

"Ma'am, are you carrying anything with you that might be of interest to law enforcement?" asked the female security officer.

"No, I don't own anything like that," said Tina.

"Anything like what?"

"Anything that would be interesting to law enforcement," replied Tina.

"Do you have any idea why the police dogs would have singled you out of the crowd?"

"I was wondering that same thing, to be honest."

"Ma'am, would it be okay if I conducted a thorough search of your person?"

"May I know why you want to search me?" asked Tina as she recalled recent media stories.

"Should I take your response as a 'yes' or a 'no'?" asked the security officer curtly.

"It was neither a 'yes' nor a 'no.' I was under the impression that the police cannot just search people randomly. Isn't that a violation of the law?"

"Ma'am, I'd like to ask you one final time whether you

are consenting to bodily search or whether you are refusing."

It took everything within Tina to hold her tongue. Having a cause was one thing, but being in jail was another. More importantly, she didn't want to be late for her meeting with Senator Cornwall.

"Yes, I will consent," conceded Tina. "It will be good for me to experience it firsthand before I submit my next article to the newspaper."

The security guard was undeterred and started her search, which was a bit too thorough for Tina's taste. When the search was complete, apparently having revealed no infractions, the security guard asked to search her carry-on bags.

"Sure. I already told you I had nothing of interest."

After a few moments, the security guard pulled a banana from Tina's purse with a look on her face like a middle-school principal finding marijuana.

"Would you like to explain this?" asked the guard.

"It's a banana. A very good source of potassium. Would you like it?"

"Ma'am, are you aware of the regulations around the transport of produce across international borders?"

"I came from Boston," said Tina with a chuckle.

"May I see your boarding pass, ma'am?"

Tina pulled out her phone and showed the security guard her flight details. The guard's face changed and looked a touch embarrassed.

"Thank you, ma'am. You are free to leave through that door. If you have any checked baggage, it will be waiting in the baggage-claim area."

"That's it? No apology for the mix-up?" Tina asked incredulously.

"Ma'am, you are free to go now. I have other passengers to check."

Tina shook her head at the woman in disgust. "I should take out my phone and record this whole sham for the world to see."

"Ma'am, the use of photography in this portion of the airport is forbidden. If you did that, your stay in this room would be much longer."

Tina was in the mood to argue, but she couldn't afford the time. "I guess my news story on this airport will have to get printed without a picture for now."

Tina grabbed her bag, made a deliberate pause to read the security guard's badge name, and abruptly left the room. She angrily made her way to the baggage claim, half hoping to find someone with whom to pick a fight. Fortunately for all of Reagan National, her bag was waiting for her on the baggage belt.

She grabbed her phone and ordered an Uber ride to the capital. Ten minutes later, she was sitting comfortably and enjoying a decrease in blood pressure. She told the driver to drop her off as close as he could to the south side of the Capitol building.

Maybe because she arrived shortly before lunch, when everyone was more interested in leaving the building than entering it, her rapid admittance through the security checkpoint both astounded her and restored her faith in authority. She wondered how security could be so different in two places run by the same government.

Tina followed the wall signs to Senator Cornwall's office. She checked in with the admin staff and was shaking hands with the senator a few minutes later.

"Would you like to take a walk and talk outside?" asked the senator.

Tina was tired but agreed. After all, he was her only contact in Washington, and maybe a walk outside would elongate the conversation.

Michael Cornwall resembled most men on the Hill, with his subdued brown hair parted on the side. He was able to hide most of his weight behind a loose-fitting white monogrammed shirt under his Armani suit. Comfortable in his uniform, he exuded confidence.

They made small talk as they walked out the front steps and found an unoccupied bench on the Mall. The air was a touch cool, but the bright sunshine and lack of wind made sitting in the warm sun enjoyable.

"So I understand you are writing an article on bitcoin?" asked Senator Cornwall.

"Yes, for the *Boston Mirror*," Tina replied.

"I haven't heard of that one, but it doesn't matter," said Cornwall. "Where are you in your research, and what is your angle?"

Tina hadn't spent a lot of time around politicians, but even she knew that she should never play all her cards at first, especially around people that made a living at posturing.

"There is a lot of hype around bitcoin, and not everyone seems to agree whether it is good or bad," said Tina. "I would like to help educate consumers as to the risks and opportunities."

"That story has been written a hundred times already, so let me save you the trouble," said the senator. "Bitcoin is a Ponzi scheme that attracts tax evaders and organized crime. It's a mobster's dream and a sex trafficker's visa. If you really want a story, then write about that. Or write about the death of bitcoin because I'm going to kill it."

"Okay, that's quite a mouthful. Can we discuss that one

phrase at a time?" asked Tina, trying to appear as impressed as she could. She knew the trick to get information from men was to play to their need to be admired. That was especially true when women were the ones admiring.

"You called it a Ponzi scheme. Why is that?"

"Bitcoin is nothing. It's like air. A couple of bits and bytes stored on a computer with a bunch of people scrambling to own it. What exactly do they own? Bitcoin's price is based on nothing but propped-up demand."

Tina made a thoughtful look, and the senator continued.

"It's like any pyramid scheme: the people who get in early make a ton of money, and the people that get in late lose all their money. Everyone is speculating right now that the price will keep going up. The only way for that to happen is for more people to buy into the pyramid. Eventually, there is no one left to buy in, and the price will drop. As more people grow weary of the empty promise, the price will drop faster. This will accelerate and end with a mighty crash. People will get hurt and lose their savings, and then they will expect the government to rescue them."

"What would you say to those that say that bitcoin is about pure supply and demand, free from government intervention?" asked Tina.

"I would say that the only people concerned with government intervention are those involved in activities that would land them in jail. If you have nothing to hide, then why are you trying to conduct your financial affairs in anonymity? And listen, it's not just bitcoin. There are hundreds of other so-called cryptocurrencies out there. Any twelve-year-old with a computer can create a new 'currency' and sell it to people."

Tina feigned surprise at his sarcasm, and Cornwall took the bait.

"It's just like it was back in the dotcom bubble, where you just put 'dot com' at the end of your company name, and suddenly your stock price jumps five hundred percent in a day. This time, however, it is worse, because the SEC is not able to step in and stop the nonsense. Not yet, anyway.

"People see some new crypto coin and they speculate, buying millions of them. The price jumps up, and someone makes a ton of money, but everyone else loses money, because it is based on nothing. Companies are using the initial coin offerings as a way to bilk money from the common investor. No regulation, no rules. No rules, and we have chaos and carnage. Everybody complains about government regulation until they need it."

"Senator, I have done some research, and many people are pointing out that the US dollar is also based on nothing. They argue that prior to 1971, when the dollar was based on gold, it had intrinsic value—but not any longer," said Tina. "These people claim that crypto is no different than government-issued currency, which also relies on everyone in the system believing it has real value."

"I categorically reject that line of thinking," Cornwall blurted. "The US dollar is the legal tender of the land and is backed by the good faith and promise of the world's only superpower. We have the FDIC, we have the Fed, and we have the central banks. We have hundreds of economists watching every aspect of the economy."

"Watching or manipulating?" Tina said before she had a chance to stop herself.

"Sounds like you've been reading the wrong blogs, young lady," chirped Cornwall.

"I take exception to the age-discrimination reference, Senator."

"I take exception to your ignorance. Do you even remember the recession of 2008? Perhaps you were too young... What happened when the government sat back and let people invent new and crazy ways to invest? The whole system almost collapsed, and everyone needed a bailout. Do you think it is the interest of the nation to allow unregulated investments again?"

"Senator, begging your pardon, but wasn't the manipulation of the investment world the very cause of the 2008 crisis? Bitcoin was literally born in 2009 as a potential solution to the inevitable evils of centralized power."

"2008 was about innate greed and rampant speculation on risky investments. Cryptocurrency takes both those traits to a whole new level," said Cornwall.

The senator glanced at his watch, and Tina decided to switch the focus of the conversation to avoid having the interview end early.

"Okay, that makes sense," Tina lied. "Getting back to your original statement, why do you say crypto investors are tax evaders? Is that because these people are anonymous?"

"See, that's the funny thing. The crypto millionaires think they are anonymous, but we just obtained thousands of transaction records going back five years. Now, we have a link between real people and their capital gains. So yes, they are evaders, but they will soon be former tax evaders."

"So why go after the crypto exchanges for that information? Wouldn't you be able to get the same records from the banks as money is moved in and out of the crypto markets?" asked Tina.

"No, because these crooks use one coin to buy another and then that new coin to buy still another. Every time they trade those coins, it is a taxable event, but almost no one is paying taxes. Hundreds of thousands of people are making investment gains and hiding it from the government," said Cornwall. "They think because they are not moving it in and out of a bank account that no one needs to worry about it. They could not be more wrong."

"Wait, so if someone buys bitcoin for a hundred dollars then uses that bitcoin to buy some other crypto coin, they need to pay taxes? Isn't that kind of like saying if you go to an arcade and buy tokens that you should pay tax when you finish playing the video game?" asked Tina.

"If the value of arcade tokens went up and down and they could sell those arcade tokens for more than they paid, then yes, it is a taxable event," explained Cornwall. "The bitcoin price changes constantly. If they sell it for more than they paid, they must pay a capital gain."

"My understanding is that some crypto traders move in and out of thousands of positions every day. Is it reasonable to expect people to track all that information?"

"If you want to be a day trader, you need to keep records and pay your tax," stated Cornwall.

"Senator, what would happen if someone paid for goods or services using a cryptocurrency? I have read that in places like San Francisco, they are doing that very thing. These people are not really selling their coins, they are using it to buy something."

"Same rules as when they donate stock. The price of the security at the time of sale is used to calculate the cost basis for the investment."

"That sounds complicated," said Tina.

"Tax evasion is a complicated business."

"Okay, you also said it was the tool of organized crime for mobsters and sex trafficking."

"I did not actually call it that, but I might borrow that phrase from you going forward," said Cornwall with a smile. "Organized crime loves dealing in nontraceable payment structures. They used to use bags of cash for its fungibility, but now they use cryptocurrency."

"Fungibility?"

"Fungibility means that the receiver of the asset has no knowledge—or need to know—where it came from. Say a drug dealer goes and buys a hamburger, and he gives ten dollars at the counter to pay. The owner of the burger joint does not know that the ten-dollar bill was received from a sale of drugs. He only knows that ten dollars is what he got for giving a guy a burger. That's fungibility. The sin is in the use of money, not money itself."

"Kind of like saying it's not guns that kill people?" asked Tina with a smirk.

"Have you heard of Silk Road?" asked Cornwall, ignoring the gun-control remark.

"Yes," answered Tina. "A big sting by the government on an online drug marketplace."

"You're damn right it was big," thundered the senator. "So the drug dealers get smart, and they start selling drugs online instead of on the streets. All the money changes hands using bitcoin instead of bags of cash. Tons of illegal and potentially life-ruining narcotics, all anonymously sold over the internet. If it weren't for bitcoin, none of that would have taken place."

"Why point the finger at bitcoin, though? If you wanted to stop the sale of drugs over the internet, why not just limit the use of the internet?" Tina managed to say with a deadpan delivery.

"Don't be stupid, lady," said Cornwall. "That's like blaming the Department of Public Works for creating the road that allowed the drunk driver to cause a crash. It's totally different to hold bars accountable for selling drinks to obviously intoxicated people. That's our position on bitcoin. You cannot create a system of anonymous payments that facilitates illegal activity because of anonymity."

"But if they were anonymous, then how did you catch them?" asked Tina.

"The government has its ways," replied Cornwall with a smirk. "As I am sure you already know, all these illegal websites are run by foreign entities who care very little about the rule of law. It's all about the money. The DEA and DOJ got involved, and we followed some leads, got a few names. Then one day, someone screws up their website, and we get the IP address of the Silk Road server. It didn't take long after that to connect the dots. You know what an IP address is, right?"

"Yes. It's like a postal address for the internet. Every computer has one," said Tina. "So how did you get the people running the Silk Road website?"

"Person, you mean. Grabbed the guy at the library in San Fran. Can you believe that?" asked Cornwall. "Some guy running a multinational narcotics ring from a public library."

"So if you can track these people down, why are you so upset about cryptocurrencies?"

"Bitcoin is one thing, but there are people working on technology to thwart all attempts at gaining insight into these anonymous identities," explained Cornwall. "It is critical that the government stop all attempts to bypass the anti–money laundering rules. These so-called 'altcoins' are the new frontier of illicit activity."

"So you are saying that there are other currencies which are untraceable and truly anonymous?" Tina asked with surprise. "I know there are lots of altcoins, but why are they any different than bitcoin?"

"These computer-hacker types are constantly improving their code. They have the advantage because we have to defend against all threats, whereas they can focus on exploiting one weakness," explained Cornwall. "There are many hackers actively developing ways for their networks to be totally anonymous. That will take this to a whole new level of stupid. Then they will have untraceable bags of virtual cash."

"You use the term 'cash' as if it's a dreaded four-letter word. Would you also say you are against the use of cash?" asked Tina with a look of concern.

"On the record or off?"

"Whichever gets me your honest answer."

"Off the record, yes, I don't like cash either. Everything should be traceable. Ironically, I actually do like blockchain, which is the technology all this cryptocurrency is based on. I would be very much in favor of putting all financial trans-actions out there where everyone can see them."

"Would that include all the financial transactions made by the US government?" Tina asked wryly.

"You seem to doubt the seriousness of this crypto epidemic. What is your opinion, then?"

"I don't have an opinion. I'm a reporter. I write about facts," said Tina.

"That's a load of crap. Reporters tell whatever story will make them and their newspapers money."

"Would this blockchain show us if the US government were to send a large sum of money to a rogue government overseas? How selective is this transparency you are proposing for the blockchain?"

"Are you suggesting that the police should announce

their plans to bust up a drug cartel well in advance of the operation, in the interest of full transparency?" asked Cornwall. "I bet the terrorists would really appreciate the advance warning."

"Transparency was something you were advocating for, Senator, not me," said Tina. "I was just checking to make sure you were only talking about transparency between citizens and not on the part of the government."

"The government is of the people, by the people, and for the people. We have the best interests of the nation in mind every single day," said Cornwall.

Tina wondered if he saw the contradiction or was blind to it. She was growing to seriously dislike the man, but she needed to get some more leads.

"Senator, I really appreciate your time today. I just have one last question," said Tina, trying to turn her charm back on. "You mentioned earlier in our conversation that you were trying to kill Bitcoin. Could you explain what you meant by that?"

"I would be glad to explain it," said Cornwall with a smile. His body language shifted as he returned to some common talking points. "As chairman of the Ways and Means Committee, I evaluate or propose measures relating to the taxation and revenue generation of the United States of America. Those who are blessed enough to have discretionary income with which they can invest are required to claim that income as taxable. Furthermore, it is our job to address situations where business and personal financial transactions are being conducted using an illegal form of currency.

"The US dollar is the only legal tender in this land, not cryptocurrency. Existing tokens should be taxed as securities and be subject to capital gains laws. Companies bypassing the SEC by raising capital through ICOs should and will be prosecuted."

Cornwall paused for dramatic effect as Tina waited for his conclusion, pen in hand.

"The Committee will be actively and aggressively pursuing legislation that shines an intense light on the world of so-called cryptocurrency."

"Senator, you've been very helpful. Thank you for your time today," said Tina, closing her notebook. "And any updates on apprehending the creator of Bitcoin so that they can face the punishment for their crimes as well?"

"Which creator would you be referring to?" asked the senator. "Bitcoin is open-source software, and the legal precedent for liability is not favorable to a punitive action against the software creators. There are hundreds of people worldwide that have contributed to that code."

"What about focusing on finding the original founders?"

"Satoshi?" asked the senator with a disinterested look. "Are you asking me about Satoshi Nakamoto? Don't be naive, young lady. He doesn't exist. If he did, he would have cashed in that pile of bitcoin a long time ago. The government is no longer looking for Satoshi Nakamoto."

"No longer looking? Does that mean that they were once searching for him?"

"Stick to the story of Bitcoin being a fraud," offered Cornwall. "Don't waste your time trying to figure out who the early players were."

Cornwall glanced at his watch, and his body language suddenly indicated he was ready to end the meeting. Sensing her window was closing, Tina thanked the senator for the meeting.

"It was my pleasure," responded Senator Cornwall.

They shook hands and parted ways. The senator walked to the edge of the trees, where a dark sedan was waiting. Tina watched him drive away and tried to gather her thoughts. She sat down on the bench and glanced back over her notes, considering her next steps.

Across the Washington Mall, a woman standing next to a large oak tree snapped several more photographs of Tina before dismantling her zoom lens and slipping into the milling crowds.

11

Tina Wood made her way through the airport security at Reagan National and awaited her flight back to Boston. She went over her notes from the lone interview with Senator Michael Cornwall, which had been productive, but she needed more contacts in Washington. She was a little fish in a big pond and would need time to get the attention she needed for her story.

Tina purchased a Washington tabloid in the waiting area and skimmed through it as she waited for her flight. She was never one for tabloid-style news because she was a "serious" journalist. But even if the stories had questionable truth threads, reading it still showed her the pulse of the chaos that politics and power create.

All the stories in the magazine seemed the same—from a politician caught having an affair and forced to resign to the latest gossip regarding the parties of the rich and powerful. Lonely men were looking for lonely women to share lives of loneliness. *These people are so blind to the bubbles their lives have become. Thousands of real problems all around them, yet they're stuck in this artificial world.* She almost started to feel sorry for them until she remembered that they had the ability to change the lives of so many people, but nothing seemed to be getting done in Washington.

When the plane landed, she immediately headed for the ground-transportation area since she did not have any checked bags. Once outside the airport terminal, she took out her smartphone to order an Uber ride to Cambridge. After submitting the request, she waited for her ride while browsing the latest news.

After a few minutes, a car pulled up to the corner, and the driver called to her, "Are you Tina? Did you order an Uber?"

Tina was surprised at how quickly the driver had arrived and shouldered her overnight bag to move toward the vehicle. When she closed the news app on her phone, the Uber app came back into focus. She quickly glanced at the app and saw that "Martin" in his white Toyota Camry was still five minutes away.

She had no idea what type of car was in front of her, but it was most definitely not white. She called back to the driver, "Are you Bill?" saying the first name that came to mind other than "Martin."

"Uh, yes. Would you like some help with your bag?" the driver said as he stepped out of his car and stood near the trunk.

"No, that's okay. I can manage." Tina gathered her things, trying to remain calm as she quickly scanned the crowd for help.

She deliberately dropped her purse, stalling for time as she glanced at Martin's progress toward her location. *Two minutes away.* "Bill" came closer, offering to help with her things. Tina didn't know what to do as she quickly scanned the crowd. She was relieved when she noticed a man in military fatigues come out of the terminal, heading in her general direction, but before she could call for help, the man stepped into a car and left the terminal.

"What did you say your name was again?" asked Tina.

"Umm, Bill. Where are you headed?"

"Doesn't the Uber app tell you where I'm going, Bill?" she asked loudly, trying to get the attention of those around her.

"It normally does, but I've been having trouble with the app all day."

Tina's blood pressure rose. She did not want to make a scene because she wasn't sure what the man would do. A dozen different scenarios went through her mind as she forced herself to make a quick decision. She was about to make a run back into the terminal when a white car pulled up about twenty feet behind the black sedan. She quickly waved at the driver, who got out and called, "Are you Tina?"

She hurried over to the car and began to explain to the man what had happened, but when she turned to point out "Bill," the dark sedan pulled away and blended into the airport traffic.

"What is your name, sir?" asked Tina.

"I go by Martin. Ready to head to Cambridge?"

Tina quickly got into the vehicle and told him to pull away. She was quiet the entire ride as she tried to figure out what had just happened. *How did they know I had ordered an Uber? Was it a random act, or did I reveal some clue that was overheard in the airport? How did he know my name? What was his end game if I had agreed to get into his car?*

She had never been targeted so specifically or come so close to being a victim of a crime. She shuddered as various news stories came to her mind. When she saw the familiar scenery of Cambridge, she asked the driver to take her to the office instead of directly home. The driver agreed for an extra five dollars, and Tina was soon walking into the office of Jack Dougan, her boss.

She gave Maggie, the front-desk admin, her typical greeting and wandered back to Jack's office and knocked on the open door.

"Tina, how did it go in DC?" asked Jack. "Did you find Satoshi Nakamoto?"

"Not unless he drives a dark, late-model sedan," snickered Tina.

Jack looked predictably confused.

"Some guy outside Logan Airport pulls up and pretends to be my Uber ride. He knew my name, but he didn't know where I was headed. Thank God I looked at my app and noticed he had the wrong color car and didn't know the correct driver's name. I stall, and the real driver shows up. I run over to the second car, and the first car speeds off before I can get his plate."

"I warned you to be careful. I knew this story might be a bad idea."

"With all due respect, I fail to see how some psycho at the airport has anything to do with finding Satoshi Nakamoto."

"Maybe you're right, but I think it is time to take you off this story. It has no legs anyway."

"Has no legs? How can you say that when you haven't even heard what I have so far?"

"Okay, fine. Tell me what you have."

"I did a ton of research, and you were right. This guy Nakamoto is like the Godfather. Everybody talks like they know him, but no one seems to have actually seen him in person. Nakamoto started the whole crypto thing. Bitcoin is his baby. Several others were involved, but he wrote the white paper on bitcoin back in 2008 when all the banks were in trouble, mortgages were failing, and people were losing their jobs. The world's financial system was in a state of collapse."

"Yes, I remember that very clearly," said Jack. "My 401(k) and I lived through it, though, thank God."

"It was more than that. The sudden collapse revealed all sorts of flaws in the system. People started to believe that the whole financial system was rigged," exclaimed Tina.

"You sound like you've been reading conspiracy novels," mused Jack.

"Those types of labels are what people in power use to try to marginalize countercultural ideas," Tina shot back as she frowned at her boss. "Nakamoto and a few other people were fed up with the government rigging the system. They proposed a new kind of mechanism for storing and exchanging value."

"You mean digital money," said Jack.

"Sort of, but it was much bigger than that. Every ten minutes, all the bitcoin transactions that have been requested worldwide get grouped together and added to the bank ledger. They call it a block of data. There are hundreds of thousands of computers on the Bitcoin network, and they each compete to add the new block. Whichever computer wins the contest for the new block receives some bitcoin as a reward. Right now, that's about ten bitcoin for each new block. The winning computer tells all the other computers across the world what they added, and they all continue competing every ten minutes.

"In the beginning, there were only a few computers on the network, so the early players got a lot of bitcoin.

Nakamoto has billions of dollars' worth of bitcoin that hasn't been touched in almost a decade."

"Okay, I get the basic concept, but why would Satoshi Nakamoto spend all that time on creating bitcoin and trying to get people to use it when he himself won't use it?" asked Jack. "That's like having stacks of money in your closet and never using a single bill. Why bother?"

"That's what I was thinking. Even more interesting is trying to figure out why Satoshi Nakamoto has always been anonymous."

"Now you lost me," replied Jack. "He's not anonymous. We know his name and all sorts of things about him."

"Not really," said Tina. "We know someone using the name Satoshi Nakamoto wrote a paper, but that same individual never filed any patents. Not only did he forgo any financial reward from creating Bitcoin, he left the whole thing wide open and free of patents so that his work could be stolen."

"Why would someone do that? It makes no sense," said Jack.

"Exactly. Then it hit me: what if Satoshi Nakamoto isn't actually a person? What if it is a group of people? Perhaps even a government or an agency of the government?"

"Now I know you're reading too many conspiracy novels," said Jack.

"Hear me out. What if the reason no one can find Satoshi Nakamoto is because their assumptions are blinding them from seeing the truth?"

"This is an interesting story that would be great for the campfire this summer, but what do you actually have that is actionable?" Jack asked.

"I had an interesting talk with Senator Michael Cornwall. During that conversation, I began to realize that I was looking at cryptocurrency with the wrong lens. What if bitcoin was a means to an end? What if the Nakamoto identity was just using bitcoin to shift the power in the financial world?"

Jack stood from his desk and looked out the window. With his hands in his pockets and no expression on his face, he seemed to be weighing choices.

"Okay, maybe you're right. This story might have some legs, but I am growing more convinced that your incident at the airport was about more than we realize. Maybe this is your big shot at a Pulitzer after all."

Goose bumps covered Tina's skin as a chill went up her spine. To be a great journalist required both skill and opportunity.

"Jack, I need more budget, and I need some freedom to travel overseas," Tina proclaimed. "Nakamoto is a Japanese name, and there is a good chance some important answers lie across the ocean."

"Let's not get too carried away with the budget just yet," said Jack with a wave of his hand. "Have you exhausted all your leads stateside? There have to be some local people with whom you can talk."

"I've hit a bit of a dead end on the political angle. I sent out lots of requests, but only Cornwall wanted to talk with me," confessed Tina.

"Politicians don't answer questions. I think that's actually in their oath of office. What about all these crypto coins other than bitcoin? Have you talked to any of them?"

"I thought I was doing a story on Bitcoin and finding Satoshi Nakamoto, not cryptocurrency in general."

"You are, but these crypto guys—"

"And girls," added Tina.

"These crypto... people... seem like they could be good resources for looking into the broader topic," suggested Jack.

Jack took out his laptop and googled "crypto currency Boston" and let out a triumphant noise after a quick glance of the search results.

"There are a couple companies right here in Boston that you could interview," said Jack. "How about you set up some local interviews and check back with me in a couple of days?"

"And what if the leads point overseas?" asked Tina.

"If you get actionable data that suggests Nakamoto's location is overseas, then you'll get the budget," promised Jack.

12

Thomas opened David's office door and sat down with a jovial greeting.

"Dude," said David. "How many times do I have to tell you to stop doing that? Knock before you enter and listen for me to invite you in."

"Knocking is for guests, bro. We're family."

"I'm pretty sure that even family knocks on the bathroom door before entering," suggested David.

"Is the bathroom metaphor a veiled confession about the quality of your code?" asked Thomas with a smirk on his face.

"What's up, Thomas?" David sighed in defeat. "I was just in the coding zone."

"I lined up an interview for you at lunchtime. Tina Wood from the *Boston Mirror* is doing a story on cryptocurrencies that are trying to take market share from Bitcoin."

"Oh, that sounds like a fun lunch topic," said David sarcastically. "Why didn't you just do the interview yourself?"

"I offered, but she wanted to talk to the man himself.

Apparently, she's read some of the other press on NuKoin and your blog."

"Interesting, because I was wondering if anyone read that blog. You know I hate taking long lunch breaks."

"I told her fifteen minutes, twenty if she agreed to meet you in the lobby at eleven forty sharp. The Red Sox have a one o'clock game today, and I told her you liked the sausage dogs outside Gate B. She said she would wait for you downstairs and be wearing red—a coincidence, she assured me."

"Fine. I guess I can't argue with free food while I soak up the pregame atmosphere."

Thomas and David chatted a little bit longer before David returned to his work. At 11:35, David received an instant message from Thomas as a reminder that the time for his interview had come. David locked his laptop and his office door and proceeded down to the main lobby. He immediately saw a young woman near the entrance, wearing a red blouse. When she saw him approaching, she seemed to recognize him.

"David Turner? I am Tina Wood, from the *Boston Mirror*," the woman said as she extended her hand for a firm handshake. "Thanks for agreeing to meet with me. I understand you like the street vendors by Fenway Park? Shall we walk down there and talk as we go?"

The spring day was warm in Boston, and David had been sitting all morning, so he welcomed the exercise. On the walk toward the baseball stadium, Tina briefed David on the story she was writing about Bitcoin, but she left out the details regarding her intent to find Satoshi Nakamoto. Instead, she focused on her need for information relating to Bitcoin and the sea of alternative cryptocurrency on the market.

Turning the conversation to David, she said, "So tell me about your company and how it is different from Bitcoin."

David had lots to say about that topic, but he didn't want the conversation to take him away from his work for too long. Nevertheless, they still had several blocks to go in their walk toward food, so he indulged her request.

"Bitcoin paved the way and started the world thinking about alternative methods of payment, but the bitcoin codebase has become too bloated over time. In the beginning, when it was just Satoshi and a few other experts, things were great, but as more people joined the team, different styles of coding started to cause the execution time to slow down."

"What do you mean by 'execution time'?" Tina asked.

"The Bitcoin network is all about the trading of a single asset between two entities. Therefore, a transaction is very small—just a sending address, a receiving address, and the amount of bitcoin changing hands. There are thousands and thousands of those transactions every second. Bitcoin can only process a finite number of transactions in a ten-minute period, so as bitcoin becomes more popular, the network becomes much slower."

"And NuKoin doesn't have that same problem?"

"Not at all. We use the laser protocol," replied David. "It's somewhat technical, but at a high level, our blocks of data get created every ten seconds, not every ten minutes, and each block is much larger than the bitcoin blocks. NuKoin has leveraged the gains made by Bitcoin, but since I control who is allowed to change the code for NuKoin, we don't have the same problems as they do."

"Has it been successful so far? Are people eager to use NuKoin instead of Bitcoin?"

"We are still in the pre-alpha stage while we test out the

security of our network," replied David. "That's one reason why we don't mind having some press coverage so that we can gain a following prior to our launch."

"So your niche in the crypto market is transaction speed?"

"That's part of it. Bitcoin is a public ledger. Everyone can see all the transactions on the Bitcoin network. NuKoin, on the other hand, encrypts the data so that each transaction is private."

"Private means that people could use it to conduct illicit activity, correct?"

"Anyone could use NuKoin to make a transfer of assets to any other party, but that is no different from the system we have in place today with cash transactions."

"Some might argue that enabling anonymous payments online is taking that to a whole new level," retorted Tina. "Wouldn't this prevent law enforcement from doing its job?"

"Law enforcement will continue to have all sorts of online tools," assured David. "They do not need to peek into every American citizen's bank account to do that."

"Do you worry that NuKoin will be used by criminals?"

"Which criminals are we talking about? The ones on Capitol Hill or the ones on Main Street?"

Tina giggled. The pedestrian traffic was increasing on the sidewalk as they drew closer to the stadium. The warm spring day caused many to be in short-sleeved Red Sox shirts, but Tina still felt a little chill from the wind coming from Boston Harbor.

"Listen, I am not a conspiracy nut," warned David, "but off the record, I do believe that educated people need to take a look at what has been going on in our country for many years now. Ever since the end of World War II,

America has been going down a dangerous road of prying into the lives of Americans in the name of national security. Back in the early 1950s, there was a school of thought that if we had been spying on Japanese immigrants in Hawaii, we would have known the attack on Pearl Harbor was coming.

"Ever since then, they have been creating all these different government agencies, largely outside of any oversight or control. The government tells us enough information to keep us scared, and we remain scared enough to thank them for keeping us safe. Our fear of the unknown foreign threat keeps us from asking our government the hard questions."

"Okay," said Tina, "but how does this relate to NuKoin?"

"Ask yourself who creates these agencies," David said with a dramatic pause. "The answer is that they are appointed by politicians, and politicians are elected by...?"

"The voters," answered Tina.

"Wrong! The candidates that run for office for the two main political parties are selected by those with large amounts of influence and capital. And what enables large amounts of capital in the hands of a few powerful people? Control of the system, top to bottom. Those in power fight to stay in power any way they can.

"NuKoin eliminates the ability for those in power to control the financial system. It is my belief that this will actually reduce crime because it will radically shift the financial power in the world to the common person."

"Wow, that's a radical perspective," replied Tina. "But how will that reduce crime?"

"Still off the record?"

"Sure."

"It goes back to the fundamental definition of crime,"

said David. "Crime is defined as breaking the law. So who makes the law?"

"Some would argue that our laws are grounded in a basic intent to protect life and property," said Tina.

"At times, perhaps," conceded David. "If we care so much about life, then why does society turn a blind eye to homelessness and other social problems? Clearly in this nation—indeed, around the world—some lives are more important than others.

"If the Super Bowl MVP dies in a car accident, it makes world news. If a single mother in South Boston dies in a car accident, no one seems to care. Do we value all life, or does our government value some lives more than others? You have to first take a step back and ask yourself if the laws of America are designed to protect all citizens or those currently in power. NuKoin was formed from the vision of getting the flow of money out of the government's hands so that the government can no longer manipulate it or manipulate our lives."

"Wow. That is quite a mission statement. Does everyone at NuKoin share your vision?"

"They all share the vision of creating a cryptocurrency that is fast and secure for those who use it, but my personal views of society are my own. I'm not forcing my political views on anyone."

"Spoken like a true Libertarian," said Tina with a smile.

"I believe that a small government is in everyone's best interest. When governments grow, it's only because people are trying to manipulate other people with self-granted power. I believe that some level of government has to be funded, but not by controlling the very system by which citizens store value."

"But don't we need someone or some organization to

make sure that no one is ripping people off?" challenged Tina. "Don't the banking regulations and the FDIC guarantee us all security and peace of mind for our assets?"

"I agree one hundred percent that we need a system in place by which people can store value without fear that their assets are going to be taken from them. What do we do, however, if the current system is the very one taking our assets?"

Tina looked a little curious, so David continued in a more animated tone.

"The average middle-class citizen stores their value in the bank and collects, what, a fraction of a percent of interest? Or maybe they manage to save a little in an IRA or 401(k). If they can make a few percentage points a year, then maybe they have a little nest egg for retirement. On the flip side, you have thousands of people in places like downtown Boston or lower Manhattan making twenty to thirty times that return by using the money of middle-class Americans."

"So you believe that the current system isn't fair to the small guys?" summarized Tina.

"I actually don't care whether it is fair or not," responded David. "I care about whether it is legally mandated that their system can be the *only* system. If it was one system among many, then people could choose. The fact that those in power *require* everyone to use their system is the problem."

He grew even more excited. "Let me ask you a question. All those people on the news that are speaking out against bitcoin and cryptocurrency—what do they all have in common?"

Tina thought for a moment and responded, "I'm not sure. Maybe they're all in a position of power?"

"You're close. All the people that are saying negative things in the media about cryptocurrency are wealthy because of the current financial system. They have managed to figure out the system and have positioned themselves. To them, the poor are just lazy or unmotivated. To them, everyone has the opportunity to be successful. The truth, however, is that the system is stacked against many people. The truth is that the system, like almost every financial system the world has ever known, is rigged to keep certain people in a place of power."

"Okay, so now I understand where you're coming from," said Tina. "Let's get back to NuKoin and how it will change the system. Can we go back on the record now?"

"Sure," said David. "NuKoin is a network by which everyone has to play by the same rules. It has inherent security, which gives people the assurance that no one is interfering in their private affairs. Society is still able to agree to a common set of rules and create laws, but the means by which we all store value should not be owned by a central entity. NuKoin brings that vision to life."

David and Tina stopped talking as they approached Fenway Park. They milled through the crowds and approached David's favorite street vendor, where he ordered two sausage dogs and a Coke, while Tina went for the hamburger and a water. After loading their food up with condiments, they stood off to one side to enjoy their meals standing up.

"So why do you love this place so much?" asked Tina. "Other than the thirty-five dollars in cash I just gave that guy. It seems like a long walk for fast food."

"I've been working really hard on NuKoin for a while now," answered David. "It's easy to get caught up in the work. Being here reminds me of my childhood and all the baseball games with my father as a kid. I've continued the tradition with my own son, and I hope he does the same with his kids someday."

"Tell me about your son. What is he like?"

"I don't like to talk about my family in public, but I will tell you that he is a brilliant kid in his own right."

"Fair enough," said Tina respectfully. "Maybe I'll get to meet him someday. Off the record, of course."

As they ate their lunches, Tina began to see the magic David saw in the ambiance outside a baseball stadium—so much history and so many memories. Tina finished her burger first, while David seemed to be elongating the enjoyment of his two sausage dogs. Tina glanced into a storefront behind where they were standing and saw the image of Senator Michael Cornwall on TV, being interviewed on a cable news station.

"He's a busy man," mumbled Tina.

David turned to see what she was talking about and cursed when he saw who was on the TV screen.

"You know the senator?" asked Tina.

"I don't know him personally, but he has sent us a few letters."

"What kind of letters?"

"Requests for information printed on congressional letterhead. The kind of letter that is supposed to make you tuck your tail between your legs and come begging for leniency."

"Why is the senator interested in NuKoin?"

"The senator is sending mass correspondence to all the cryptocurrencies," explained David. "I doubt very seriously that he has any idea about the technology or the real issues. He's part of the problem, so I take his letters with a grain of salt."

"Are you nervous that regulation could be coming?"

"I think 'nervous' is a strong word. I'm 'concerned' when the government forgets that they serve at the pleasure of the citizens. I think all the congressmen—"

"Congresspeople," Tina interrupted.

"I think they have the spectrum reversed. They are supposed to be public servants, not treating the constituents like their minions. They're scared to lose their power, so they keep the public at bay in a little fish bowl."

"That seems a little strong, don't you think?"

"Too strong? You think my disdain for government control is misguided? Then why has that woman been taking photographs of us since we left my office?"

"What woman?" asked Tina, glancing around in sudden curiosity.

"If you keep looking around like that, you'll scare her away," warned David. "Pretend to be looking at the vendors selling the Red Sox clothing, but pay attention to the lady standing outside the bar on the corner."

Tina took David's advice and noticed a woman with a camera taking photographs of the baseball park.

"I see a tourist taking photos," said Tina.

"Yeah, then why isn't she dressed in tourist clothing? How many photographs of the outside of a stadium does one person need? One would think she might change positions and get some different angles. She followed us down here from my office, keeping a slight distance away."

Tina considered David's words and stared at the woman more directly. The woman put down her camera and walked away into the crowd.

"She could have been anyone," said Tina. "What makes you think she's taking pictures of us?"

"Because this is not the first time it's happened to me,"

said David. "Wait until you try going through airport security now that we've been seen together."

"That's weird that you say that," replied Tina. "On my flight to DC, the TSA gave me the hardest time getting through security, and on the way back, a random guy tried to impersonate my Uber driver."

"Good for you," said David. "Seems you've already made their list."

"Their list for what? And who is 'they'?" asked Tina.

"The people that are really running this country. The money train. Stay off their radar, and you're fine—the system seems to work great. But once you are a person of interest, you start to understand the problem firsthand."

"Person of interest? Like a criminal?"

"'Criminal' is the word they use to justify their harassment and control," said David as he finished the last bite of his lunch. The TV was silent behind the glass of the store, but they both groaned out loud when the TV showed an image of Brian Parker, the president's son-in-law.

"Talk about a criminal," said David. "The fact that Parker is allowed to see confidential government documents is grounds for someone to be fired."

"You don't like Parker either?"

"I can respect the criminal that earns his jail time from being good at his law-breaking craft," mused David. "But nepotism is a special category. Let's get going. I need to get back to work."

The two made their way back toward the office, and gradually the crowd seemed to decrease. Soon, they were almost alone on the streets as they made their way back to the NuKoin offices.

"So we didn't talk too much about NuKoin," David

conceded. "Do you think you have enough information for your story?"

"I already had a lot of research on NuKoin. I just wanted to meet you and get some personal insight into the company. I appreciate you talking with me today. I would like to use you as a sounding board for some of my upcoming tech articles if you don't mind."

"Thanks. I do appreciate being able to look over articles before they are published. Especially ones relating to NuKoin."

"That's not a problem," agreed Tina. "While we still have a few minutes, what do you know about Satoshi Nakamoto?"

"I see you've read the Wikipedia article on Bitcoin." David chuckled. "Why do you care about Satoshi?"

"With all this cloak-and-dagger stuff you're trying to get me to see, wouldn't it make sense to know who started the fire?"

"This is not Satoshi's fault. He was never interested in that stuff anyway."

"You sound like you know him."

"I worked with Satoshi on the bitcoin code many years ago. Back then, there were just a handful of us with noble ideas to change the world. We put thousands of hours into that code, only to see it get wrestled from our hands."

"Where is Satoshi now?"

"That would be the ten-thousand-dollar question," admitted David.

"You mean the one-billion-dollar question."

David laughed out loud more than he had during their whole conversation. "Yeah, I suppose, but don't forget that Satoshi could never move any of his bitcoins without spooking the entire market. I'm pretty sure he has moved on to other things. He hasn't been heard from for years."

"I read online that some people have come forward to claim they are Satoshi."

"I'm not even going to address the imposters," said David in a dismissive tone. "Satoshi has an account where he has commented from time to time. When the latest imposter got media attention, Satoshi posted to his public blog that it was not him. I still can't figure out why people believe these guys."

"What do you have to say to those people that think that Satoshi Nakamoto is just a pseudonym for some group of people?"

"I say that's a dumb idea," replied David. "Listen, I know Satoshi from my Bitcoin coding days. No, I never actually met him face-to-face, but I can guarantee you that he was a single individual. If he had silent partners, what do I care? Satoshi is brilliant, and he is not a group of people... and because he is brilliant, that rules out the idea that he somehow worked for the government."

Both Tina and David were laughing as they neared the end of the interview. The two professionals were about to shake hands when Nicole walked out of the office and stopped short when she saw them.

"Oh, hello, David," said Nicole. "I didn't know you were out here."

"This is Tina Wood, a reporter from the *Boston Mirror*. We were just finishing an informal interview."

"Well... I was just on my way to go get a Starbucks," said Nicole, somewhat frazzled. "Do you want anything?"

"No, thanks," said David. "I'm just going to finish up with Tina and then get back to work."

Tina waited for Nicole to get across the street before

speaking again. "She seemed a little jealous. Did I upset your girlfriend?"

"No, Nicole and I are co-workers. Nothing more than that."

Tina decided to let that go but filed it in her memory bank. She thanked David again and let him return to his work.

13

———

David woke to Lucie's muffled bark from the corner of the room. He glanced at his clock as he rose from bed. He knew he would have a late night, so he'd decided to sleep in. Lucie, of course, had not been informed.

"Come on, girl. Let's get you outside and get you something to eat."

David made his way downstairs and found Owen nearly ready for school.

"I thought your sleeping in was permission for me to stay home today," said Owen with a hopeful smile.

"You know me better than that," replied David. "I have a fundraising dinner to attend downtown tonight. It will probably be a late night."

"A fundraiser for what?"

"Some boring banking thing, but at least the food should be good. I have to go and make an appearance so that NuKoin gets some brownie points from the financial sector."

"Why don't you get someone else at the company to go

instead? You're the CEO. Can't you just force someone to represent you?"

"Nicole is coming with me, so I guess I kind of did."

"She is *going*, or she is going with *you*?" asked Owen.

"She is my guest for the evening."

Owen didn't respond right away, so David let the comment sit a moment while Owen processed.

"Why do you need a date? Can't you just go alone?"

"I could go alone, but these things are much better if you have someone with you," explained David. "Then you have someone to talk to if all the other conversation gets too boring."

"Do you like her?"

"Nicole is pretty easy to get along with, yes. But are you asking if I have feelings for her?"

"Is it a real date, or are you just friends?" clarified Owen.

David's fatherly intuition kicked into high gear as he tried to imagine the real intent and emotions in his son. He decided to probe.

"Would you care if it was a real date?"

"I'm just curious," said Owen in an evading tone.

"Well, Nicole is an attractive woman—I'm not going to lie. But so far, our relationship is strictly business."

"So far?" replied Owen with a raised eyebrow.

"Meaning we have a business relationship, but we have shared a drink after work on occasion."

"Mom has only been missing for less than a year."

There it was, just as David suspected. That type of emotion was natural in a child who'd lost one of their parents. Grieving was a natural process, but people had to move through the process and not get stuck in one spot.

"Owen, Mom isn't missing—you know that. She would want both of us to be happy and move on with our lives."

"I don't think it is a good idea for the CEO to be dating one of his employees," said Owen.

"Well, I already told you that we are not dating. But thank you for your professional opinion. Somehow, I think this is about more than your assessment of business etiquette."

"Whatever."

"Come on. Don't get all 'whatever' with me."

"Dad, we need to stick together and look out for each other," said Owen in a voice that made him seem a few years older. "You don't have time for someone else right now. You're working a lot as it is, and I don't want to give up what little time we have together. Besides, you're going to be rich soon, so you need to be suspicious of people latching onto your success."

"Nicole is the CFO of NuKoin. I hardly think you need to worry about her latching onto our personal finances."

Owen didn't seem comfortable with the topic of David having dating aspirations, so David decided to change the subject. The two talked about sports and a few stories in the news before he dropped Owen off for school.

That evening, David left the office early to avoid traffic and get some quiet time before he had to overcome his introverted nature by socializing with strangers. He picked up his black dinner jacket from the cleaners on the way home and stopped at the barbershop near his house.

The fundraiser started at seven, so he allowed enough time to pick up Nicole on the way. He parked along the street in front of her apartment and buzzed the intercom. Moments later, she opened the door, wearing a black evening gown that caught him off guard.

"Wow," David managed.

"Oh, thank you, David," Nicole responded with a smile. "Do you like the dress?"

David knew he was staring for too long, but he couldn't resist the temptation to take a long gaze at his date for the evening. Nicole was his co-worker, but that night, she was breathtaking. She was wearing her hair up, which only accentuated her delicate shoulders. Her dress hung as if suspended in midair, perfectly forming lines that were both simple and inviting. Her legs were toned and tan, precluding the need for stockings.

"I will take that as a yes," said Nicole with a giggle.

David offered his arm, and they walked to the car. He opened the door for her, and they drove to the fundraiser. They were quiet for a few minutes, as both seemed lost in thought. Nicole finally broke the silence.

"So what's the game plan tonight? Do you want to work the room together or divide and conquer?"

Nicole was back in business mode, and David liked a woman who could keep him on his toes.

"The bankers will all be there, so I guess we have to schmooze with them a little bit. I'm most interested in the politicians. We need their support to keep the law on our side."

"Do you want me to cover the bankers, then, while you find the politicians?" asked Nicole.

"I think we need to leverage that dress with both groups," said David without thinking.

As Nicole smiled, David quickly said, "I'm sorry, Nicole. That was out of line."

"No, it's okay. I took it as a compliment. Don't worry."

When they reached the hotel, David pulled up to the valet and turned over his keys. He walked to the passenger side and took Nicole's arm. They strode up the steps and into the hotel like they had been together for decades, and David was overwhelmed by the happiness growing inside him. They told the host their names and were invited inside.

The fundraising dinner was in the Liberty Hotel, the renovated nineteenth-century Charles Street Prison. The ground floor was busy with hotel guests and patrons at the bar, and the ninety-foot ceilings gave the building an elegant reverence. Three upper levels of balconies allowed for private parties in the space once occupied by jail cells. The cell walls had since been removed, giving the venue a unique open feel.

The fundraiser was occurring on all three upper levels, so David and Nicole made their way to the top floor and ordered drinks from one of the satellite bars. They took in the crowd and silently planned their angles of pursuit.

Nicole turned to David in a whisper, and he leaned in. "By the way," she whispered, "you look pretty good tonight too."

David felt his face go flush as the two proceeded to move from group to group. They took turns introducing themselves to each new cluster, but Nicole seemed to relish the stage. She used her dazzling looks and keen mind to command respect from men and women alike. Only after she left each group did many of the women scold their dates for gazing at Nicole's figure as she walked away.

David and Nicole improved their presentation of NuKoin with each new group, always probing for the influencers in the room. David collected all the business cards, even those given directly to Nicole, much to the chagrin of men who were apparently hoping for a relationship of some kind.

As the night went on, David found himself increasingly distracted by Nicole's charm. Without realizing it, he was letting her do more of the talking. After a couple of hours and a few drinks, Nicole leaned in toward him.

"You seem to be staring a little bit more as the night goes on," she said softly. "Don't get too distracted, David. We haven't finished our work here."

David took a sip of his wine and smiled into the distance. He noticed a familiar face coming toward him, and Nicole sized the woman up as she approached.

"David Turner, good to see you," said Tina Wood. "I was wondering if I might see you here tonight."

"Well hello, Tina," replied David. "Nicole, this is Tina Wood, a reporter from the *Boston Mirror*. She interviewed me the other day."

"Why yes, of course," recalled Nicole. "I remember meeting you outside the office. How are you doing?"

"I am doing well, thank you," said Tina. "How about you two? Is the event going well for NuKoin?"

"Yes, we're making some good connections," replied David. "A lot of these people are influencers in the financial space who need to understand the important future role of cryptocurrency. What brings you here, Tina?"

"Just tracking down some new interview opportunities in the cryptocurrency space."

"Anyone we would find interesting?" asked Nicole, always searching for competitive intel.

"No one like NuKoin," said Tina, to Nicole's obvious satisfaction. "But there's no shortage of opinions in the room regarding where crypto will or should go. Lots of nervous and greedy bankers, and it's hard to tell which ones will win."

"Bankers always think they will win," retorted David.

"This whole world is run by a select few who see themselves as the gatekeepers for everyone else."

Nicole rolled her eyes in a playful way that made David laugh. Tina rolled her eyes in response, put off by the gratuitous flirting. Tina gulped down the wine she'd been sipping and waved to someone across the room.

"Cornwall is here?" said David.

"He is indeed. Is that good news or bad news?"

"I hate all politicians," said David quietly. "I'd prefer to keep them as far away as possible."

"Too late, I'm afraid," said Nicole. "I do believe that is Senator Michael Cornwall over there."

Tina brightened as she placed her glass on a waiter's tray and waved the senator over to the group.

"Senator Cornwall, good to see you again so soon," she said. "I'd like you to meet some friends of mine. David Turner, CEO of NuKoin, and Nicole..."

"Mancini," interjected Nicole, "I am the CFO of NuKoin."

"Ah yes, NuKoin," replied the senator in the precise but vague manner of a politician. "Interesting business model."

"Just living the dream," said David in a youthful tone.

"Senator, David is one of the leading experts in blockchain technology," said Tina. "It's the technology that runs Bitcoin."

"I am aware of what blockchain is," replied the senator. "But I don't think Mr. Turner would appreciate the comparison between NuKoin and Bitcoin."

"Quite correct," conceded David. "NuKoin is an antipattern, in fact."

"Indeed," said the senator. "Tell me more."

David refused to take the bait and simply said, "We still

have a lot of research and development to get under our belts."

"I have read a few of your blog posts, David, and in your writing, you don't seem shy about the value NuKoin can bring to the market."

David instantly tried to recall which posts the senator might have read. "You can't believe everything you read on the internet, Senator. Everyone knows that. Sometimes, you just have to stretch people a little bit and add some passion to your points."

"Tell me, David, how do you feel about anonymous financial transactions that facilitate criminal activity?"

"What types of criminal activity are you referencing?" asked David with a sparkle in his eye.

"Drug cartels, human trafficking, illegal gambling—"

"Senator, people have been selling drugs and sex for thousands of years. Cryptocurrency is not responsible for that activity. And I think it is interesting that you used the phrase 'illegal gambling' instead of just 'gambling.' Isn't the only real difference whether the government are the ones who profit?"

"The government regulation protects the average citizen from scams," replied the senator. "We keep the markets free and open but also safe for the average investor."

Nicole tried to diffuse the tension and shift the discussion. "Senator, the leadership at NuKoin shares your desire to ensure organized crime cannot use cryptocurrency for nefarious purposes."

"Perhaps I misread the NuKoin white paper," Cornwall said with a trace of sarcasm. "Is NuKoin not trying to create completely anonymous financial transactions?"

"NuKoin provides a payment gateway that offers security to both sides of the transaction," explained David in a calm tone. "The identity of the transacting parties may or may not be the government's business, but that is not something that the NuKoin network handles. Currency is fungible. Currency is not good or evil on its own."

The senator seemed placated for the moment, and the four of them continued talking for several minutes. David had shifted into salesman mode thanks to Nicole's subtle prodding. They were there to sell NuKoin—and cryptocurrency in general—not to debate their personal political views.

The senator excused himself and continued to another group of people that resembled bankers. They watched him leave before continuing their conversation.

"Well, that was interesting," remarked Tina. "Are you here tonight looking to stir up trouble or quench it?"

Nicole beat David to the punch. "Sometimes the best defense is a good offense."

David smiled and took another draw from the drink in his hand. After a couple of moments of awkward silence, Tina excused herself. Both David and Nicole seemed to enjoy the privacy.

"Do you want to call it a night?" asked Nicole.

"Yeah, good idea," replied David. "My extroverted energy level is getting low anyway."

David offered his arm to Nicole, and the two walked to the exit to get their coats. David escorted her to the sidewalk then toward the parking garage and the car. He started to realize how much he liked the feeling of Nicole's arm in his. They walked slowly toward the car, partly because Nicole was in heels and partly because they both seemed to be enjoying the slow pace.

"I thought we worked well as a team," David suggested.

"It's amazing what can happen when you include me in your plans."

David glanced over and saw her smirking at him. He laughed and looked into the distance. Out of the periphery of his vision, he could see Nicole still looking at him.

"David Turner, you are a mystery," said Nicole. "Why don't you let people into your world more often?"

"I don't know. Maybe it's because I don't like asking anyone for help."

"Why not? Everyone needs help once in a while. Asking for things is not a sign of weakness. It's a sign of being secure in who you are and who you are not."

"How exciting... Nicole the therapist is back."

Nicole chuckled, and David could tell he should be the one driving that night. Nicole changed the subject. "Did you decide yet if you are going to the blockchain conference in St. Petersburg next week?"

"I should go, but I can't leave Owen alone. I was thinking of sending one of the lead developers instead."

"We should definitely send someone, but it really should be you. The real value of that conference will be making connections."

"Yeah, I know, but Owen comes first."

"How about I watch Owen then?"

"The trip is five days, Nicole."

"I don't mind. Besides, it would give me someone to cook for every night, a reason to go home at a normal hour of the day."

"If you get Owen hooked on real food, he might make me cook for him."

"Maybe when you get back, I can teach you a few dinner tricks."

The two walked for about a block while David seemed to consider the offer.

"Come on, David," Nicole finally said, "Owen is a teenager. He just needs someone at home each night. Let me help you. And let me help NuKoin get you to this conference."

David glanced over and finally said, "Okay, let's give it a shot. I'll book my itinerary tomorrow, as long as it's okay with Owen."

"Great," Nicole responded, seeming to hold his arm a little more tightly than earlier.

They reached the car, and David opened her door. They rehashed the events of the night as he drove Nicole back to her apartment. He pulled up outside and got out to escort her to the front door.

He stopped on the lower step as she ascended to the front door and unlocked it.

Turning back to him, she said, "I had a great time tonight, David. Thanks for taking me."

He hesitated, perhaps a bit too long, before responding, "I had a great time too. I have to admit it was a lot more interesting than I thought it would be."

"I better get inside and get some rest for tomorrow," said Nicole in a slightly more distant tone.

He suddenly wondered if he had misspoken. *Did I offend her? Was she hoping that the evening would be extended a little longer?* "Nicole, I didn't mean—"

"David, I know what you meant. Work parties are not all they're cracked up to be. I'm glad it was endurable for the both of us."

As Nicole walked through the door, David said good night then got into his car.

On the ride home, he thought about Nicole and how

they'd worked the room together. He thought about his company and some of the challenges government interference could bring. He thought about how the night might have gone had Nicole invited him into her apartment.

He also thought about her offer to watch Owen for a few days. He needed to get to that conference in Russia, and she had given him a perfect solution.

David pulled into his driveway and parked. He made his way into the dimly lit house and paused after putting his things down. The house was dead silent.

He began thinking about Mia and how perfect their life had been together. Silence could bring peace or emptiness, and he suddenly felt both. Quietly, he made his way upstairs and toward Owen's room.

David gently opened Owen's bedroom door and smiled when he saw the form of his son sleeping peacefully. Ever since Mia's death, his protectiveness of his only son had only increased. He winked at Lucie, who was curled up in a corner, wagging her tail. Then he closed the door softly and got ready for bed.

Owen waited until his father closed the door before getting out of bed. He returned to the computer he'd been using all night and continued his research. Despite the fact that Lucie was mostly asleep, Owen continued to explain to her what he had found, but now in a whisper.

"Lucie, this Nicole Mancini is up to something sinister," Owen told the dog. "I can feel it."

He brought up a few more websites and toggled back and forth between screens as only a teenager could do. He alternated between trying to track down facts about Nicole and studying the world of Bitcoin.

"Lucie, check this out... This website will show us all the transactions associated with Mom's bitcoin wallet. We can see all the activity and use the dates to correlate Mom's activities."

Owen copied the bitcoin wallet address into the website's text box and pressed Find. Several dozen transactions were listed on the screen, and Owen gasped, which caused Lucie to lift her head up and look at him.

"Oh my... Lucie, this wallet has over three thousand bitcoins! That's worth, like, thirty million dollars."

He sat there in stunned silence. He had on his computer a bitcoin wallet worth tens of millions and had absolutely no way to access the funds. *How did she keep this secret for so long?*

"Lucie, there hasn't been any activity on this wallet in years. The first transaction is from summer 2009—a few transfers in and a few out—then nothing since July of 2010. That is really weird. Why would Mom use bitcoin for almost eighteen months and never mention it to Dad?

"Wait. In July 2010, Bitcoin jumped up in value from being worth less than a penny to being worth eight cents each. Even if we assume that Mom knew about that price jump, this wallet was still worth only two hundred forty dollars at that time. That's hardly enough to get her attention. I guess she really could have just forgotten about it."

Lucie wagged her tail a few times then put her head back down on the bed and closed her eyes.

"But Mom knew about cryptocurrency. She worked at NuKoin. She would never have forgotten she owned some. Maybe she didn't tell Dad because she knew how much he hated Bitcoin... It doesn't make sense, Lucie. Dad says he actually liked Bitcoin until a few years ago, when he started calling it a bubble.

"And what are all these transfers? Where was Mom sending the coins? And what are these other wallet addresses giving her bitcoin?" Owen shook his head as the light from the monitor danced in his eyes.

"You see, Lucie, the Bitcoin ledger is public, but we can only see the amount that was transferred between two parties. We can't tell the true identity of either person. That's what keeps Bitcoin anonymous. As long as the people trade outside any of the public exchanges, no one will ever know who they are.

"And where does Nicole Mancini fit into all of this? She has to be after my Dad's money, after his company, or maybe she's somehow connected to this bitcoin wallet. I guess we'll wait and see if she makes a move. But until then, we better keep this bitcoin wallet safe."

14

Owen woke from a sound sleep to his father calling his name.

"Owen, wake up! You're late for school."

Owen buried his head in his sheets, secretly hoping he could magically squeeze a couple hours of sleep out of the blanket. Rubbing his face, he tossed his feet out from the covers and onto the cold floor.

He rushed through his shower and breakfast but had just enough time to reach the car as his father was getting into the front seat.

"Owen, I was hoping I'd have more time to talk to you this morning. I have a business trip I need to take in a couple of days."

"Where are you headed?"

"It's kind of far away, actually. St. Petersburg."

"Florida isn't that far."

"St. Petersburg, Russia."

"Wow. What for?"

"It's a blockchain conference, and all the major cryptocurrency players will be there," explained David. "It's something NuKoin needs to participate in, and I'll be gone for almost a week."

"Sounds pretty cool," said Owen. "Any chance I get to go too?"

"I wish you could, but you have school. You can't miss an entire week."

"You trust me to stay alone by myself?" asked Owen, surprised.

"I do trust you, but I'm going to ask someone to stay here while I'm gone, just to give me peace of mind that everything is okay."

Owen's expression sank a little as he began to see what was coming.

"Nicole Mancini offered to stay here and watch the house while I'm gone. I hear she's quite the cook."

Owen rolled his eyes and stared out the window before replying. "I don't want your new girlfriend staying here with me. Why can't I stay with a friend or something?"

"If it was only a day or two, that would work. But a week is a lot to ask, and I want you to keep your normal routine. Besides, Nicole offered, and I think it makes the most sense. You've already met her, so why the sudden animosity?"

"I don't trust her. We don't really know her, and she suddenly has all this interest in you."

"She has been the CFO of my company for the past six months. I hardly think she's a stranger. And by the way, she is not my girlfriend."

"Six months is not a long time. You have no knowledge of her life prior to NuKoin. Don't you think it's a bit of a coincidence that she just appeared on your doorstep?"

"Appeared on my doorstep? She was recommended for an executive position by the NuKoin investors."

"Trust is earned, not given," said Owen. "That's what Mom always said."

"I'm beginning to think this is about something else. No one is ever going to replace your mom. I've told you that. Nicole offered to help me out while I go to this conference, nothing more."

They continued to Owen's school in silence as both men contemplated the gravity of the conversation. When David parked in front of the school, Owen spoke first.

"I don't have to talk to her, right?"

"I expect you to be polite, Owen. But no, you don't have to sit down in the living room and share your life story."

"Maybe I could get more information about her that way," said Owen with a slight smirk.

David pulled out of the school driveway and continued to work. He made his way up to the office and sat down at his computer to register for the conference. Only three days were left, but he managed to get one of the last tickets.

Then he booked a business-class plane ticket to St. Petersburg via Amsterdam because no other itineraries were available in economy. "Thank you, William DeFrost." David laughed aloud as he used his company charge card to purchase the flights and hotel.

Nicole knocked on his office door just as he completed the purchase. "Booking your tickets, I hope?"

"As a matter of fact, I am," replied David happily.

"I take it Owen was okay with me watching him, then?" asked Nicole.

"Owen is a teenager. He shows muted responses that take on a wait-and-see posture whenever possible."

"That's an interesting nonanswer," said Nicole. "Don't worry. I didn't expect him to be excited. He doesn't even know me. I embrace the challenge of winning him over."

"I really appreciate this, Nicole. This conference is going to be great for NuKoin."

"And for you, David. You need to get away."

Nicole went back to her office, and David got busy reviewing computer code written by some of the developers. Soon, he noticed some changes to the code from the new developers at Danzi Consulting. He grew more frustrated and angrier as he looked more closely at their code.

He considered making another appearance at their desks but decided on an alternative approach. He sent both an instant message asking them to come to his office right away.

Averting his eyes from his screen, he tried to settle down by looking out the window at the Boston skyline. He took a long pull from his lukewarm coffee and consciously tried to calm himself.

The knock at his door pulled him out of his happy place and back into the moment.

"Satish, Ramesh, please come in and close the door," said David in a deliberately calm tone.

"Yes, sir. Thank you for inviting us," said Satish with a large grin on his face.

"Guys, I have been looking at your code again."

"Are you happy with our work, sir?"

"I tell you what," said David with a pause. "Before I answer that question, I'd like you to walk me through your code and explain to me what you were trying to do when you wrote it." He'd become convinced the two developers did not possess the skill to write complex blockchain code.

Satish's and Ramesh's faces immediately brightened—they were obviously very proud of their work. David brought up the code changes on his large triple monitors, and Satish and Ramesh took turns explaining their work.

David could see that they had tried very hard, but he still was frustrated at what he perceived to be a general lack of expertise. This was his baby, and he wanted only experts touching this code.

"Guys, I want to learn about your background," said David abruptly. "How did you end up here writing blockchain code? Talk to me about your coding experience."

Satish began his story much further back in history than David had anticipated. And before David could interject to insert a fast-forward in the verbal resume, Satish began relating some very personal details.

"Ever since I was a little boy, I dreamed of coming to America. I am one of twelve, and all my brothers and sisters have remained in India in our ancestral village. A few of my brothers tried to move to the city but ended up living on the streets. They returned home in ruins, and from then on, my father commanded us all to remain where he could keep us safe.

"But my mother always pushed me to become more. She was the one who paid for my first computer course, making dresses by candlelight and selling them to the village girls. She and I are very alike—her drive and passion are inside me.

"When I got older, I began working at the college in the town near our village. I would work in exchange for food and free courses. I was in charge of cleaning the entire college after everyone left for the day. Many nights, I worked until almost dawn, and then I took my courses, often getting no sleep. But I wasn't about to lose the opportunity.

"I eventually graduated with high honors and got a scholarship to one of the big schools in the city. My father forbade me to go—he wanted my help in the fields. But my mother eventually convinced him with the hope that I could one day help support the family with a good job.

"After graduating with my master's degree in computer science, I got a good job in India, but I dreamed of coming to America, the land of opportunity. So I did some research and landed a job at a consulting firm called Danzi, which specialized in contract work for American companies. The first couple of years, I worked on a team made up of Americans who gave us all the details on what the code should do. We would write the code from India while they were sleeping in America."

"Satish, I know how outsourcing works," David interjected. "This is an inspirational story, but what does it have to do with your background in blockchain and your current role at NuKoin?"

"I was just getting to that, sir," replied Satish. "One day, my boss called Ramesh and I into his office and asked us what we knew about blockchain. I had done some research but had never written any code."

David didn't realize he had rolled his eyes, but both Satish and Ramesh saw it.

"Sir, our manager offered us a chance to come to America and write blockchain code," explained Satish. "We could not pass it up. We both worked late into the evenings and learned blockchain on our own time. Ramesh has a story very similar to mine—he is also the first in his family to have a chance to come to America. Ramesh and I have worked hundreds of hours developing our skills."

"Where do you live now? Are you both renting apartments in Boston with your families?"

"We stay with some other consultants from Danzi. There are six of us altogether," explained Ramesh, "all developers from India. We share a two-bedroom apartment just outside the city. We each send most of our wages home to our families in India."

"Six people in a two-bedroom apartment?" remarked David. "Is that even legal?"

"Back home in India, that would be considered more than enough room," said Satish casually.

"Once we got to America," said Ramesh, "we continued to study night and day. We even contributed to several open-source blockchain projects."

David was beginning to soften. Both developers had overcome tremendous obstacles in life and were thousands of miles away from home, struggling to be successful. These guys had no plan B—this was their one shot. Their families were counting on them to succeed and to send the fruits of their labor home.

"What happens if it doesn't work out here at NuKoin?" asked David.

"Then we return to India," replied Satish flatly. "Our families are counting on us."

"Okay, let's get back to the code," said David. "Explain to me what you are trying to do."

Satish and Ramesh went through every line of code they had written for NuKoin, and David gave them some pointers. David began to see they were not as clueless as he'd first thought—they just didn't possess some key information about the NuKoin codebase. They simply needed a mentor.

They spent most of the day going over code and exchanging information. Periodically, Satish or Ramesh would tell a story from his life in India, and David would give a lesson on a particular coding technique. When the day was over, everyone in the room had been both teacher and student.

"Guys, this has been a good day," said David. "Get some rest tonight, and let's see what you can do tomorrow."

"Thank you, sir," said Satish. "You have helped us so much. We will not forget what you have done for us. We will make it up to you."

The three men shook hands, and David was left alone in his office. He stood and stared out the window, thinking about everything that had gone on. He decided to leave a little early so he could have dinner at a decent hour with Owen.

He sent Owen a text message and told him he would pick up some Chinese food on his way home.

David and Owen spent the evening in front of the TV, watching sports in quintessential boys-bonding style. They stayed awake until they both started nodding off on the couch.

Before turning out the light, David took his habitual walk to Owen's room to say good night. Owen was almost asleep but stirred when he heard his father at the door.

"Dad, I like when you're home early."

"It was fun. Spending time with you is my favorite thing to do."

"Good night, Dad. I love you."

"Love you, too, buddy," said David as he turned out the light. As he was closing the door, he quietly said the refrain from the family song, "And if the road is too hard to pass..."

Owen pulled the covers up to his face as he quietly hummed the rest of the tune that his father had started. David quietly closed the door and started back to his room but then heard Owen jump from his bed.

"That's it!" yelled Owen.

David rushed back into the room. "Owen, are you okay?"

"Dad, that's it," repeated Owen. "We'll fly like ponies in the sky!"

"I know the song, Owen, but why are you yelling?"

"The bitcoin passphrase. That's Mom's bitcoin passphrase!"

Owen was already sitting at his computer, typing.

David walked over to get him back into bed. "Owen, I told you this was a long shot. I warned you about getting too emotionally attached to this."

David was silent as he watched Owen getting more frustrated as each attempt at cracking the passphrase was rejected as invalid on the computer screen.

"Owen, it's late. Let's talk about it in the morning," said David calmly.

"No, Dad, I know this is it. It has to be it... This was our song. It's the perfect passphrase. I know this is it."

"Which combinations did you already try?"

"We'll fly like ponies in the sky... Fly like ponies in the sky... Ponies in the sky... In the sky like the ponies..."

"Did you try with and without capitalization?" asked David.

"Yes, and I even tried 'we will' instead of abbreviating it."

"Did you try punctuation at the end?"

"Yes, I tried with and without the period."

"Try an exclamation mark or a question mark," suggested David.

Owen tapped a few more times before standing up abruptly from the desk.

"Oh my God..." whispered Owen. "Ponies in the sky... with an exclamation at the end. We're in."

They looked at each other for a long moment before tears appeared in Owen's eyes. They hugged tightly for a couple of minutes, each giving in to his emotions. Owen was reliving the loss of his mother, and David was realizing the depth of hurt that his son still carried. She might have been gone, but she had left them a puzzle, and they had solved it. Both of them could almost sense her looking down at them with pride.

After several minutes, they loosened their grip and stared at the computer.

"Dad, you know more about this. You take a look."

David sat down and started typing and clicking... clicking and typing. He put his hands in his lap and let out a long breath.

"This wallet has just over three thousand bitcoin," said David.

"That's over thirty million dollars, right?"

"Yes," replied David in shock. "That's exactly what this is worth." He just sat there, shaking his head in disbelief.

"I knew we could figure out the passphrase," said Owen excitedly. "I just can't understand why Mom had a bitcoin wallet that she never told us about. She created it a long time ago, before bitcoin was worth anything—that I can understand. She probably was just messing around, but after bitcoin was going up in value, how could she keep that from us?"

"Maybe she just forgot," said David. "But it won't do much good wondering, because we will never know the answer."

"What do we do now with all this money?" asked Owen.

"Well, let's get this one detail straight," replied David. "This is not money. However, there are plenty of people that will give us money for these bitcoins, so your question is a good one. For now, we need to keep this a complete secret. No one can know about this, Owen."

"You can trust me, Dad. I'm not telling anyone."

"I mean it, Owen. None of your friends, not a single soul. Absolutely no one."

"Dad, seriously, you can trust me with this secret. This was my mom's wallet. I'm not letting anyone spoil the legacy she's left us."

David spent the next thirty minutes teaching Owen how to back up a bitcoin wallet in several different ways. They gave each other a hug, and Owen got back into bed.

Owen started to sing the song but stopped suddenly. "Maybe we can just hum the tune for the foreseeable future and not say the words out loud."

"I think that would be a great idea."

David turned out the lights and walked to his room in disbelief that Owen had guessed the passphrase. He'd been counting on it, although he would never admit that to his son.

15

Nicole Mancini arrived at the Turner home at three in the afternoon, about an hour before David had to leave for his flight to St. Petersburg. Owen answered the door and was anything but quiet.

"Hello, Ms. Mancini. Please come in."

"Hello, Owen. Please call me Nicole."

"Please, let me take your bags and show you to your room," he offered.

"Thank you," agreed Nicole. "Such a gentleman."

Owen led Nicole upstairs to the guest room with a smile on his face. His mother had always told him to "start off the way you want to finish." He had already solved one puzzle, and next, he would unmask this Nicole Mancini and determine her true motives for entering the life of his father.

"Nicole, thanks for coming early," said David as he entered the guest room. "You never know what traffic will be like on the way to Logan Airport."

"It was no problem at all," replied Nicole. "Owen and I were just getting to know each other. You have a very polite young man."

"Indeed," said David as he smiled at Owen. He was proud of his son's effort but gave him a look that made it clear he knew his son was up to something.

Once David had finished packing, he said goodbye to them both, careful to give Owen a hug and Nicole a handshake. She went to her room to unpack while Owen went to work on his new computer.

After a few hours, Nicole called Owen for dinner. He came into the kitchen, surprised to see pots steaming and smells coming from the oven.

"What's going on in here?" asked Owen.

"This would be dinner," replied Nicole. "I made you my famous chicken casserole."

Nicole brought some bowls to the table and sat down, motioning for Owen to join her. The table was all prepared for the meal, complete with a tablecloth and place settings.

"What's wrong, Owen?" asked Nicole nervously.

He was quietly standing and looking at the table. "Nothing. It's just that I haven't seen the table set like this since my mom passed away."

Her heart sank. "I'm sorry, Owen. I just wanted to make you a nice home-cooked meal. I didn't know it would—"

"It's okay," said Owen. "It just took me by surprise. Dad and I usually eat by the TV, that's all. It'll be nice being back at the table again."

Nicole smiled reflectively as Owen sat down. They talked about a wide range of subjects over dinner, and Owen ate enough for two boys his size. Nicole enjoyed having her cooking received well and did not mind cleaning up the dishes when Owen went to his room to use his computer.

Owen was researching Bitcoin feverishly, trying to get insight into his mother's secret world. When he realized it had gotten late and he'd lost track of time, he went to look for a snack. He expected to find Nicole in the kitchen, but the house was silent. He got curious and walked around, looking for her. Finally, he heard her quietly talking on her phone inside the guest room. Being careful not to be noticed, he moved closer to see if he could overhear.

"I can wait, there's no rush... Yes, sir, I was thinking the same thing... No, not yet. But he will."

Owen grew more curious and wished he could hear the voice on the other end of the call.

"How about we meet and discuss it in person? I'm not comfortable talking about this over the phone... Yes, tomorrow will work."

Owen heard Nicole moving toward the bedroom door and was thankful he only had socks on his feet, allowing him to jog away quietly.

A few moments later, Nicole appeared in the kitchen. "There you are. I was wondering if I would see you before you went to sleep."

"I was just getting a snack," replied Owen, still a little nervous from his eavesdropping. "I'm probably going to head to bed soon."

"Okay. Sounds good," said Nicole. "What is your plan for tomorrow? It's Saturday, but I need to head into the city, so I thought you might need a ride somewhere."

If Nicole was going to meet someone mysterious, he had to follow her. Thinking on his feet, he replied, "Could you drop me off at the library? I'd like to do some research on a project I'm working on."

Owen wasn't exactly lying, but the project had nothing to do with his schoolwork. He was definitely going to be doing some research of his own.

"Sure, we can take the T into town, and I can walk to my appointment from the library. That will work out fine."

They agreed on a departure time, and both headed to bed.

In the morning, Owen was up early and showered. He made himself some breakfast and went back to his room to finish getting ready. As he made his way past the hallway bathroom, he heard the shower turn on and concluded that Nicole was about to get in. He paused outside the door and decided to get a little daring.

He gently pushed open her bedroom door and peered inside. The bed was still unmade, and the door to the en suite bathroom was half open. Steam was coming out, and he could hear sounds from inside, telling him that Nicole was in the shower. He concluded that he had at least ten minutes, if Nicole was an average woman. So he glanced around the room, looking for anything suspicious.

After a few moments, he defied all sense of good judgment and stepped into her bedroom. Her nightclothes were on the floor near the bathroom, and her suitcase was open on a table near the bed. He looked in the suitcase and gently pushed some of the clothes back to see if anything else was inside.

Her purse was leaning against the suitcase, and her phone was charging on the nightstand. He quietly walked toward the bed and pressed a button on the phone and noticed it was not PIN locked. Nicole must have checked her phone just prior to getting in the shower and had not bothered to lock the screen.

He didn't know how much time he had left, but he navigated to her recent-calls list. He saw the call from the previous night and pulled out his own phone to take a picture of the phone number. But before he could unlock his own phone, the shower turned off. *What happened to ladies taking a long time in the shower?* he thought.

Panicking, he put his phone back in his pocket and raced across the room. He opened the door and gently closed it behind him, trying not to make any noise.

A moment later, Nicole walked out of the bathroom in a towel and made her way to her suitcase to get ready. She paused for a moment as she stared at her clothes. Then she continued getting dressed and did her makeup for the day.

When she was ready to leave, she called Owen, who joined her near the front door. He got into her car, and the two headed to the parking lot near the subway station. They took the T downtown and got off at the stop near the library.

"How much time do you need at the library?"

"A couple hours, I guess."

"Perfect. I have a couple of errands to run and will come back to get you in a few hours."

Nicole walked off, and Owen pretended to walk into the library. He ducked behind one of the exterior pillars and watched Nicole from a distance. He pulled off his coat and switched it with another one from his backpack. After he added a baseball cap, his disguise was complete. He crossed the street and followed her from a distance.

Nicole walked for a few blocks and onto some more populated streets. Tourists were all around, along with various street vendors selling food and souvenirs. Children were playing in the park, and Owen was sure he was moving unnoticed.

When Nicole's pace slowed, he ducked into a small group of trees and peered between them. She stopped at a hot dog stand on the edge of Boston Common and placed her black hobo bag on the ground. The man in front of her had done the same thing, but when the man received his hot dog, he picked up Nicole's bag instead of his own.

Owen's pulse increased, and goose bumps formed on his arms. He knew Nicole was up to something, and he had proof. He pulled his phone from his pocket and took a picture of the man walking away from Nicole. The man crossed the road and disappeared into the subway station. Owen looked at his phone and cursed aloud when he realized his picture was too blurry to determine the man's identity.

Owen turned back toward the hot dog stand and realized he could no longer see Nicole. He had turned out to be a terrible private detective and had lost track of his suspect. Dejected but unwilling to give up, he started searching the nearby streets.

After he departed, Nicole emerged from a doorway and shook her head at the sight of Owen jogging down a side street. "He certainly has his father's passion," she said to herself.

Nicole wanted to follow Owen to make sure he was okay, but she couldn't let Owen know he'd been found out. So she decided that Owen would have to make his way back to the library on his own. She continued to her appointment in the opposite direction, heading into the dense streets of Chinatown. She doubled back twice to make sure she was not being followed by anyone else then stepped into a small coffee shop with only a dozen seats. A man was sitting by himself, busy on his mobile phone, but the restaurant was otherwise empty.

Nicole took the seat opposite the man. "I am beginning to have some second thoughts as to whether you have everyone's best interests in mind," said Nicole.

"I always have everyone's best interests in mind," said

William DeFrost, "especially mine. We have some things we need to talk about."

"I have done everything you asked me to do, and it's all going according to our plan," said Nicole.

"So it's *our* plan now, is it? I seem to recall having to convince you to get on board with this," reminded DeFrost. "And I need to make sure you are still on the team."

"I have David under control."

"That is what the last CFO told me too. And how did that work out for me?"

"I'm not sure how to answer that, because you never wanted to talk about the last CFO."

"Those details are not important. What is important is that I get full control of NuKoin, with or without Turner."

"You underestimate him. David is not going to just give up control of his company and let you take over."

"Everyone has a price, and this is a lot of money."

"I did my research before I agreed to work for you. Delphi doesn't have that kind of capital."

"Let's just say I have some new and powerful friends in this part of town."

"You already told me about the Chinese funding," said Nicole.

"Yes, but you have no clue just how much."

"Go ahead—impress me."

"The less you know the better," said DeFrost. "Leave those details to me. Just make sure you get leverage with David in any way you can. We are talking about life-altering money here... for both of us."

"I told you I'd get it done, and I will," said Nicole.

"I'm just making sure you're fully committed," said DeFrost. "Fully."

"What's that supposed to mean?"

"Use every asset at your disposal," answered DeFrost.

Nicole resisted the urge to kick him in the groin under the table. She simply stared at him until DeFrost averted his eyes.

"If we're a team, then why did you blindside me in that meeting the other day and agree to David's ICO idea?" asked Nicole.

"I didn't agree to anything," responded DeFrost. "And let me remind you that if you had done your job in getting him on board with Chinese funding in the first place, we wouldn't be in this mess."

"I'll find what you need, then you'll have your leverage."

"Yes, I heard you had moved in for a few days," said DeFrost with an obnoxious grin. "Playing house. Nice touch."

"I will get you the leverage you need. There is no need to involve the boy," said Nicole sternly. "Just remember that."

"Now you think you can give me the orders. Just remember that it was me that found you. People that start feeling entitled end up getting hurt."

"Is that a threat?"

"It's whatever you need it to be to make sure you get the job done. David agrees to my terms, or we get a new CEO. Do your job, or I'll find someone who can."

"Keep the boy out of this," repeated Nicole, staring directly into DeFrost's eyes.

She stood without another word and left the small restaurant. After walking back to Boston Common, working off her frustration with a fast pace, she searched for Owen.

After ten minutes, she saw him and his baseball-cap disguise emerging from a side street. She raced ahead and into the middle of the Common and sat at a park bench where she could be seen. She put on her sunglasses so that she could watch for Owen.

She could tell from his sudden return to slinking among the trees that he had seen her, so she rose from the bench and started walking slowly back toward the library. She made sure to feign talking on her phone or texting to give Owen time to take a shortcut back to the library.

Nicole headed up the front steps and into the main sitting area, searching for Owen. She found him with a book in his hands and sitting near the back stairs.

"There you are, Owen," said Nicole. "Did you get everything done that you needed to do?"

"Yes, I did. Thank you," said Owen, trying to catch his breath.

"Ready to leave, then?"

Nicole let out a slight smirk as she noticed Owen wiping sweat from the sides of his head. She couldn't resist. "Homework is hard work, huh?"

"Um, yeah. I have some tough classes at school this year."

Nicole and Owen caught the T back to their car and headed back to the house. She made some chicken soup from scratch with grilled-cheese sandwiches, then Owen retired to his room to continue his Bitcoin research.

16

———

David woke from a nap to the stewardess asking him to raise his seat while they made their approach into Pulkovo Airport, about a dozen miles outside the center of St. Petersburg, Russia. He had been required to get his travel visa prior to his flight and now only needed to fill out a migration card as he waited for the plane to land.

Walking through the airport, he thought it seemed like a typical American airport, but he couldn't shake the feeling of being watched. He had grown critical of his own government, but at least in America, he knew the rules of engagement. In this foreign city, he would be on his best behavior.

That was not the first time he had been overseas, but several years had passed since his last trip. Mia was the world traveler in the family. David used to tease her about her living out of a suitcase and how many frequent flyer miles she was racking up. But that all ended when she left her public relations gig at the tech firm.

David was surprised at how easily he made his way through Russian immigration, which put his mind at ease.

He made his way past the lines of taxi drivers ready to take advantage of foreign travelers. Public transportation from the airport was not easy, so he was thankful he'd reserved ground transportation in advance.

After verifying that his driver knew the correct destination, he relaxed in the back seat and took in the sights.

St. Petersburg had been the capital of the Russian Empire since the early 1700s, named after its founder, Peter the Great, who relocated the capital from Moscow. It remained the capital until the early 1900s, when it was renamed Leningrad after the leading voice of the Russian Revolution. The seat of Russian government was then moved back to Moscow, where it remained up to the present.

The blockchain conference was fittingly located in the quintessential east-meets-west city, drawing attendees from at least five continents. Some of the best software-developer talent in the world was located in Eastern Europe and Asia, and David was looking forward to meeting some of them. Fortunately, he was tired enough from his trip to get a decent night's sleep, despite the jet lag.

In the morning, he was able to check into the conference quickly since he was so early, and he grabbed some pastries and a cup of coffee. Taking a seat at one of the small tables in the lobby, he looked through the various items in the bag of swag he'd been given during registration.

The room gradually filled up as the start of the opening keynote address drew closer. He decided to go and look for a seat in the main auditorium but felt compelled to first consume a second cup of coffee. As he savored the caffeine, he became firmly convinced that Nicole would be ruined from her expensive American coffee for good if she were able to experience what St. Petersburg had to offer.

Just as he was finishing, he heard a familiar voice.

"David Turner, how interesting it is to run into you."

He recognized the journalist's voice before he even turned around. "Tina Wood, what brings you to St. Petersburg?"

"I think you remember why I'm here," said Tina in a coy tone. "Same story, same goal."

"Ah, right," said David with a nod. "Your Bitcoin research—how's that going?"

"I'm learning some very interesting information. And I'm looking forward to getting some new contacts."

"Anyone in particular? I might be able to introduce you to some people."

"How about Satoshi Nakamoto?"

David started to both laugh and choke on his coffee and struggled to regain his composure. "I'm pretty sure that's one interview I cannot arrange."

"You don't think he's here?"

"If he was at this conference, that would be quite a compliment to the organizers. Revealing himself at this conference would be quite the event."

"Well, if he does," said Tina, "this journalist will be present to capture the moment."

"You're wasting your time looking for him. If he wanted to be found, then he would have been found already. Not all who wander are lost."

"Ah, Tolkien," said Tina. "Interesting choice in metaphors. Will Bitcoin be the one network to rule them all? Or maybe it will be NuKoin?"

"This is a blockchain conference, not a Bitcoin conference, and certainly not a NuKoin-promoted event. You're a bit feisty. Nicole was right about that."

"Speaking of Nicole, is she here too?"

"No, it's just me from NuKoin."

"And what interests does NuKoin have here in Russia?"

"This is a blockchain conference. Blockchain is what we do," replied David with a slightly condescending tone.

"You don't have to get testy with me, David. I'm a reporter, and the asking of questions is pretty common in my business. I was just curious what specific impacts this conference might bring to NuKoin."

David furrowed his brow and looked away, timing the rolling of his eyes so that Tina wouldn't see. Then he quickly got over Tina's mock interrogation and prepared for a real one. She picked up on his change in demeanor and followed his eyes to see a young man approaching.

The man started speaking while he was still ten feet away. "David, how good to finally see you at a conference," said Demetri Kornechiv. "I was beginning to fear that NuKoin had bought the digital farm."

"Thank you very much for your concern, Demetri," David said, disdain filling his voice. "I actually just came here for a hug."

"If I squeezed you any harder, NuKoin wouldn't be able to breathe," retorted Kornechiv.

Tina had been quietly taking all that in, smirking at the two geeks exchanging barbs like a pair of playground children. "Wow, is this like MMA? Menacing Men Arguing—"

"We're not arguing," said David. "We're just discussing a mutually interesting topic."

"I agree, and I'm hoping we can continue our conversation at my panel discussion tomorrow," said Kornechiv. "We had someone drop out, and I'd welcome the opportunity to adjust your thinking in front of an audience... That's if you are up for it."

"You want me to give a presentation on NuKoin and why it's superior?"

"Don't get carried away, Turner," replied Kornechiv. "This is a panel discussion. I just thought you'd want to be on stage to comment in case you get mentioned as an example of crypto failure."

David knew the man was baiting him. He knew Kornechiv just wanted drama to entertain the audience, but he wasn't going to back down from a challenge—especially not a challenge from his nemesis, Demetri Kornechiv.

"I want a list of the questions ahead of time," said David. "And a list of the other presenters, complete with full bios."

"Of course, of course," responded Kornechiv. "The panel is this afternoon on the main stage."

David mumbled some unspeakables as Kornechiv walked away, smiling. Tina was sipping her coffee, enjoying her glimpse of a different side of David Turner, who saw her amusement and felt the need to explain.

"Demetri Kornechiv... Russian but born and raised in Canada. He is the cofounder of a blockchain company that has been fairly mute when it comes to disclosing many details. He has some very interesting personal beliefs that would scare me if I didn't have so much doubt in his ability to pull off an actual product."

David's summary was cut short by an announcement over the lobby speakers that the conference would begin soon. Putting down his coffee, he wished Tina well and went to find a seat.

The conference was well attended, and David recognized several faces. All the key stakeholders from the cryptocurrency world were expected. Bankers, venture capitalists, entrepreneurs, and plenty of developers were in attendance, each with resumes and CVs in hand.

David sat through several presentations and was starting to feel the effects of being in a new time zone when lunch arrived. As they were walking out toward the area where lunch would be provided, David was handed a folder with a few papers inside. Glancing quickly at the contents, he realized that his panel discussion was directly after lunch.

He decided to skip the meal and study the panel questions and information on the other presenters.

In addition to Kornechiv was a lawyer, an official from the United Nations, and a bank executive. The lawyer was a product of Stanford Law, a fitting place to find someone specializing in the legality of cryptocurrency, David thought. He forgot the lawyer's name seconds after reading it.

David had little patience for the United Nations in general, so he skimmed quickly over the credentials of Asha Tinibu from Nigeria. Her apparent focus on cross-border payments seemed pretty innocuous.

Vitalik Grune was the head of the Russian Federal Bank, and his biography was a bit vague. David paused for a few minutes, wondering if Grune was supportive of blockchain or against it. Despite what many Americans believed, the Russians were fairly open-minded about technology and new ideas.

David shifted gears and went over his notes, which he often used to remind himself of various talking points he might need to discuss. The hour-and-a-half-long lunch break passed quickly, and he gathered his things to set off for the panel discussion.

David arrived about ten minutes early, but the other

panel members were already in the room and had claimed the prominent seats at the table. That was fine with David, as he preferred to be off the radar anyway. Taking the last seat at the table also had the added advantage of placing him far away from Kornechiv, who was acting as the moderator.

At precisely one p.m., Demetri Kornechiv asked the growing crowd to take their seats as he introduced the people on stage.

"Welcome to this panel discussion on the Global Legal Challenges for Decentralized Identity Management. Today, you will hear from Sam Wisener, Doctor of Law, specializing in crypto legality, and adjunct professor at his alma mater, Stanford University.

"Next, we have Asha Tinubu, Deputy to the Assistant Secretary General at the United Nations, focusing on global finance in Africa, and best-selling author. Seated next to Dr. Tinubu, we have Vitalik Grune, Vice Chairman of the Asian Financial Council and head of the Russian Federal Bank.

"And at the far end of the table, David Turner, cofounder and CEO of NuKoin, an American-based anonymous crypto currency."

"I am Demetri Kornechiv, author, adjunct professor, and advocate for the global identity movement. I am also the founder of an exciting new crypto tech firm, poised to usher in the era of Bitcoin 2.0."

David hoped his face didn't reveal his true feelings for Kornechiv and his gross self-aggrandizement.

"The first question will be for Dr. Tinubu..."

David sat patiently for the next thirty minutes as he listened to Kornechiv engage his fellow panelists in question after question. He found the topics largely boring, so he was glad he was not forced to feign the interest that a direct question would bring. He waited for a question leveraging his expertise to come his way but began to sense a ruse when the main part of the session concluded and the audience was invited to ask questions.

He decided to make an impression in the room at the earliest opportunity and was delighted that the first question offered him that platform.

"This question is for you, Dr. Kornechiv," the audience member said into a microphone. "Are you saying that, in the future, the government-issued identifications that we all rely on every day will no longer serve a purpose?"

"Thank you for your question," replied Demetri Kornechiv. "When I look at the world, I see a global marketplace that is too reliant on the government to provide safety to the markets. There are vast amounts of untapped capital sitting on the sidelines in fear. They fear the con man. They fear losing their store of value.

"If we could give everyone a single identification that we knew was accurate and that could not be altered in any way, it would enable us all to trust each other in open commerce. We would create digital identities and store them on the blockchain, where they cannot be altered or deleted. That is the strength of blockchain. It gives us a global database that no one can alter, providing a shared trust among those who use it."

"If I may interject," said David as he addressed Kornechiv directly, "it seems that you and I have a drastically different view on what decentralization means. Anyone familiar with your company knows that you're seeking to replace dozens of different government-sponsored identifications with a single global identification, with your company software firmly in the middle. Why would any government or individual want to trust that your intentions are not nefarious in nature? Why would we swap one regime for another?"

"Mr. Turner," said Kornechiv, "let's try and keep this conversation civil and free from false representations."

"Dr. Kornechiv," David continued, "you've also suggested that maybe the digital key to accessing the global identity should be embedded in the physical body of the identity holder. You claim this helps the security, but would the technology you propose also allow governments to track the physical movements of its citizens and visitors with well-positioned sensors?"

"Mr. Turner, your fearmongering threatens to betray your own bias. Blockchain will usher in a new world of equality and free trade."

"Freedom, by definition, cannot be restrained. Trade has never really been free because it has always been subject to the manipulations of those that control the system. The real value of blockchain is only realized when each identity is verifiable but also anonymous. Blockchain without anonymity becomes the worst kind of centralized control."

"It is precisely the anonymous transaction that has allowed those in power to operate unrestrained," countered Kornechiv. "Your American government, for example, has long cloaked its so-called black ops through brokers and third parties, in an intentional strategy of obfuscation. What makes you think anonymity will preclude state actors from using your system to up their game?"

"Nothing prevents anyone from being anonymous. It is the nature of the level playing field that removes the self-granted power of the state actor," explained David. "On the surface, we both seem to want the same thing, Dr.

Kornechiv. The difference is whether the system we espouse can meet our stated objective or whether it is a secret and alternative agenda."

Kornechiv was visibly annoyed as he glanced around the room to see heads nodding in approval of David's ideas. His plan to embarrass David had come back upon him instead. "Let's take the next question," said Kornechiv.

"This question is for Mr. Grune," said a middle-aged white male of average height. "The Russian government has been somewhat outspoken on the topic of whether cryptocurrency is viable and legal as a digital method of payment. Can you elaborate on your personal thoughts and the position of the Russian government?"

Vitalik Grune wore a permanent frown on his face that made him look angry even when he was smiling. His face was weathered with wrinkles that seemed to each tell a tale of its own. He was cautious in his response, with a deliberate tone.

"The Russian government has allowed bitcoin miners free range for many years. Russian-based computers make up a large portion of the Bitcoin network. If Russia was against bitcoin and other altcoins, why would we allow the miners to continue?" asked Grune. "We do, however, have a responsibility to make sure that no one can prey upon unsuspecting victims by taking their life savings. There is a future role for the state to bring stability to the digital marketplace."

David had heard bankers attempt to discuss this before, so he gradually tuned out the Russian. The question-and-answer discussion ventured into the world of legal matters and patents, took a turn into whether governments possessed the sole right to issue currency, and finally headed back toward the potential evils of anonymous financial transactions. David entered into a few lively discussions and was even able to plug NuKoin by name on several occasions.

After the session concluded, many people approached David to get his business card or, to his delight, to give him a resume and a personal sales pitch. He was distracted by the commotion and did not notice Tina Wood close her notebook and slip out the back door.

David spent the rest of the day being something of a celebrity at the conference as word got out about his confrontations at the session. He turned down several invitations for dinner or drinks and chose to go to bed early to try to beat the jet lag.

The next morning, he woke before dawn and noticed a new text message on his phone from Tina Wood. He tapped out a quick response.

> **David**: *How did u get my personal number?*
> **Tina**: *I'm an investigative journalist, remember? Need to talk asap*
> **David**: *Urgent and important or just important?*
> **Tina**: *You need to hear what I have to say.*
> **David**: *Fine. Meet in lobby 10min*
> **Tina**: *Too public. Coffee shop near side entrance to hotel?*
> **David**: *k*

David took a quick shower and got dressed. Then he locked his personal valuables in the room safe and put his laptop in his backpack just in case... In case of what, he wasn't sure. It just seemed appropriate for a clandestine meeting with a somewhat unknown woman in a foreign land.

Tina was waiting for him at one of five tables in the coffee shop. David sat down in the small chair opposite her but sat sideways so as to have a sight line to the door.

"I feel like I should talk in whispers or code," said David with a twinkle in his eye. "What's this all about?"

"I was in your session yesterday and did some follow-up research."

"Oh, that. Well, I can get a little excited about certain topics."

"It's not you that I researched. It's a couple of your fellow panelists."

"Really? Do tell."

"First of all, Vitalik Grune... Did you know that he's former FSB?"

"Russian Federal Security Service?" asked David. "That's basically the rebuild of the KGB."

"I know what it is. I am asking if you knew he was FSB."

"I didn't have time to research all the panelists. I only got the list about an hour before the session started. I guess I am not completely surprised, though. Appointments in Russia come to those that play the game."

"Okay, how about Demetri Kornechiv?" asked Tina.

"I know a lot about him, and I can promise he's not FSB."

"Indeed, but did you know he is an advisor to Ginsick Capital?" asked Tina.

"The Chinese VC firm?"

"Yes, that Ginsick Capital," said Tina.

"That is annoying on a few levels," said David in disgust. "The Chinese have lots of capital, but it comes at a price."

"Such as?"

"Such as the fact that even if the money is 'private' VC money, it always connects back to the Chinese government somehow, and that's one set of agendas that's best avoided."

Tina took a few sips of her coffee and let the information sink into David's mind. She was acting casual with him but was studying his mannerisms and reactions intently. She would need more information about the darker side of cryptocurrency if she had any hope of flushing out Satoshi Nakamoto.

She finally spoke. "What do the Chinese and Russians want with cryptocurrency?"

"The same thing that every state actor wants. Control the flow of money. In the world banking system, the US dollar is still king. You can clearly see that on the commodities trading markets. If the Chinese or the Russians can supplant the US dollar, that would be a huge financial blow to the United States."

"I thought you were hoping for the same thing?"

"Don't trade the devil you don't know for the devil you do," responded David matter-of-factly. "I may have issues with the US banking policy, but I am not naive in regard to some of the other options."

A woman walked over to their table with a mug and coffee pot in her hands. David didn't understand Russian, but the context clues indicated that he was expected to purchase a drink if he intended to sit inside the shop.

After the woman left, David added a small amount of milk to his coffee and took a couple small sips. As he drank, a thought crossed his mind.

"Tina, why are you really here in Russia?"

"I'm beginning to see how big my story could become. If

I want to meet the big players in the game, I need to go where they congregate."

"There are many sides to the crypto world. Make sure you're not digging into the darker side."

"Like drugs and illicit sex?"

"Just be careful how deep you try to trace the money flow. These are powerful people that prefer to remain anonymous," warned David.

"I'm a big girl. I can take care of myself."

"I'm not talking about organized crime. I'm talking about powerful state actors," said David, pausing for dramatic effect. "Did your research on Ginsick Capital reveal that they are financing video-surveillance software that can recognize thousands of faces in a crowd at the same moment?"

Tina shook her head slightly.

"Ask yourself what China or Russia would do with such technology," said David.

Tina took the last sip of her coffee and placed the mug between herself and David. She thought about all the photos on social media, linked to limitless personal information. She thought about suspected terrorists in crowded train stations. She thought about what the endgame might be for an anonymous identity known as Satoshi Nakamoto, who had not shown interest in the vast and growing value of bitcoin.

"Promise me you'll be careful too," said Tina as she buttoned her coat and slipped into the deserted alley.

17

David paid for both coffees and returned to the hotel. He had just enough time to grab a quick pastry in the lobby before taking his seat in the main auditorium.

The rest of the day, he listened to several different speakers in a variety of rooms. As the day wore on, he found himself listening less and paying more attention to the other attendees. He studied their faces and observed their expressions, becoming increasingly curious about what roles they played in this evolving game he was caught up in.

He found himself getting more suspicious of a growing number of people. He imagined they were attending sessions just to spy on him... or maybe it wasn't his imagination.

He began choosing seats that offered the best viewpoint of the entire room, especially the entrance. He started paying attention to exactly who was in attendance and became convinced the same group of five or six had been with him for almost the entire day.

His frustration finally hit a climax shortly after four in

the afternoon, when David left a session early in an attempt to throw off any would-be followers. He crossed the main lobby and was about to exit the building when he was approached by a man wearing sunglasses. David suddenly changed directions and ran toward the restrooms. Seeing his exit path was blocked and fearing for his safety, he ducked down a hall and into the ladies' bathroom.

He quietly closed the door behind himself and ducked down, peering under the bathroom stalls, checking for legs. He was relieved that no women were in the stalls, but that also meant he was alone.

He opened one of the doors and stood on the toilet after quietly shutting the latch behind himself. He waited for what seemed like hours until sufficient foot traffic could be heard outside the restroom. Sensing that he had to take a chance, he left his hideout and headed toward the exit.

On his way out, he passed two startled women but didn't stop long enough for them to protest. The conference session had ended, and lots of people were milling around. He decided against the seclusion of his hotel room and headed for the lobby, the most crowded place he could imagine.

As he mingled among the small crowd in the lobby, David began to relax, feeling secure among the sheer numbers of people. As he looked around for someone he knew, someone grabbed his arm.

"David Turner," said a man in sunglasses, "someone would like to have a word with you."

Speechless, David followed the man's pressure on his arm toward the side of the room. Two other men in sunglasses were standing in front of the door, now open. David's mind was working overtime, but he felt he had no choice but to follow the man's lead.

Once he was inside, the door closed, and he was left alone except for one other person sitting at a table. Vitalik Grune motioned for David to take the seat opposite him. David quickly scanned the room and slowly took the seat.

"I can assure you that we're alone and not being watched," said Grune.

"Can you explain to me why I've been kidnapped and thrown into a locked room?" said David incredulously.

"We thought it best to make sure our meeting stayed a secret. There are lots of prying eyes that jump to incorrect conclusions."

"Did you happen to consider simply talking to me after our panel discussion yesterday?"

"We didn't decide to talk to you until today," explained Grune.

"You could have easily just sent me a note asking to meet in private and spared yourself all the antics. And why are you talking in the first-person plural?"

"I'm not here on behalf of myself, Mr. Turner. I'm here on behalf of a larger interest."

"And who might that be?"

"It's probably best for me to remain vague on that point for now."

"I know about your ties to the FSB, so I assume this connects back to the Kremlin?"

"You can believe what you wish," mumbled Grune. "You Americans are—how do you say it—free."

"Free to believe what I want in regard to the FSB connection or in regard to the Kremlin?"

Grune let a frown grow on his face. "I'm a banker, not a spy. I represent the banking interests of the Russian Federation. I'm here at this conference to make connections with those involved with cryptocurrency. We've been watching your company with great interest, David, and we wanted to see if we could discuss ways that we can help your project."

David tried very hard not to let his face reveal what was going through his mind. *Has NuKoin really gotten the attention of the Russian Federation?* David was both flattered and nervous. He had been so focused on deflecting the interest of his own nation that the thought hadn't occurred to him that other state actors might be watching him.

"Mr. Grune, I'm an American citizen, and my country might think it unwise to even be talking with a Russian official."

"I think you're beginning to understand the need for this meeting to be private," replied Grune. "But surely you have the freedom of speech in America. Is it a crime to talk to someone?"

"I think the 2016 US elections proved that it might be," answered David before he could stop himself.

"Fake news," said Grune with a wave of his hand and a look of dismissal. "I expected you to be more informed and pragmatic."

"Pragmatic?" said David with a raised eyebrow.

"Was I wrong in assuming you were a businessman?"

"Mr. Grune, what exactly is it that you want?"

"Ah yes, you are a businessman. Just as I thought."

David suddenly became aware of the sweat on his palms and casually wiped them on his pants. He shifted slightly in his chair and could feel his pant legs sticking to the seat.

"I think if you would suspend your innate suspicion, you would find that we have quite a bit in common."

"I very much doubt that," said David.

"Well, we both believe in the power of the people," replied Grune. "And we both believe cryptocurrency is a way to put the people back in control of their financial transactions."

"You said you were a banker. Now you expect me to believe that bankers want to give financial power back to the people?"

"You believe too many of the lies that are written in your primary school textbooks, and you confuse the motives of our two countries. Russia does not live by the mantra of capitalism and the inequalities that it produces. We're a nation run for the people."

"Now it's you trying to spread fake news."

"Don't avoid the facts. I have read your blogs personally. I know how you feel about what is going on in your country and the world. Again, I invite you to be willing to suspend your distrust and consider the truth of what I'm saying."

David stared at Vitalik Grune and considered his options. He suspected that trying to exit the room before hearing Grune out would not end well for him. Even if he did escape the room, the Russian government had tremendous resources and could kidnap him in many other places. On the other hand, if he did hear Grune out, he might learn details that would make it hard for David to remain alive if he failed to agree to work with Grune.

He decided to play along and hear what Grune had to say but to try to limit his exposure to information.

"Okay, please elaborate on your thoughts, but understand that I'm still obligated to my country should our discussion stray off the rails."

"Oh, I assure you our conversation won't be breaking any of your laws," responded Grune. "I just want to talk about your company."

"You want to talk about NuKoin?" said David with obvious reservation.

"My countrymen have invested lots of time and energy in Bitcoin."

"Lots of energy, that's for sure," said David, referencing the amount of electric power needed to run the Bitcoin network.

"Bitcoin was the pioneer, paving the way to a more advanced view on creating a global system of value transfer. But Bitcoin is deficient in its speed and security. We are actively seeking to partner with those who can solve those problems."

"There are literally hundreds—even thousands—of cryptocurrencies out there. Why the interest in NuKoin?"

"We recognize leadership when we see it. This blockchain movement will require leaders that speak their mind and aren't afraid of anyone's opinions. Yesterday, you showed us that you might be that kind of leader. So we did plenty of research last night to get a greater context on the life and beliefs of David Turner."

"You mean you deployed your agents to track down all my family, friends, and neighbors?"

"You watch too many spy movies. But no, we aren't interested in your neighbors."

David struggled with a slight smile, unsure of whether Grune had deliberately omitted "family" from his list of noninterests. Nonetheless, David relaxed just enough to talk to Vitalik Grune about the fundamental differences between NuKoin and Bitcoin. Grune was especially interested in how NuKoin handled anonymous financial transactions. David was very careful to keep the conversation at a high level, not giving any details of the exact methods used by the code. That would eventually be open source anyway, but he couldn't shake the feeling that he should go very light on internal technical details.

"What if NuKoin was being used by a terrorist organization to overthrow the American government?" proposed Grune. "Is there a way for the government to protect itself in advance? In other words, have you designed any methods of oversight? Any ways to prevent bad actors from hijacking the network?"

"There can be no bad NuKoin actors because the system is neutral. It's just a means of value storage and transfer," explained David. "It does not judge the actions and moral intentions of those who use it."

"Of course. But is there a way for NuKoin to assist those that do?"

"Do you mean by turning over log files to law enforcement?"

"I was probing a little deeper than that," answered Grune.

"How much deeper?"

"What about a special piece of code that could help proactive monitoring?"

"You want to know if I would put a back door into the software to allow you to see into all the transactions?"

"It was just an idea and a question around the boundaries of possibility," replied Grune.

"Back doors are just vulnerabilities and viruses used by those in power, a means to manipulate by—what did you call it?—by those who are 'for' the people."

"Government oversight is inevitable. To deny that reality is to be stuck in a world of dreams."

"NuKoin was born from a dream of a world free from the kind of 'oversight' you speak of," lectured David. "What governments call oversight people call oppression."

"That may be the case in America, but in the Federation, the ruble provides that safe and secure transfer of value inside the borders of our nation. What we lack is that same system of safety on the global scale. I already know you agree with me that the US dollar has become a vehicle of control and oppression worldwide."

David was beginning to see where the conversation was going but decided not to jump to any conclusions without hearing it said out loud. Against his better judgment, he continued to probe.

"Exactly what are you suggesting?"

"The crypto ruble."

"What does that even mean?" asked David with laughter in his voice. "The banking world is already online. No one is getting paid in stacks of paper bills anymore. Blockchain is all about decentralized control, so how does a central government issue and control a cryptocurrency?"

"With cryptocurrency, the government doesn't control the currency. The laws of supply and demand are in effect. But the government needs administrative access to prevent abuse," argued Grune.

David Turner and Vitalik Grune spent another hour arguing over conflicting government theory. Finally, Grune gave David an exit option, and he seized it.

"David, I want you to think it over," said Grune as he slid a white business card across the table with a single email address embossed. "When you send the email, just mention the headline from that day's *Washington Post* in the body of the email. We'll find you."

David took the card but later would regret doing so. The two men shook hands, and David exited the room. He crossed the lobby of the hotel and went to his room. He did not scan the room or even care who might be watching him. For that reason, he did not see Tina Wood or notice that she lingered just long enough to see Vitalik Grune leave the room five minutes later.

Then the man working the concierge desk used his smartphone for a few brief moments, proving that Tina wasn't the only person observing the conversations in the hotel that day.

18

David used the long flight home to think and get some much-needed rest. He was looking forward to getting back and seeing Owen. His flight was uneventful, and he landed on time at Logan Airport.

When he made it through customs and immigration in record time, he was surprised, and his faith in the system was briefly restored. He made his way toward the public transportation that brought him to the garage where his car was parked.

After throwing his bag into the back, he settled into the familiar feeling of the leather seats. Gripping the steering wheel, he felt a sense of control seep back into his bones. He loved his country and the freedoms it afforded. Being over-seas always reminded him of that basic point.

He pulled out of the parking lot and headed onto Interstate 90 West, away from the oceanside concourses. He cranked up the heat and decided to open the windows, the simultaneous heat and cold providing an additional metaphor for freedom.

As he exited the tunnel and drove toward Back Bay, he

picked up speed, trying to avoid the inevitable traffic of the approaching evening commute.

As he saw the brake lights forming ahead, he eased his foot on the brakes but noticed the pedal felt different. Within seconds, he was pumping hard, trying to slow his vehicle, to no avail. Averting his eyes from the road, he frantically searched for the lever of the emergency brake and pulled... He thought he pulled it in time. Recalling was hard. He just wanted to sleep, and for once in as long as he could remember, his thoughts slowed down. He was aware of voices somewhere far away.

NICOLE MANCINI WAS NOT one to curse out loud, but when she heard the voice of a doctor on the phone, she did just that. She had left work early to make sure the house looked nice for David's return. Owen had gone home with a friend from school and was due back at the house at any minute. She felt the situation spinning out of control, and she questioned her motives for the first time.

Nicole heard the key in the front door and quickly wiped tears from her eyes before Owen walked in. He was talking on his phone as he made his way through the front door but stopped cold in his tracks. Nicole just stared at him, unsure of what to say.

Owen stood motionless, the door still ajar, trying to assess the expression on Nicole's face. "It's my dad, isn't it?"

Nicole could not utter a reply and instinctively moved closer to give Owen a hug.

"Get away from me!" yelled Owen. "What happened to my dad?"

Nicole was startled but composed herself quickly. "Your

father has been in a car accident, Owen. The doctors are taking really good care of him even as we speak."

"Everything was fine until you showed up!" stammered Owen, his lips starting to quiver.

A chill flooded Nicole's body as she struggled to hold back her emotions. "Let's go see him. I'll drive."

Owen just nodded, and they both hurried out of the house.

Fortunately, the traffic on the way to Mass General Hospital was very light, and they arrived in less than ten minutes. On the way, Owen sat in the passenger seat, silently staring out the window while nervously bouncing his knees up and down. Nicole forced herself to focus on the task at hand, pushing her emotions out of her mind. She blinked back tears, trying to focus on getting to the hospital safely.

They parked near the ER, and Owen sprinted to the check-in desk. Nicole arrived moments later and helped Owen talk to the nurse on duty. They were assured that David was in good hands and responding well to treatment. After a few minutes, a doctor emerged from a door and took them into a side room.

"He is stable and doing well, considering," stated the doctor.

"What happened?" asked Nicole.

"All we know is that he was involved in a very serious car accident and that his vehicle was totaled," said the doctor. "He sustained some pretty serious bruising, but as far as we can tell, no broken bones or head trauma. Like I said, he's doing quite well, considering the description of the car."

Owen began to sob.

"He needs to rest," explained the doctor, "but I think it

would be okay for you to visit for a few minutes. He's in room one twenty-seven when you're ready."

The doctor gave Nicole a sympathetic smile and excused himself. She sat with Owen, wanting to give him a reassuring touch but remembering his previous reaction. Owen collected himself, and they rose to find David's hospital room.

The door to the room was already open, so Nicole and Owen slowly walked inside. A nurse was tending to David, who was thoroughly bandaged but conscious.

"Hey, buddy," managed David.

"Dad, are you okay?"

"I'll be fine... but you should see the other guy."

Nicole chuckled as Owen went around to his father's bedside and gave him a gentle hug.

"Do you need anything?" asked Nicole.

"No, I'm fine. They have me drugged up a little bit, so it looks worse than it really is."

They caught David up on all that had happened in Boston while he was away, and David told them a few brief stories from Russia, but he chose to leave out the details of his clandestine meetings with Tina Wood and the Russians.

After about thirty minutes, a nurse arrived, escorting a Boston police officer. The nurse told Nicole and Owen they would have to leave, but David played some emotion cards to get Owen permission to stay.

"Family only, miss," the nurse told Nicole.

"Not a problem. Owen, I will wait for you in the lobby. Take your time."

The nurse escorted Nicole from the room and closed the door behind her.

"Mr. Turner," said the officer, "I'd like to ask you a few questions about the accident if that's okay."

"Sure, but I don't remember a whole lot."

"No problem. Just tell me what you can remember. Let's start with where you were coming from and where you were going."

"I was leaving Logan Airport and headed home," said David. "I remember coming out of the tunnel and seeing traffic..."

David seemed to reflect a little bit before continuing. "I think I pulled the emergency brake... Yeah, my brakes weren't working all of a sudden. I tried to slow down, but... it all happened so fast."

"Were you traveling too fast, Mr. Turner?"

"No, I really wasn't. I remember having the windows down and the heat on and just enjoying the drive. I really wasn't in a rush."

"Okay, you said the brakes weren't working. Did you have any ability to slow the car or just reduced stopping ability?"

"There was nothing. It was like the pedal wasn't attached to the car."

Owen started to get restless and acted like he wanted to interject. David cast a knowing glance in his direction that generated an inquiry from the officer. "Is there something else you want to tell me, Mr. Turner?"

"No, that's about all I can remember."

Owen could not keep his tongue. "Dad, you have to tell him!"

The officer looked back and forth between Owen and David.

"Sir, is there something you want to tell me?" repeated the officer.

"Officer, my wife passed away in a car accident a year

ago, and I think my accident has brought back some bad memories for my son."

"I understand," replied the officer. "Were there any details from that accident that seem relevant to this one?"

"Yes, Officer," Owen blurted out. "Her car couldn't stop either. It crashed, and the car caught on fire."

The officer seemed more interested and pressed David for more details.

"The car was burned pretty bad, and the body... Well, it was hard for them to make a positive identification. But they were able to tell that the brakes had not been engaged, based on some physical evidence and recreation at the scene."

"The brakes failed," interjected Owen. "Mom wouldn't have just forgotten to hit the brakes."

The officer was quiet for a few moments, making some quick entries into his notebook. "Did they ever discuss the reason the brakes failed?"

"No," responded David, "not really. Just that the brakes had failed and that she was likely unable to stop the vehicle from going off the edge of the road."

"Mr. Turner, there is some evidence that your brakes may have been tampered with."

David sat motionless on the bed and took in the full meaning of the officer's words.

"You didn't engage the emergency brake because it had been disconnected. Your SUV veered out of your lane and got pinched between a pickup truck and a van. Witnesses said that appeared to slow down your SUV quite a bit, which is why we believe you didn't sustain more life-threatening injuries. The airbag malfunctioned, and the bruises you sustained are mostly due to your seatbelt also failing."

"Officer, that's a lot of mechanical failure happening at the same time," responded David in disbelief.

"That's exactly what we thought as well. Now that I've heard about your wife's accident, it has me even more suspicious. Do you know anyone that might have cause to wish you harm?"

"Like murder?" said David without thinking.

"There are all sorts of reasons people might benefit from someone no longer being around."

"I can think of someone," whispered Owen, to the surprise of both David and the officer. "Nicole."

"Owen! That's rude. Why on earth would you accuse Nicole of something like that?"

"Because I heard her talking to some strange person on the phone... and I followed her to this super creepy meeting—"

"You eavesdropped on her? You followed her? Owen—"

"Dad, hear me out," pleaded Owen. "It's like I've been telling you all along: Nicole Mancini isn't who you think she is!"

David just looked away, shaking his head. "Officer, please forgive my son. Nicole is the CFO of the company I run."

"As in the woman that was just in this hospital room?"

"Yes," responded David, casting a disappointed look toward his son.

"You're a CEO of a company?" continued the officer.

"Yes, sir. A small tech firm here in Boston."

"Why were you at the airport?"

"I was returning from a short business trip to St. Petersburg."

"Okay, you were in Florida on business?"

"No. St. Petersburg, Russia."

"You do business in Russia?" asked the officer with eyebrows rising.

David and the officer talked at length about NuKoin's business and the various employees, executives, and investors in the company, but he did not tell the officer about any of the strange things that took place during his trip to Russia. Those details he kept close to his chest.

"Mr. Turner," asked the officer, "was there any evidence of foul play regarding your wife's accident?"

"No, none at all. It never even came up."

"Well, that doesn't surprise me, given the fire. But I think it's an angle we need to keep an eye on. The two incidents might be related."

Owen's head was spinning. He had always been suspicious about the details of his mother's accident. *Had the police suspected foul play and not revealed it to my family? Was it really possible for two cars owned by the same family to have brake failure?*

Owen shifted his thoughts to Nicole. *Did she have access to Dad's car before he left for the airport? What about tampering with the car while it was sitting in the airport parking lot?* The garage surveillance cameras might have captured some footage.

"Owen?" said David, bringing his mind back into the room. "Owen, is that going to be a problem?"

"Sorry, my mind was wandering."

"The officer wanted to know if you would be okay having Nicole drive you back to the house and stay with you overnight," repeated David.

Owen thought quickly. If Nicole was involved in his father's crash, they would need proof, and that might take time. Owen could not afford to let Nicole realize that he suspected her. If someone was attacking his family, he knew he'd have to step up his game.

"That would be fine," said Owen.

"What about those terrible accusations you made earlier?" asked David.

"This has been a lot for me," Owen exaggerated. "I guess I was just freaking out at seeing you in a hospital bed, that's all."

The officer rose from the chair and closed his notebook. "Gentlemen, I'd like to keep our discussion to ourselves. Will that be a problem?"

"No, sir," said Owen.

The officer left the room while Owen and David were silent for a few minutes. Finally, David spoke.

"I need you to try to control your emotions."

Owen nodded silently and gave his father a hug. They both held on for a good bit longer than usual.

"Dad," whispered Owen, "I can't lose you."

Tears formed in their eyes as David gripped the back of his son's head, drawing it close to his. With his other hand, David gave him a few pats on the back then let Owen stand.

He was overcome by the feeling that his son had grown up too quickly, but he was proud of the young man standing before him.

They said their goodbyes, and David promised to be home the next day. Owen found his way into the waiting room and briefed Nicole on David's status.

"What did the officer want to talk to you about?" asked Nicole.

"It was no big deal," answered Owen. "I'm not even sure why you had to leave. He asked some basic questions about my Dad's memory before and after the accident."

"I did think it was a little odd that he wanted a private

audience with your father," replied Nicole, "but I thought perhaps he didn't want to embarrass him. Do you think the officer was satisfied with your father's answers?"

Owen was careful with his words, not wanting to make Nicole nervous or suspicious of the true nature of the conversation with the police. For the time being, she seemed to think his father was the subject of the inquiry, not a witness to it. That was just fine with Owen.

"I think the officer was satisfied," said Owen. "He's a great driver, so he has nothing to worry about."

Nicole and Owen left the hospital ER and walked to the car, and he noticed she was particularly careful driving home, slowing the car at all crossroads and being extra cautious looking for other vehicles.

"Did your father talk about how the accident happened? I hope they catch whoever crashed into his car," said Nicole.

"Yeah... but he said it all happened so fast, so he didn't see the car that started it," said Owen, thinking on his feet. "When cars are traveling on the highway, it doesn't take much."

Nicole just nodded in silent agreement, and Owen was relieved when her questions stopped. He was eager to continue his investigation of Nicole but didn't want to seem too anxious. He was smart enough to know that he needed to continue to be concerned with his father's health or Nicole would suspect he was holding information back from her.

He also couldn't appear to be suddenly warm toward her after the way he'd spoken to her earlier. That would be too dramatic a switch to go unnoticed. So when they got back to the house, Owen told her he needed to be alone.

She said she understood and let him go off toward his bedroom.

"I'll be staying here until your father is able to come home, Owen. I hope that's okay with you."

Owen turned and gave her a somber smile. "Yes, that would be great, Nicole. Thank you. And thank you for your help tonight. I know it means a lot to my Dad."

Nicole smiled and seemed relieved to hear his kind words. She puttered around the kitchen for only a few minutes before Owen heard her close her bedroom door.

19

Tina Wood deplaned at Reagan National Airport later that night. She was thinking about her discussions with David Turner and didn't notice the throngs around her. If she had been aware of David's car accident, she would have changed her plans for the evening and been more cautious. She had not been able to get a direct flight into Boston because of the budget limitations that her boss, Jack Dougan, had placed on her trip overseas.

Washington, DC, was her port of reentry into the country, and she had to go through immigration, collect her bags, and pass through customs before boarding her flight to Boston.

Tina made her way to the immigration checkpoint area and took some time to study the other passengers. Businessmen in suits were there, as well as a few moms with baby strollers and a couple teenagers fully enraptured with their earbud-tethered smartphones.

She chose one of the many lanes designated for American citizens. Her time with David Turner had impacted her more than she'd realized, and she shook her head in annoyance when she noticed the area for foreign travelers largely deserted. *How about spending some time and money on your own citizens?* she thought.

Then she noticed a couple of men walking in a peculiar fashion. Their deliberate gait caught her eye as they crossed the room toward the immigration agents. She followed them with her eyes and noticed a third man with them that looked familiar. *Is that the guy from the conference? From that panel discussion David was on... What is he doing here in the States?*

As the men passed easily through immigration, Tina became convinced that it was indeed Vitalik Grune. All three men progressed through the checkpoint quickly and headed toward baggage claim.

She grew more curious as she considered what business interest Grune might have in Washington, DC. When she noticed an agent opening a new line to her right, she sprinted to get to the line before the other passengers in front of her.

"Seriously, lady?" remarked a businessman who strolled up behind her. "I'm so glad to be back in America, where everyone thinks they are the most important person in the room."

Tina just ignored the man and walked up to the desk when the agent beckoned her forward.

"Are you in a rush to get somewhere, ma'am?" asked the agent.

"Just anxious to get back to my family, sir," said Tina, giving the agent a semiflirtatious smile, the irony of her statement and body language suddenly dawning on her.

Tina answered the standard questions, got her passport stamped, and quickly headed to the baggage area to find

Grune. Her bag was already moving around the belt, and she grabbed it without having to break stride.

She spotted Grune and his companions moving toward the customs exit and tried to appear nonchalant as she picked a line. As she got to the front of the customs line, she decided to try her dumb-tourist act in an attempt to divert attention.

She smiled quickly at the customs agent, handing him the declaration card.

"Anything to declare?"

"Just that I'm so happy to be back in America!" said Tina, managing her best cheesy grin.

"Never heard that one before..." mumbled the agent in a grumpy tone.

Tina picked up her pace as she scanned the crowd for a glimpse of Grune, and she spotted him and his cronies getting into a limousine just outside the door. On impulse, she decided to follow them despite the fact that she had a connecting flight leaving in ninety minutes. Eyeing the waiting taxis, she again cut the line and jumped into a cab, bags in tow.

"Lady, there's a freaking line!" yelled the cab driver, seeing the angry expressions on the faces of the people outside.

"There's an extra twenty in it for you," offered Tina.

"Twenty?" replied the driver incredulously. "You want me to violate the rules of being a normal human being for twenty dollars?"

"Make it fifty."

"Okay, then. I was never big on rules anyway."

As they were speeding away from the terminal, Tina commanded the driver to follow Grune's limousine.

"I think you watch too many movies, lady," the driver said mockingly, obeying her nonetheless.

Apparently, the taxi driver had watched his own share of movies, for he kept a safe distance behind the limousine, more motivated by the promise of fifty dollars than the avoidance of detection.

They traveled north along the banks of the Potomac River and passed Arlington National Cemetery before crossing over the Teddy Roosevelt Bridge. As the evening darkness obscured their journey on Interstate 66, Tina could see the outlines of the iconic Jefferson and Lincoln Memorials. The world seemed quite different than it had back in her grade-school days, and she wondered if she, too, would make her mark on history.

They exited the freeway and headed east down Pennsylvania Avenue toward the heart of downtown Washington. Tina wondered about their ultimate destination and realized she had no real plan should the limousine suddenly stop and empty its passengers.

When they got to the roundabout at Washington Circle, the limousine traveled nearly a full revolution and headed due west, back toward Georgetown.

"Lady, this guy is either really lost, or he's trying to see if anyone is following him," the cab driver said toward the back seat.

"Make sure you stay back, then," replied Tina, "I don't want them to spot us."

"I can try my best, but on this salary, it's hard to muster the strength," teased the driver.

"How about we make it double or nothing, then?"

"I'd say that'd do it," the driver agreed.

The cab driver was true to his word and distanced himself from the limousine like a professional. As the cab came to a stop near the river beside a park, Tina was nervous they'd lost them.

The cab driver pointed. "They're parked right over there, ma'am."

"Wow, nice job. Seems like you've done this before."

"This is Washington, DC, the home of quite a few politicians. Helping people go unnoticed is my specialty."

The cab driver tapped the meter that read "34.75" and was slowly rising. "I'm happy to wait, but I'd like to settle up part of this fare now, if you don't mind."

Tina dug into her pocket and pulled out fifty dollars in cash and handed it to the driver. "This should buy me a little time."

"It feels about a hundred bucks light," replied the driver.

"Oh, right," mumbled Tina, digging into her pockets for more cash.

Tina had a dilemma. She could always put it on her credit card, but that would leave a trail. She was growing increasingly paranoid, and her gut told her to err on the side of caution.

She found a hundred-dollar bill and noticed she would only have another fifty left after handing the driver the remaining cash. As she gave the money to the driver, she realized that if she waited too much longer, she would not have enough money to get back to the airport.

"When the meter reaches fifty dollars, I'll need to end this ride," Tina told the driver.

Several minutes passed as Tina glanced back and forth between the limousine and the running meter. Just when it seemed Tina was going to have to make a tough choice, the headlights of another car appeared in the distance.

Both Tina and the cab driver stared into the night and

saw the doors of the limousine open as two men exited. They walked a short distance into the park and toward the river.

Tina glanced at the meter and said, "It seems that I'm getting out of the car."

"Lady, this isn't the safest place at night for a young lady like yourself to be alone."

Tina just smiled and quietly closed the door.

The driver lowered the car window. "I'll hang out for a bit to make sure you don't need a ride back. At least until I get another fare."

Tina barely heard the offer as she attempted to plot her path across the park without being seen. She let her eyes adjust to the light as she crept from tree to tree, a task made more complicated by the overnight bag she was carrying.

About three hundred yards in front of her, Vitalik Grune walked with his bodyguard toward the edge of the Potomac River, stopping at a small bench near a few trees. A small group of men joined them and took up positions around the area. Tina was still too far away to see the identities at the meeting, which also meant her presence was not yet detected. It also meant that Tina could not hear their private conversation.

"Brian Parker, good to see you," said Grune to his new companion.

"Let's skip the pleasantries and get straight to business," replied Parker. "Why did you request this meeting? This isn't protocol."

Brian Parker was in his mid-thirties. He had tried and failed at many business ventures before being appointed to a high-level White House staff position by virtue of his marriage to the president's favorite daughter. He was tall and very thin, with boyish features that prompted him to wear his hair and clothes like someone two decades older. He didn't need opinion polls to know that he needed to prove something to Washington.

"You make it sound like we're not partners, my friend," answered Grune.

"I already have enough friends. I don't need any more. Answer the question."

"There has been some increased attention that needs to be taken care of. This was supposed to all be under the radar and away from the media spotlight."

"Do you think we have a problem?" asked Parker.

"There are no problems, my friend, only opportunities for solutions."

"Please skip the Confucius and Yoda crap and make your request."

"There was a reporter scouting around at the conference. She seems to be on a mission."

"You're talking about the cryptocurrency conference in Russia? There are supposed to be reporters there."

"Yes, but she's not interested in the currencies," replied Grune. "She is looking for people."

Parker considered Grune's words before replying. "And you think she's a threat to the mission?"

"No, not a threat, rather an opportunity for solidarity between us."

"I don't think we have to worry about any threats to the mission," replied Parker. "We've put some things in motion to deflect any unwanted interest."

"Now it's you that's speaking Confucius and Yoda."

"You'll find out soon enough," cautioned Parker. "You know how this goes—plausible deniability and all that."

"We need assurances that this is under control," Grune challenged.

"We're in full control. Don't worry about that. You just do your job."

"And what about the reporter?"

"Tina Wood? Is that who you mean? Give me a break. If that's all you're worried about, I could have saved you a trip to Washington. But by coming here, you've led her right into her next lead."

Tina could almost make out the faces of the two men, but the lens on her camera couldn't focus in the darkness of the evening. She reached into her bag and fumbled for a low-light lens that would allow her to take a few photographs.

As she did, she felt cold hands on her shoulders pull her back and onto the ground. Handcuffs were placed on her wrists, and she felt a stinging sensation in her back.

"You have the right to remain silent..." someone said behind her.

"Who are you? What are you arresting me for?" demanded Tina.

"Crimes against the United States of America," said another voice.

Tina Wood protested the entire time as she was forcibly dragged and placed into a dark SUV. Once inside the vehicle, she switched into full-blown journalist mode and tried to observe as much about her surroundings as possible. But within a few seconds, a hood was placed on her head, and the vehicle started to move.

A short distance away, Vitalik Grune and Brian Parker continued their conversation.

"This is our last face-to-face meeting. If you need to contact us, you know the proper channels," said Parker.

"You tell the president that if he wants our cooperation, then he'll have to start acting like we're truly partners," replied Grune, who was no longer holding back his disdain for the American in front of him.

"What makes you think the president is involved? You were fully aware of the risks when you signed up for this," Parker shot back. "Don't go trying to rub your crap in our faces."

Grune glanced at his Russian comrades then back at Parker. "You tell your father-in-law that he better choose his words and actions more carefully, or it might not be only one reporter he has to worry about."

Vitalik Grune rose and walked away. Brian Parker was visibly annoyed but chose to let him leave without responding. Instead, he pulled out his mobile phone and made a short phone call. As he put the phone back in his pocket, he was escorted by his Secret Service detail back to his car for his next appointment.

Tina Wood was terrified. She had seen this sort of thing play out in the movies, but the reality of her condition came crashing upon her as she began to shake. In all her years of journalism and investigative pieces, she had never been in this much danger.

The SUV slowed to a stop, and Tina heard the door open. The door shut again, and the hood over her head was removed. The inside dome light of the car was right above her head and shone into her face. She could see the knees of someone seated in front of her, but their identity was shielded by the complete darkness on that side of the car.

Tina tried to look up at the faces attached to the sets of legs on each side of her, but she was quickly admonished to keep her eyes straight ahead. Finally, the man across from her spoke, but he was using some sort of audio device to avoid being recognized.

"Why were you in the park today?"

"Just out for a walk," replied Tina smugly. "Is that a crime?"

"For someone who just skipped their connecting flight after returning from a country of interest, you should be making smarter choices."

Tina hesitated. "Who are you, and what do you want?"

"Unless you want that hood back on your head, I suggest you let me ask the questions. What were you doing in Russia?"

"I was reporting on a cryptocurrency conference that was being held there. I'm a journalist, and I'm researching a story."

"A story on what?"

"A story on whatever I want to write about," she protested, once again ignoring her present circumstances.

"Ms. Wood, there are many ways this can go, and not all of them are pleasant for you."

Tina was still scared, but she was also stubborn. She was in America, and they had no right to be questioning her or detaining her.

"Am I being arrested?" asked Tina.

"No, Ms. Wood, that would be far too easy for you. They told me that you wouldn't cooperate, but I wanted to give you a chance. Am I wasting my time here?"

"You have no right to detain me without cause, and you can go to hell if you think I'm going to talk to you about anything!"

The man motioned to the two others sitting next to Tina, and the hood was placed back on her head. She was taken from the car and pushed onto the ground. As she fell, the hood was pulled off her head as the men got back into the car. The vehicle sped off before she could make out the license plate clearly.

She picked herself off the ground and cursed out loud, both for the way she had been treated and for the realization that she no longer had her bag. She put her hands to her chest and was relieved to discover her research journal was still in its special compartment in her coat. *They might have my suitcase, but they didn't get my research,* she thought.

Looking around, she no longer recognized the area and pulled her mobile phone from her pocket to order an Uber ride. Within ten minutes, she was headed back to the airport, where she was able to purchase a one-way flight to Boston. The woman at the airline counter saw her ruffled condition and took pity on her, issuing her a discounted ticket for a missed connection despite the deadline being long past.

Being out of cash, she used her credit card to purchase the ticket and boarded the flight to Boston, beaten down and penniless. She used the time on the flight to document her adventure in the nation's capital. But in that and future journal entries, she used code words and euphemisms as the reality sank in that the game had drastically changed.

20

———

David was glad to be headed back to work after two boring weeks of recovering from his car accident. Nicole had stopped by a few times to give him office updates, but that didn't prevent his feeling of losing control of the company.

The bright spot in having time off work was spending extra time with Owen, who soaked up the alone time with his father. Owen was grateful for being given a second chance and was determined to take advantage of the opportunity. They were bonding on new levels and talking about things they had never discussed. The one topic they did not discuss, however, was the bitcoin wallet.

Owen understood his father had to go back to work, but hiding his disappointment was still hard. "Dad, you need to ease back into your work schedule. You can't work long hours from day one."

David couldn't hide his smile. "You're right, Son. And I am looking forward to hanging out with you tonight."

After David finished getting ready, Owen met him at the car for the short ride to school. When they stopped in front of the entrance, in sight of some other kids who were arriving, David offered his son the customary fist bump, but Owen leaned over and gave his father a hug. The sight of his son entering the building made him peaceful and reflective.

When David walked into the office, he was greeted by balloons and a large Welcome Back sign. About a dozen employees broke into applause, cheering their CEO's fast recovery. Thomas and Nicole were off to one side, smiling at David's surprised expression. William DeFrost stepped forward and gave David a firm handshake.

"Welcome back, David," he said. "Everyone here at NuKoin and at Delphi Capitol is happy to have you back in the saddle again!"

David showed the obligatory gratitude and made sure he personally thanked each person in the room. Many of those people had sacrificed much for their shared vision, and having had a brush with death made him even more grateful.

After the party died down, Thomas, Nicole, and DeFrost gathered in David's office.

"We've all been pulling for you during the last couple of weeks," DeFrost said, "and it's good to see you back. The guys from Danzi have made some great strides while you've been away, and I know you'll be impressed."

"Thank you, William," David managed, but with a slightly cold tone.

David had done a lot of thinking over the past couple of weeks, especially about the information from Tina Wood that Delphi had connections to Chinese government funding. David wanted to bring Thomas and Nicole in on this information before confronting DeFrost, so he was holding his tongue.

"It feels great to be back at the office, and I'm looking forward to getting caught up on all that's been going on," said David.

"And we want to hear all about the conference in Russia," said DeFrost.

"Oh, right. The conference... It was really great. I made some great connections and learned a lot of interesting things." *Some very interesting things.*

"I tell you what," replied DeFrost, "I'll let you get acclimated again and catch up on some emails, and I'll take you out for lunch."

"Thank you. You'll be sticking around the office today, then?"

"Yes, I've actually been working from the conference room during the time you've been out, so I've grown quite used to it."

David shot glances at Thomas and Nicole, both of whom gave a quick eye roll back.

"Oh, well, thank you for holding down the fort, but you didn't have to do that. Thomas and Nicole have my full confidence."

"Indeed they do," said DeFrost in a tone that was hard to read. "Well, I'm going to get some things done myself, but let's touch base around lunchtime."

The three NuKoin execs sat quietly until DeFrost left the room. David motioned to Thomas, who quietly closed the office door.

"Has it been a nightmare with him around?"

"He's been okay, I guess," responded Thomas. "He always thought he was in charge anyway, so this gave him an opportunity to convince the staff."

"I think we've all learned how to give him his space," offered Nicole.

"How about the two Danzi consultants? How have they been doing?"

"Pretty well, actually," said Thomas. "I asked a couple of the tech leads to keep an eye on their code quality, and it's been fine. They've even contributed to the core."

"What?" exclaimed David. "You let them alter the core module?"

"David, don't get all worked up," responded Nicole. "Like Thomas said, every line of code they write has been reviewed before it has been merged into the production version."

"What about DeFrost?" asked David. "Has he been interacting with them a lot?"

"Yeah, a fair bit," answered Thomas. "I don't blame him. He wants the Danzi move to work out well."

"I bet he does."

"What's going on, David?" asked Nicole. "It feels like you're holding something back from us."

David hesitated for a moment and then said, "Guys, my trip to Russia was... enlightening on a number of levels."

"Let's hear it," Thomas said.

David peered out the window, considering his thoughts.

"I learned that Danzi Consulting is funded by the Chinese government."

"What? Who the hell told you that?" asked Thomas.

"I'm going to keep that close for now."

"Give us a break," replied Nicole. "It's us, for the love of God! Why would you keep that information from us?"

"I'm not sure, to be honest. There were a lot of things that happened while I was away that have given me reason to be careful. We all need to be more cautious."

"So you think Danzi is a plant from the Chinese to steal our code?" asked Nicole.

"I'm not sure," replied David. "But if the Chinese are interested in NuKoin, we need to be extra careful, especially until we find out why."

"Do you think DeFrost knows?" asked Thomas.

"About the Chinese funding? Again, I'm not sure, but I wouldn't be surprised. Money is money to him."

"Dude, let's slow down here," said Thomas with his hands raised. "Industrial espionage is a serious accusation. Confronting DeFrost on this will not go well, regardless of his awareness."

"If he's camped out in our office and his cronies have full access to our code, what is to stop him from doing something sinister? I knew this whole Danzi thing was a mistake from the beginning."

"Okay, let's back up and think about this," said Nicole calmly. "If you're the Chinese, why do you need the NuKoin code? It's going to be open source anyway. You don't need to steal it since it will be freely available once it is released."

"Maybe you want to steal the algorithms in the code before it's released so that you can compete with it," said Thomas.

"Okay, maybe," conceded Nicole, "but wouldn't the Chinese government have an army of developers to write all the crypto code they want? Why would you need access to a small startup in Boston?"

"Unless you were sabotaging the codebase," answered David, "and the goal was to destroy the project."

"That would mean that DeFrost has no idea," said Nicole, "because he wouldn't want to risk his own investment by destroying NuKoin. He may be a dolt, but he's not that stupid."

"But how could they sabotage the code if all the changes

are reviewed?" said Thomas. "They can't even delete all the code since we have it backed up in several different places."

"Now you understand what I've been thinking about these last couple of weeks," said David. "I still can't figure it out."

"Yeah, this is a bit of a puzzle," said Thomas. "And you're sure that your information is solid?"

"Am I certain? No," conceded David, "but with everything else going on, it rings true."

"Everything else?" asked Nicole.

"Like my 'accident,'" said David, using air quotes.

"What do you mean," asked Thomas?

"I mean it wasn't an accident."

Both Nicole and Thomas stared at David in disbelief.

"You believe someone tried to hurt you?" asked Thomas.

"You need to relax," Nicole chimed in. "You're going to delay your recovery time if you get all worked up."

"I'm just saying that the police aren't convinced it was an accident. They are seeing a pattern."

"What kind of pattern?" asked Nicole.

"There are similarities between my car accident and Mia's car accident," said David.

"Dear God, David. Mia's death was not a homicide," protested Thomas.

"There seem to be some growing opinions to the contrary," responded David.

Nicole remained quiet, her facial expression hard to read. David had observed that she grew a little distant whenever Mia's name came up.

"I'm starting to think it might be better for you to take some more time off," said Thomas, shooting a quick glance at Nicole for approval.

"You've been under a lot of stress," said Nicole, "and then the accident."

David quickly processed how the conversation was going and decided to take a more pragmatic approach. "Yeah, I guess you're right. I really have been enjoying my evenings with Owen. I was thinking of making today a short day anyway."

"That's a great idea," responded Thomas. "And one of these nights, I'll join you, just like old times."

The truth was that David and Thomas had grown more distant since Mia's death. Hanging out with the Turners had been a lot easier as two couples, but with Mia gone and both men much older than they'd been in college, that just didn't happen anymore. They both chalked it up to the fact that they saw each other at the office every day and didn't need to hang out after work, but both men realized their relationship had changed.

The three coworkers spent about an hour catching up on various aspects of NuKoin business, and David shared a couple benign stories from Russia. He was trying to seem engaged in the conversation as best he could but was distracted by his thoughts regarding DeFrost. He finally played his "tired" card and was left alone in his office for the remainder of the morning.

Shortly before noon, William DeFrost knocked on David's office door. "Ready for some lunch?"

David looked at his watch. "Sure. Where did you have in mind?"

"How about sushi?" asked DeFrost with a smile.

David hated sushi and contemplated whether DeFrost knew that and was being intentionally antagonistic.

"How about burgers?" responded David.

"Only if we can go to that gourmet burger place."

"It's your dime," said David.

The two men grabbed their coats and headed down the street for lunch. DeFrost did most of the talking, listing off all the work he was busy doing. When they reached the restaurant, DeFrost took the lead and requested a quiet table in a section not currently being used. David noticed him slip the hostess some money to secure the preferential seating request.

They sat down, and the waitress took their orders right away since neither of the men needed any extra time to order a cheeseburger. DeFrost continued the small talk for a few minutes before getting to his agenda.

"David, while you were recovering from your car accident, I was doing some thinking. NuKoin is very vulnerable without its top development mind in his office."

"I'm not sure if I should take that as a compliment."

"It wasn't meant to be anything more than a statement of fact," said DeFrost. "You and I have obviously had our differences in the past, but I'm hoping you can see my sincerity today."

David was tempted to tell DeFrost what he really saw when he looked into his eyes, but he chose the high road instead, just sipping his water and waiting for DeFrost to continue.

"I think we need to shift some of the technology oversight pieces to some other resources, building a little redundancy to shield NuKoin from being too closely tied to one or two individuals. That will give you some help, and it will help you balance your work and family life."

"I didn't know you cared so much about my family."

"David, why do you get so confrontational with people? I'm bringing up an important discussion in a nonthreatening way and in a neutral place. Is there really no discreet way to have an adult conversation with you?"

"I have no issue having any discussion with you. The real issue is that you have trouble being honest with what your real agenda might be. So I tell you what—you be honest with me, and then we can have a real discussion."

The waitress came to the table and delivered their drinks, giving a momentary pause to the conversation. When she left, David took a long pull from his Coke, content to wait to see what cards DeFrost would play. David was more suspicious than he had ever been but felt it important to let DeFrost make the first move.

DeFrost said, "The delay in delivering something to market has the board at Delphi nervous that we're lacking the proper leadership at NuKoin."

There it was. DeFrost had played his card. Delphi wanted David out as CEO. Normally, David would take an attack like that head on, but his experience in Russia had introduced new caution into his world.

As they sat across from one another, the big question in David's mind was whether DeFrost was the one with the agenda or whether he was merely the messenger. David also wondered if anything linked his trip to Russia with the board's desire to have him removed as CEO.

"I'm sorry to hear the board wants new leadership," responded David. "Do you need me to put a good word in for you?"

"You're such a self-righteous fool! You're like a little boy in a man's world. Are you really that blind to the obvious facts circling this company?"

"I know a lot of things, William. I know that I started this company. I know that I'm the main contributor to the product that this company is developing. I know that I single-handedly hired eighty-five percent of all the employees at NuKoin."

"Do you also know that without Delphi, this company wouldn't exist?"

"Yes, William, Delphi Capital. But where in this puzzle does William DeFrost add unique value?"

DeFrost held his tongue as the waitress brought the burgers to the table and asked the two men if they needed anything else. Once she left the room, DeFrost returned to the verbal confrontation.

"You don't get it, David. I'm in control of the interests of Delphi when it comes to NuKoin. You work for me."

"Last time I checked, Delphi only owns a twenty-five percent stake in NuKoin, whereas I own thirty-five percent. So it sounds like you work for me," said David before picking up his burger and taking a large bite.

"Thirty-five percent of zero is zero. Without more money, your precious company goes insolvent... and Delphi owns the assets."

David took another bite. He just stared at DeFrost, trying to act unfazed. But inside, David seethed with anger. He was tempted to cash out the newly discovered bitcoin and buy Delphi out, but DeFrost was unpredictable and might just up the price. He also knew it might attract the wrong kind of attention.

DeFrost was correct that in the Series A funding contract, Delphi had insisted on total ownership of assets if the company was dissolved. David had reluctantly agreed to that clause, but only because he had no choice and because he believed that he and Thomas would succeed in building a company.

In the beginning, Delphi was largely hands-off, but after the first year, the VC firm was increasingly focused on when the company would turn a profit. That was when William DeFrost was inserted into NuKoin's day-to-day operations as an "advisor," but he always seemed more like a chaperone. DeFrost knew absolutely nothing about their product or the crypto industry, and his presence at the office adversely affected staff morale.

David said, "I'd like to remain focused on delivering a product to market and not get distracted by bureaucratic political jockeying. Off the record, from the very first day I met you, it was clear you were a sleazy executive, just out for yourself."

"Let me be very clear with you," said DeFrost, who still hadn't eaten a bite of his lunch. "The board at Delphi has agreed that you need to step down and that a new CEO needs to be appointed. You'll become CIO, in charge of all things engineering but accountable to a delivery timeline."

"You really think that the best use of time is to pause and find a new CEO?" questioned David.

"No, we don't. That is why I will be named interim CEO while the search is conducted."

David laughed out loud. "Delphi wants to make *you* the CEO? You know absolutely nothing about this industry."

"I don't need to be an expert in crypto to understand that companies are supposed to make money. Delphi is alarmed that you call yourself a CEO and don't seem to understand you're a for-profit business."

"I couldn't disagree with you any more than I do right now. But I'm not going to waste my time arguing with you about it, because you have no power to make it happen."

"Ah, but I do. Effective immediately, Delphi is pulling all funding from NuKoin," DeFrost said.

"That would be a boneheaded move. You freeze the funding, and your twenty-five percent becomes worthless.

Once staff walks, your timeline is shot forever," countered David.

"Well, we hope it doesn't come to that. We're confident you'll take the high road, even if only for the sake of your precious company's future—your little dream," DeFrost said with scorn in his voice.

"Delphi is contractually obligated to fund NuKoin for the specified term length. Do you really want a lawsuit?"

"Lawsuits take years, David. What becomes of your little company then? Will there be any value left in your idea if dozens of other companies deliver to market while you and your lawyers are on the sidelines? That is, if you can find lawyers that will work pro bono for a couple of years."

David had lost his appetite but kept eating, trying very hard to hide his growing rage. DeFrost had already been an idiot, but he was becoming a bully. And the best way to treat a bully was to punch them in the face. Not literally, for that would just play into DeFrost's plan.

"William, are you really in charge of this little bluff of yours, or are you just a puppet?"

"Let me assure you I'm not bluffing. I'm the voice, but I'm also on the board. We're united in this decision, and I have the task of getting you on board. It will be safer for everyone."

"Safer? That's an interesting choice of words, William."

"People keep their jobs, families have employed parents, and you get spared the public disgrace of failure."

"Yes, it's unfortunate when the public learns about financial details that people wished were private."

"What the hell is that supposed to mean?" asked DeFrost.

"Only that the public likes their families with employed

parents and companies being honest about how they're paying them," answered David. "Crypto is such an international phenomenon, we need to be careful to get funding from pure wells."

DeFrost stared at David, expressionless, trying to read his thoughts. "You see, that's exactly why you need me. Focus on your code and let Delphi manage the rest. Step down as CEO and tell the press you want to focus on the technical details of the project. We issue a press release, the market gets excited about an imminent beta, and we all win."

David finished the last bite of his meal and wiped his mouth with his napkin. He rose from the chair and excused himself. "Thanks for lunch. I always enjoy the conversation."

DeFrost watched him leave and sat thinking for a couple minutes after David disappeared from the dining room. He used his corporate charge card to pay for the meal and grabbed his coat to leave. When he got into his car, he dialed his mobile phone and gave a summary of the meeting to a frustrated individual on the other end of the line.

21

Tina Wood made the brisk walk to the *Boston Mirror* office to meet with her boss, Jack Dougan. A few weeks had passed since she had updated him, and she needed to check in.

The last couple of weeks since her return from Russia had caused a growing sense of paranoia as she went slinking around Boston. That wasn't the first time one of her stories had generated some negative attention, but that usually happened only after the article was published.

For instance, in the summer of 2011, James "Whitey" Bulger had been apprehended in Santa Monica, California, after being on the run from authorities for eighteen years. He was extradited back to Massachusetts to stand trial as the mob boss behind numerous racketeering and murder charges. Tina had been a fixture at the courthouse throughout the end of 2013, often waiting all night for one of the handful of seats open to the public at the trial.

She had been obsessed with the case once she learned Bulger had been an FBI informant in the late 1970s.

Convinced the feds had contributed to his money-laundering schemes, she zeroed in on a chain of mattress stores prevalent throughout the Boston suburbs. They were always empty, and the salesmen were more than a bit shady. She was very proud of her piece, "Sleeping with the Enemy," which she sold to the *Boston Globe* in early 2014.

Convinced that this would be the next Pulitzer for the *Globe*, she waited anxiously for her shot at the Sunday cover, only to be buried deep within the pages of a midweek edition. She was stonewalled by the editors when she asked for an explanation but was confident she had her explanation when her federal tax return was randomly selected for audit five years in a row.

Even in that type of case, though, she had never been kidnapped and never feared for her life. But though she was scared, an iron resolve was growing in her mind.

The walk should have taken her about five minutes since she chose to do without the stop at Starbucks—not because she didn't need it but more out of the growing habit of avoiding a predictable routine. After crossing the street several times and even doubling back twice, she stepped into the office twenty minutes after leaving her apartment.

Maggie, the receptionist, greeted her warmly but with a facial expression that revealed her time with Jack Dougan might be a little overdue. Silently mouthing "thank you" to Maggie, she continued back to Jack's desk.

Tina stepped into the open doorway and quietly knocked on the doorframe to get Jack's attention.

"Tina Wood, I was beginning to wonder if I would ever see you again," said Jack.

"You knew I was busy with this story. I would have sent you an email, but you told me to only update you in person."

"Yes, you have been very busy," said Jack sarcastically.

"What is that supposed to mean?"

"Why don't you close the door."

Tina obliged by slowly closing the office door as she braced herself for another one of Jack's attempts to manipulate her research progress.

"Is something wrong?"

"Yes, Tina, something is very wrong. And I have to admit that in my thirty-four years in this business, this ranks as one of the most awkward conversations I've ever needed to have."

Tina could not hide her confusion as she just stared at Jack.

"What have you been doing these past few weeks?"

"I've been researching the Satoshi Nakamoto story. Boston, Washington, and even Russia. You knew where I was going, and you even approved the overseas travel in advance."

"Okay. Anything else besides researching?"

"Definitely not any personal time. Lord knows I have no life."

Jack opened his desk drawer, removed a manila envelope, and slid it across the desk, motioning for Tina to open its contents.

She slowly reached for the envelope, casting a curious look at him. She opened the flap and pulled out some photographs. Her eyes bulged as she glanced at them, quickly thumbing through as many as she could. "What the hell is this?" she blurted out as she tossed them back into the envelope.

"You know, I had the same reaction when I received them in the mail. You can imagine how awkward it is to even be in possession of those photos."

Tina picked up the photos again, carefully studying one or two of them. "I have no idea where these even came from. This cannot be me."

"Yes, I thought the same thing, but I have to admit it is a bit awkward, staring at naked photos of one of my reporters to make sure that it is really what it seems to be."

"I don't recognize the men in the photographs... This isn't me! I don't even recognize them. And let me promise you my personal life isn't this interesting."

"Those are not casual selfies between two consenting adults. That is multiple men. Those are business photos, not personal ones," said Jack.

"I've already told you that isn't me in the photos. Do you think I'm the type of person that would do this?"

"I know this type of journalism doesn't pay the best, but if you needed money or something..."

"Shut the hell up. Don't you dare even suggest that I was involved in something like that for money."

"Tina, we're a small publication with some very conservative subscribers. If it gets out that one of our reporters is moonlighting as a... Listen, what you do in your own time is your business, but if it negatively affects this newspaper, it becomes my business."

"Did you ever consider that these might be photoshopped or something?" Tina picked up a photo again and examined it closely.

Jack just sighed and leaned back in his chair.

"Here, look at this. This isn't me. Well, the face is mine, but that is not my body!" Tina said as she slid the photo back toward Jack.

"Tina, please! This is awkward enough without us studying these photos under a microscope."

"Well, gee whiz, so sorry you're uncomfortable," said

Tina with disdain, "but if someone is trying to ruin my reputation with fake photos, I think I deserve the chance to prove it."

Jack rolled his eyes. "I did study a few of those photos, I'm ashamed to admit. And they are not printouts. These are printed images, and none of them look altered."

"Well, not to get more awkward with you, but there are definitely a couple easy things I could show you to prove that naked body isn't mine."

"Okay, that was way over the top. I'm going to have to record this conversation from here on out for my own protection."

"Where did these photos even come from?"

"US Mail with no return address or a note."

"And that didn't seem suspicious to you, Jack? Random photos from an unknown source?"

"I don't think I would call them random, Tina. They seem quite specific... You're a reporter. We get anonymous stuff all the time."

"This is different," pleaded Tina. "Did it cross your mind that someone is trying to get me off the Satoshi trail?"

Jack remained silent, letting out a few sighs and looking pained as he thought about Tina's angle of defense.

"I'm getting really close. This isn't the time to back down," said Tina.

"Some weirdo posing as an Uber driver does not equate to something like this."

"A lot has happened since then."

"Okay, prove it to me," challenged Jack. "Prove to me that you are close enough to Nakamoto for someone to go through all the trouble of producing perfectly fabricated porn photos of you."

"When I was coming back from the conference in St.

Petersburg, I had a connection in DC. I recognized a Russian banker from the conference and decided to follow him from the airport. It didn't make sense why he'd even be in DC, especially right after the crypto conference."

Tina could tell Jack was not impressed.

"He gets in a limo and does all sorts of backtracking through the streets of DC, clearly not in America for a normal reason. He finally stops at a park in Georgetown and has this clandestine meeting in the dark, surrounded by his cronies."

"So a Russian comes to America and acts weird?" said Jack sarcastically.

Tina ignored his comment. "I pull out my camera to take pictures, hoping the night lens can make out the identity of the person he is meeting with. Then all of a sudden, someone grabs me and throws me into a dark SUV."

Jack's facial expression betrayed a belief that Tina's story was a fabrication.

"They mumble some crap about being arrested and hold me in this SUV, like out of some crazy movie. The middle seat is turned backward, and some guy gets in. I can't see his face, and he uses this voice modulator. Tells me to back off and ends up throwing me on the grass as the vehicle speeds away. They even took my bag. And now that I think about it, those clothes in the photos are some of the clothes that got stolen, Jack."

"Interesting. I wasn't aware there were any clothes in those photos."

"Down here at the bottom of this photograph. Making them look like they were ripped off," said Tina, her voice trailing off and betraying a little shame.

"That's a really good story, and I applaud your creativity, but I don't have a choice here."

"Obviously, we are getting somewhere with this story. We cannot stop now!"

"I'm not talking about the story. I'm talking about you being fired."

She was stunned. "Fired?"

"What am I supposed to do? If these photos get sent to the wrong place, the media is going to have a field day with this. The *Boston Mirror* can't afford to have a scandal like that. We'd lose our subscriber base."

"This is wrong, and you know it."

"This is business. I cut ties with you now—whoever sent these photos gets what they obviously want."

Tina was fuming and struggling not to let herself cry in front of him. She picked up the photos and put them back in the envelope and into her purse.

"What are you doing?" asked Jack.

"Making sure no one else sees these pieces of fabricated slander," exclaimed Tina.

"I need to keep those for legal reasons."

"Hell no, you little pervert. I bet you looked at these photos for a lot longer than you want me to know."

"Give me a break and don't try and flip this around on me."

"After all the years I worked for this place, you're going to treat me like this?"

"Like what? I am going to pay all your Nakamoto expenses incurred to this very moment, and I'll pay you for the story as if you completed it. That's very generous, considering these circumstances. But I need to keep one or two of those photos for the sealed legal record, and I need to keep all of your research on the story."

"Wait a minute. Why do you want my research on a story that will never get published?"

"The Mirror paid for all that research, and it belongs to this newspaper. Again, for legal reasons, I need to keep it as part of the file."

"No, something else is going on here. What else was in that envelope? Did someone contact you?"

"Stop trying to turn this into something it's not. Just give me the photos and the research, and let's part ways somewhat amicably."

"Is someone blackmailing you off this story? It's more than these photos, isn't it?"

"We need to stop this conversation before it goes places we'll both regret."

"The only thing I regret is not quitting this job years ago. After all I have done for this place, you throw me to the wolves at the first sign of trouble. You never had any real guts, Jack. You were always too soft to go after the big story."

"I warned you that these people were powerful. This isn't just about you anymore. There are lots of other lives that are being affected by your actions."

"You were the one who gave me this assignment, and now you're blaming me for being too good at my job?"

"You're right—I did give you this assignment—and now, I am telling you that it is over. Take your money and move on, Tina. It's over. Send me all your research, or you'll find a court summons in your mailbox."

Jack stood up and pointed to the door. Tina rose, shaking her head.

"I think I will just keep these photos. I am sure if you need more copies, your new friends will be glad to photoshop you some new ones. Maybe if you ask them nicely, they'll put you in there too."

Tina stormed out of the office as Jack kept demanding

the pictures. She flew past Maggie's desk without a word. She went straight to the post office and paid for a safe deposit box then placed the photos under lock and key. She was tempted to destroy the photos, but since the game had escalated, she needed to keep a paper trail of evidence.

22

David Turner made good on his promise to Nicole, Thomas, and Owen by leaving a little early on his first day back to work, enjoying the lack of traffic on the way home.

Owen greeted his father at the door with a hug, clearly pleased to have his father–son time survive the first day back to work.

"How was it?" said Owen.

"The first day back is always a little overwhelming, but I'd say it went okay."

"Was everyone at the office glad to see you?"

David pushed the thoughts of William DeFrost out of his mind. "Yes, they were. They even threw a little welcome-back party in the lobby when I walked in."

David and Owen continued talking about their days, and both eventually realized they were hungry.

"Do you want to go out to eat tonight?" said Owen.

"That sounds like a great plan. How about a movie afterward?"

"Perfect," replied Owen. "I could use a little restaurant

action after so many home-cooked meals while you were away."

They both laughed and grabbed their coats. They stopped for pizza before the movie, splitting their time between casual conversation and watching various sports on the large TVs.

When Owen was walking back from the restroom, David noticed he had a new pair of sneakers on.

"Where'd you get those?" asked David, pointing at Owen's new kicks.

"Oh, these? I went shopping while you were on your business trip."

"Those look like expensive sneakers. Where'd you get the money to buy them?"

Owen didn't answer right away and looked a little embarrassed. "Well, I guess you could say that Mom bought them for me."

"Owen, what did you do?" David asked with a look of concern.

"I didn't tell anyone, just like we agreed. I just was experimenting with how you sell bitcoin."

"Owen, what were you thinking? We agreed to keep that bitcoin wallet a secret," whispered David.

"I didn't tell anyone. I just moved some of it around—that's all."

"Oh, that's all, huh?" David was visibly irritated, which clearly dampened the mood at the table.

Owen sank his head, and the two remained quiet for a few minutes.

"There are ways people can track bitcoin transactions," David said. "By connecting the bitcoin to a bank account, it creates a trail. We have to be really careful with this. There is too much going on to draw attention to either of us."

"I'm sorry. I didn't think about that. I thought that since no one knows we had that bitcoin wallet, it wouldn't be a big deal to use one of those ATMs downtown that let you get cash for bitcoin."

David knew otherwise, but he decided that scaring Owen had no benefit. "Promise me you will not move any more of that bitcoin around or attempt to change it for dollars."

"Okay," Owen replied.

"I don't want there to be any connection to either of us. There will come a time when we can figure out what to do with that bitcoin, and we will do it in a safe and, hopefully, anonymous way."

The two finished the large pizza and left cash for the waiter. David owned only one credit card but rarely used it. Cash was still king.

They left their car in the parking garage and walked to the movie theater. David purchased two tickets to the latest action movie and bought two sodas and a large popcorn. They chose two seats in the front row of the upper section and pursued their goal of finishing the snacks before the movie even started.

Halfway through the movie, David leaned over and asked Owen how much bitcoin he had sold.

"Well, probably a little too much, to be honest. I still have, like, six hundred dollars in cash in my piggy bank at home. They only let you take out eight hundred per day from the ATM, as it turns out."

"You paid two hundred dollars for those sneakers?" exclaimed David in an animated whisper.

They got shushed several times by the people around them but continued whispering for a few more minutes. Finally, a security guard appeared and asked them to leave the movie. Owen was sure his father was about to make a scene, but to his surprise, he just got up and obeyed.

"I blame the movie," said David to the security guard. "If it was mildly interesting, we wouldn't have had to entertain ourselves."

David and Owen left and headed toward the exit. The security guard followed them into the hallway, and David began to get annoyed.

"We agreed to leave the movie, and we're going," said David. "Why are you following us?"

"I'm just making sure you leave, sir."

"Don't harass us," said David, "or I might need to file a complaint with your manager."

The guard ignored David and continued following. Owen could tell his father's blood pressure was rising, a clear sign of an impending incident.

"What's your name? I need to speak to your manager immediately," threatened David.

The guard was silent as David looked for the name badge to identify the guard to the manager. He didn't see it coming when the security guard pounced on David and overpowered him.

David was pushed into a wall and fell to the floor. Owen jumped back in horror and scrambled to the opposite wall as his father let out a deep groan from a blow to the stomach.

"Somebody help us!" shouted Owen, trying to get someone's attention. He had seen his father in many verbal confrontations but never had he witnessed any physical fighting.

David instinctively went for the attacker's face but only connected with a glancing blow. The guard had experience.

David was facedown, struggling to keep his hands from being zip-tied.

Owen could no longer watch and jumped on the attacker, temporarily catching him off balance. The surprise move was just enough to give David a moment to roll over and get to his feet. Footsteps approached down the hallway as voices grew louder.

Seeing the advancing people, the attacker ran out the exit door. David and Owen both shrank to the ground, exhausted and inventorying their wounds.

"Are you guys okay?" asked a uniformed woman.

"What happened? Did he hurt the boy?" asked someone else.

"That security guard just attacked us," said David, pointing a finger toward the open door. "He asked us to leave the theater, and we did, but then he bullied us and attacked me."

People were talking over each other, creating quite a commotion, but David and Owen tuned them out. They were bonding once more, albeit in a way that neither would have chosen.

"Sir, we don't know who that man was, but he doesn't work for this theater. We'll look at the security-camera footage right away."

David and Owen got ushered into the employee lounge and were given some towels and ice packs. The manager apologized several more times and arranged for them to give statements to the police.

The security tapes were examined, but the attacker's face was never in full view. Even when he fled, he had covered his head with a hood. Despite the many camera angles, the intruder was never able to be identified. The police agreed to do some more research and continue the investigation, but David knew enough about the larger issues around Boston to know that the case would go unsolved and be closed before lunchtime the next day.

When the police offered to drive them home, David turned them down. "The guy had nerve, but we have nothing for anyone to take. We'll be fine. Besides, I have plenty of protection at home," he said in an empty reference to his Libertarian views on gun control. The truth was that David did not own a gun, but talking as if he did made him feel safer somehow.

David's mood improved when the manager gave him a fifty-dollar gift voucher to the cinema. They even managed a couple of laughs on the way to the car.

By the time they reached the house, they had almost forgotten about the theater incident, but their chattiness ended when they saw their front door was slightly open.

David was brave, but he wasn't stupid. He took out his cell phone and dialed 911.

"What about Lucie?" cried Owen. "We have to make sure she's okay."

"Once the police get here, we'll find Lucie. She's a smart little dog. She can fend for herself." He remained outside with Owen for the twelve minutes that passed before the police arrived.

The officers quickly determined the house was free of intruders and asked David and Owen to examine the situation.

Someone had ransacked the house, leaving open drawers and cabinets everywhere. They were in a hurry and had made no attempt to disguise the intrusion. David and Owen wandered around the house in a state of bewilderment, looking for anything that might be missing.

"Are you sure nothing has been taken?" asked the police officer.

"There's really nothing to take," answered David. "The flat-screen TV is still there, and I left my laptop at the office."

Owen had been searching the house, calling for Lucie. He finally emerged from his room, holding the scared little beagle in his arms.

"I found her under my bed, shaking like a leaf. She's nervous but otherwise fine."

David came right over and gave the dog several loving strokes.

"You're a good girl, Lucie. You did the right thing, hiding from these awful people."

"By the way, Dad, my new computer is missing."

David and the officers followed Owen to his room and stood by his desk, where a lonely monitor and printer sat unconnected.

"It was right there," said Owen.

They spent about an hour going over the rest of the house with the officers, but nothing other than Owen's computer was missing. The officers told David they would watch some of the local stores for the computer, but they didn't seem optimistic.

"That's it? You're not going to dust this place for finger-prints?" demanded David.

"Sir, this seems like simple petty theft. It's not exactly a murder scene."

"Officer, my son and I were attacked in the movie theater tonight, and then we came home to find our house robbed. You don't think that makes this more serious than petty theft?"

The officers interviewed the pair for almost an hour,

taking additional details on both incidents. David was animated throughout.

"Sir, I think you're going to need to stay in a hotel for a couple of days," said the officer as he was leaving, "just until you process through the emotional side of what happened tonight."

"Don't worry about that. We're not staying here. And I want you to make sure you check this place thoroughly for fingerprints and DNA." However, something was telling David they wouldn't find anything.

As David and Owen headed toward the front door, Owen looked concerned. "Dad, you'd need to use a credit card to stay at a hotel, right?"

"Probably. Hotels don't like cash. They want to be able to charge you if you damage the room."

Owen was quiet, and David knew something else was on his mind.

"What is it? I know that computer meant a lot to you, but we can build another one. Don't worry."

"It's not that. They have our bitcoin wallet now. Do you think this all has to do with me getting that money out of the ATM?"

David thought about it for a moment before responding. "It does seem weird they only took the one computer, but then again, that was really the only portable thing of value in the house. They'd have to be pretty sophisticated to even check for a bitcoin wallet. Besides, you and I both know that without the passphrase, they'll have no use for that file."

"We backed up that wallet, right? We didn't lose all that money, did we?" asked Owen.

"No, we're good. It's safe and secure and out of the reach of anyone trying to steal those coins."

"We need to stay somewhere secret, somewhere we can't be traced," said Owen.

"How about I call Nicole. Maybe she will let us stay with her for the night."

"No, I don't trust her! For all we know, she was involved in this," said Owen.

"Why do you keep saying stuff like that? Nicole has always been helpful to both of us."

"Okay, maybe she has been helpful, but how do we know she's not playing us? All this weird stuff going on. Someone messes with your brakes, and then we get attacked. We have to think outside the box from now on. At least until this starts to make sense."

The two talked it out for the next twenty minutes before they agreed to stay at least one night at a motel that would accept cash and dogs. They parked their car behind the motel, out of sight from the main road. They made sure to deadbolt the door, and Owen insisted on sliding the dresser in front of the window.

David and Owen shared the queen-sized bed, but neither got much sleep that night. That might have had something to do with Lucie sharing the bed with them, but it was mostly because their minds wouldn't stop racing.

David was nervous about Owen. Adults could choose the challenges that came their way, but not children. David being targeted was one thing, but coming after Owen was taking it to another level.

Ironically, Owen's biggest fear that night was for his father. He had been through so much, and Owen wondered at what point his father would snap. As he trickled in and out of sleep all night, Owen had several dreams in which he needed to save the world from certain doom, none of which he would remember in the morning.

23

Tina was fuming when she left Jack Dougan's office, so after leaving the photos in the safe deposit box, she decided to walk around Cambridge to blow off some steam. She also felt somewhat violated that someone was in possession of what people might believe were illicit photographs of her. She knew they were fabrications but still felt her privacy had been compromised.

As she walked, she tried to tune out all that had transpired in the last couple of months, dwelling on happier times. But she was a journalist, which was all she had known. Good journalists got personally involved in every story—that was the key to producing gripping material. If something didn't grab the author, it wouldn't impact the reader.

The story on Satoshi was no different, but it was proving to be much more dangerous than she'd ever imagined. The blockchain technology itself seemed fairly benign, but when applied to create cryptocurrency, it attracted a wide assortment of suspicious characters.

As Tina walked, she sorted through everything she had learned, trying to determine who might be responsible for the photos.

David Turner had warned her about people watching when they met for the first time at Fenway Park. He didn't seem like the type of person that would do something like this, nor did it seem to her that the interview with David was incriminating. Yet he was the one who first tipped her off to the presence of a photographer in the crowd. He must have been connected to these pictures somehow.

David's presence at the fundraiser was also innocuous on the surface, but Tina wondered if she should have kept her distance from him. He had taken his CFO, Nicole Mancini, as his date that night, and a streak of jealousy clearly existed there. She didn't know much about Nicole, but maybe those photographs had nothing to do with the blockchain story at all. Perhaps Nicole just felt threatened by Tina's presence in David's life. But Tina had never given David or Nicole the impression that her interest in David went beyond a simple interview.

The third time Tina had bumped into David was at the conference in Russia. They had talked a few times, and she was the one that tipped him off to some of the secrets of his fellow panelists. Tina suspected the Russian banker most. But if Vitalik Grune's ties to the Russian FSB were indeed fresh, incriminating photos were nothing compared to what she should be fearing. Perhaps they were just a warning shot across her bow.

The more Tina considered that last thought, the more nervous she became. She started looking into the crowds for strange behavior and walking in more random patterns. After a few minutes of playing "spy," she realized that if professionals were really on her trail, she wouldn't be able to avoid whatever fate they had for her. Showing signs of knowing she was being followed might even make it worse. Her thoughts drifted back to her puzzle, and she stopped trying to walk undetected.

Vitalik Grune had met with David Turner in Russia, and she had no idea why. She had warned him of Grune's identity, but Turner had still met with him. *Did David see me watching when he left the room? Did he learn something in that meeting that he needed to keep from me? Was David Turner more than just a computer geek on a business trip?*

Or maybe Grune was the one that needed Tina to stay away from David. *Were the photos meant to get me to stop interacting with David Turner? Did Grune know the real topic of my story, and if so, why would Grune fear my story of Satoshi Nakamoto?* Tina broadened her thought process.

She thought about Demetri Kornechiv, the moderator of the panel discussion. He was the reason David was even up on stage in the first place. David said Kornechiv was creating a company to rival NuKoin, one with nefarious intentions. *Could David's information be trusted?* If David was correct, that panel moderator might have known David had tipped off Tina and been afraid that the details of his plan would be revealed in her blockchain story. If Kornechiv had enough power to put together a panel with the likes of Grune, he might have friends that could apply leverage on Tina.

The more Tina thought about it, every possibility always had Grune as a thread. He seemed to be the key to understanding the source of the photographs.

As she walked, she nodded and said out loud, "Who was Grune meeting with in Georgetown?"

Being kidnapped while trying to take photographs of her own was too coincidental. Vitalik Grune seemed to be at the center of it all. She cursed to herself, recalling that she hadn't discovered the identity of the person meeting with Grune that night she was taken by those men.

Her thoughts went back to David Turner and the possibility of a second meeting with Grune, but this time stateside. Why would Turner and Grune meet a second time so quickly after the first? That didn't make sense. Grune had no reason to risk coming to America when he could have just extended his meeting with Turner in Russia. A different explanation had to exist.

She assumed for the moment that Turner wasn't in the park that night with Grune. "Okay, so what about the guards?" Those men that had taken her bag and thrown her in the car didn't seem like thugs—they seemed more like trained police than hitmen. They had even used the word "arrested" when she was first apprehended, which their boss later contradicted.

The thought occurred to Tina that perhaps the "boss man" that questioned her in the car was the person meeting with Grune in the park, but that would seem rather brash if the duo were truly in a secret meeting. No one seeking the cover of darkness would reveal themselves plainly to her and risk being recognized, even using a voice modulator.

Nicole stopped walking and sat on a park bench. She tilted her face up into the sunshine with closed eyes and let the rays warm her skin. Then she lowered her head and opened her eyes. After taking a few breaths, she rubbed her head with her hands.

What kind of person has access to their own bodyguards? One either needed to be rich or protecting oneself from people that had money. Grune was probably a bit of both but would have no reason to have a nighttime meeting with a fellow banker. That meant the meeting was for the sake of the other party.

Washington, DC, was full of powerful people that dealt in secrets, politicians being at the top of that list. But her list of contacts on Capitol Hill totaled only one.

Senator Michael Cornwall had given her a very robust interview during the early days of her research. At that time, she would have come across as a vanilla journalist with a tired story. When she met Cornwall again at the fundraiser, her questions still wouldn't warrant his trying to get her to stop the story. But then again, he hadn't known the true subject of her research.

What if he was working with Grune and discovered my true goals and that I was much further down the trail than the last time we'd met? Would that be a reason for him to deploy his resources to frame me and take me off the story?

Tina didn't think that made sense. Grune had met with David, and David hated Cornwall—she was sure that kind of distaste couldn't be faked—unless Grune was trying to persuade David of something on behalf of Cornwall and reporting back to Cornwall on the status of that meeting.

Again, that didn't make sense. Grune had no reason to travel to America to talk to Cornwall when senators had access to all sorts of video and audio chat technology that couldn't be traced—not to mention that Cornwall seemed to be trying to kill the very technology that Grune was promoting.

And what about the trouble I've been having with the TSA officials at the airports? Putting me on a TSA watch list would be an easy task for a senator to call in. Or what about the Uber driver trying to capture me before the meeting with Grune in Russia? Too many loose threads still existed to tie this mystery together. Someone wanted her to stop trying to find Satoshi Nakamoto.

She still felt Grune was a piece to this puzzle, but the circle seemed much wider and much closer to home. David Turner again entered her mind.

David's company had funding connections to the Chinese government through what appeared to be a shell company in Danzi Consulting—NuKoin, Delphi Capital, Danzi, and back to the Chinese government.

David had claimed to have no knowledge of the Chinese involvement in his company, and he even seemed visibly annoyed at the revelation. Was David really out of the loop, or had others given him plausible deniability? As CFO, Nicole Mancini clearly had to know the money trail, and Tina wondered about David's other partners at NuKoin. Maybe she needed to pay another visit to David Turner.

Tina was calm now and tired of walking. She was refocused on the task at hand, and nothing Jack Dougan could say would stop her. He could fire her from her gig with the *Boston Mirror*, but he could not forbid her from tracking down Satoshi Nakamoto. Photos or no photos, she had to keep going.

The only thing that seemed clear was that she was getting close to this mysterious Nakamoto, and he did not want to be found. The photos had to be about getting her to stop trying to uncover the mystery.

Suddenly, another thought crossed Tina's mind, causing goose bumps to form on her skin. Perhaps she no longer needed to find Satoshi Nakamoto. Perhaps she had already met him.

24

———

Senator Michael Cornwall was a disciplined man who accounted for every minute of his time. Like many of his colleagues, he prided himself on long workdays filled with meetings and discussions. Being a congressman came at a cost, but it also came with a few perks now and again.

Having access to the White House was both a blessing and a curse. Meetings there could make one feel important, but the mystique quickly wore off. Meeting anyone from the executive branch usually left him with more work than when he arrived, so Senator Cornwall preferred to meet outside the walls of 1600 Pennsylvania Avenue whenever possible.

He had earned an office close to the Senate floor, based on his years in office and his power within the Democrat party. That was extremely convenient for photo ops and being recognized as a powerful man in Washington, but it also meant that clandestine meetings in his office were a nonstarter. Therefore, that day's meeting with Brian Parker needed to find an alternative location.

Brian Parker was the son-in-law of the president of the United States of America, and the fact that Cornwall could even get Parker to meet outside the White House meant he had leverage in the relationship. Parker knew that, but Cornwall was useful to him, so he didn't mind pumping up the senator's ego a bit. Parker was shrewd and knew that egos could blind even the biggest personalities, so he used that to his advantage whenever possible.

Both men's official calendars that afternoon listed an anonymous fundraising lunch, which was partially accurate. The meeting was in fact a discussion about large sums of money, but not the kind that most people would even understand.

Café Minalvo was quiet enough to allow discussing business but also had limited seating and enough ambient noise so that conversations would not be overheard. Also, the restaurant had no CCTV or security cameras that might accidentally capture the presence of anyone wishing to remain undetected.

Brian Parker arrived first and was escorted to his usual table, and his Secret Service detail sat at a table around the corner with clear visibility of both the kitchen and the front door. Cornwall preferred to arrive a few minutes late to emphasize his importance, but Parker played the part of the waiting don well, causing Cornwall to regret his timing.

Secret Service personnel were not normally assigned to any White House staff, not even the chief of staff, but Brian Parker was classified as being in the president's immediate family. Parker was not embarrassed by this tradition of Secret Service nepotism and often flaunted the presence of his detail.

The two men were very familiar with the restaurant

and had no need for menus. They both had things on their mind, so the conversation needed no warmups.

"Do I have the president's support for the crypto bill?" asked Cornwall.

"Which one? I've lost count of your budding legacy lately," answered Parker.

"Let's skip the crap, Parker. SCATTA," replied Cornwall. "The Securities and Cryptocurrency Tax and Transfer Act."

"You boys love creating acronyms, don't you?"

"It helps the voters to recognize landmark legislation," said Cornwall.

"Yes, and perhaps the media too," said Parker. "The president is open to supporting it as long as it fits into his greater strategy. Give me the talking points."

Cornwall knew Parker was posturing for a starting point in the negotiation. He knew Parker was already familiar with the goals of the bill.

"Cryptocurrencies will be treated as securities, both for taxation and for asset transfer. If cryptocurrencies are purchased with other cryptocurrencies, that is a taxable event. ICOs will be fully regulated by the SEC, just as stocks and commodities are."

"I thought you wanted to ban initial coin offerings altogether," replied Parker.

"I don't really care what companies use to raise funds. I just want our piece of the pie," answered Cornwall.

"You mean you want the good people of this nation to be protected from Ponzi schemes and tax evaders?"

"I thought we agreed to cut the crap," replied Cornwall.

"Fair enough. So what does the president get for supporting your bill?"

"I was under the impression that the president supported these same goals."

"The president has lots of goals, Senator. For instance, he is up for reelection in two years. How would supporting this bill help him get reelected?"

"The number of voters involved in cryptocurrency is small, but the amount of money in play is very large. This is an opportunity for a tremendous increase in revenue from the hands of a very small number of fringe voters."

"But there are all sorts of small businesses that use ICO funding. How can a probusiness president reconcile these details?"

"The tech startups using an ICO are not the kind of small businesses that hire Joe the Electrician from North Carolina or Bob the Farmer from Kansas. These are a bunch of millennials working from their parents' basements who don't like supporting their government," countered Cornwall.

"So supporting this bill will decrease his approval rating among young voters?"

"Fringe voters, Parker, fringe. I'm not even sure they vote."

"Okay, so how much money are we talking about?"

"We estimate fifty billion dollars annual taxable income if we assume that the thirteen million Coinabee users are American citizens," answered Cornwall.

"And doesn't that assume that Bitcoin will produce a capital gain and not a loss?" asked Parker. "What happens if it crashes and all of a sudden we've given people billions in write-offs?"

"The bill will be retroactive to 2009, when Bitcoin first launched. That kind of capital gain would offset any short-term write-offs from the crypto dabblers. The total tax revenue will easily top one trillion dollars for the past decade."

"You plan to go back over a decade? People have destroyed their records after seven years. IRS Rules 101."

"Tax evasion has no statute of limitations," countered Cornwall. "Criminal Justice 101."

"There is a great amount of anonymity with cryptocurrency. Do you expect these digital millionaires to just voluntarily reveal themselves?"

"We continue to put pressure on Coinabee to get all their member records, and we will tie those identities to the Bitcoin wallet addresses. The entire history of Bitcoin transactions is public record. It's a tax ledger just waiting to be used."

"So you are just going after Bitcoin, then?"

"Not at all. Bitcoin is just the beginning. All the crypto has public ledgers that can be investigated. But once people see the IRS unmasking a few notable examples, the rest will fall over themselves to cut deals to stay out of prison. While we are at it, we will find trails that lead to organized crime. Would the president also like to be seen as tough on crime?"

"Indeed, he already is tough on crime. That's why he favors getting rid of cryptocurrency altogether, not trying to baptize it with new regulations. Your bill embraces the legitimacy of crypto as a new type of value transfer. You're not going to prevent the use of cryptocurrency for laundering money unless you get rid of cryptocurrency."

"As much as I would like to think we had the power to eliminate cryptocurrency, the more we try to squash it, the more entrenched it'll become. Regulation is the best answer."

"I agree regulation is an answer, but I disagree that it's the best one," teased Parker.

"Okay, I'm listening."

"What if we were able to create a better cryptocurrency than what is on the market today? One that would give the appearance of protecting the average investor while at the same time preventing its use in crime."

"The only way to prevent crypto from being used in crime is to not let it be anonymous at all," replied Cornwall. "Once you remove the anonymity from any given currency, then it'll lose popularity."

"I agree. That's why we need a digital currency that maintains the features that law-abiding citizens value while still making it possible for the government to track down crime."

"And how exactly are you going to allow government control of a decentralized blockchain? The whole point of things like Bitcoin is to take control of the currency away from a central power."

"Indeed." Parker raised his glass and took a drink. "That would be the rub, wouldn't it?"

Cornwall decided to eat some of the bread that had been brought to the table as he considered how much deference he wanted to give Brian Parker. Crypto legislation was to be his legacy, not the legacy of the current administration, but he was curious to hear what Parker had up his sleeve. If someone was making a crypto play in Washington, he wanted to know about it. "So do you have anything firm in motion?"

"Of course we do," replied Parker. "We just need to keep the circle tight."

Cornwall was tired of beating around the bush and decided to go blunt. "Am I inside the circle, then?"

"That depends on you, Senator. And it depends on

whether you consider yourself a supporter for the president's reelection in two years."

"What about SCATTA?" asked Cornwall, speaking of the legislation he was sponsoring.

"The president would gladly support SCATTA. It sounds like some important legislation, despite the idiotic name. You can count on the president's support and signature, provided we find ourselves on the same team on the other matters we're discussing."

"I think we have an agreement," replied Cornwall. "Are there any other partners in this that I need to be aware of?"

"The less you know about the partners, the better," said Parker, "but I do need your assistance with a few things."

Of course you do, you little snake, thought Cornwall. "Absolutely. How can I help?"

"In order for the right horse to win, we need to pick some losers," explained Parker. "There are some crypto companies out there with some pretty good technology but with the wrong leadership vision. I need them tied up and distracted for a little while to pave the way for the most beneficial cryptocurrency to get some momentum."

"It sounds like you already have a couple losers picked out."

"Have you heard of NuKoin?" asked Parker.

"As a matter of fact, I have," replied Cornwall. "David Turner, Nicole Mancini, and Thomas Randall, if I'm not mistaken. I've bumped into them a couple of times recently. Turner is a real arrogant jackass, if you ask me. I have no problem with them being a loser, but what exactly did you need my help with? You have direct access to the DOJ. You don't need me to tie up Turner."

"Indeed I do not," agreed Parker, "and you will be seeing us move very soon. When we do, I need you to make sure that the media storm has some congressional fire poured on it."

"Ah, you want me to publicly lambast NuKoin and kick them while they're down? I could do that... I'd be most happy to do that."

"Oh, you won't have to kick him too hard," said Parker. "Once they find out their rival blockchain company is the chosen winner, they'll snap and take themselves out of the equation forever."

Cornwall was taken aback. He knew a lot about NuKoin and David Turner, and he was nearly certain of the identity of the company Parker had in mind. But if he was correct, that added a new layer of risk.

"Are there any state actors in play here?" asked Cornwall.

"What the hell does that mean?"

"It means exactly what I asked. I would like to know if there are any other state actors other than the United States government involved in this little plan."

"I told you the less you knew, the better."

"Yes, you did, but if the Russians are involved, I need to know up front. I'm not going to be caught off guard by something like that."

"Why the hell would you think the Russians are involved in this?"

"Because there are only two or three companies in the same space as NuKoin that would need David Turner out of the way. I'm not going to mention names, but the best guess hails from Russia."

"You've been on the Hill for a long time now. You know that the relationships between the world powers are complicated. We need them just as much as they need us. Rest assured that we're in control, and whatever state actor may or may not be involved can be controlled. We hold the cards."

"The Russians are not just going to roll over and give up their mining control in Bitcoin and let some other cryptocurrency take root," said Cornwall.

"The Russian Federation doesn't like Bitcoin any more than we do," said Parker.

"You confuse the Russian people with their government. Moscow needs to control the currency just like any nation state does. If a government doesn't control the flow of money, then it doesn't control anything."

Cornwall was nervous and tried to take a few drinks to give himself time to think. But when he noticed his hand was shaking slightly, he decided to put the glass back down.

"So whose idea was it to take out Turner? Yours or the Russians?" asked Cornwall.

"I never said the Russians were involved in this. I only clarified the well-known position of the Russian government on cryptocurrency," said Parker. "The world needs a digital money system that can be transferred across borders, but it doesn't need that system to be controlled by a couple of hackers in a basement. It needs a steward. We are the leaders of the free world. We will usher in the new system."

Cornwall was taken aback by Parker's arrogance or, perhaps, ignorance. Parker was no more in control than the president. The world was run by big money—Cornwall knew that. He aspired to be one of the power brokers and that was why he needed his legislation passed through Congress—so that currency would remain in safe hands like his.

"I want to be ready to pounce on Turner," said Cornwall. "What are you going to get him on?"

"Like I said, we like to keep things close to the chest,

Senator. But let's just say that one of his funding sources is going to get him in trouble."

"Turner is using private funding, not ICOs. Believe me, if he'd tried an ICO, I would have nailed him already."

"Private funding has its own pitfalls, Mr. Senator. You should be well aware of that."

"Turner is laundering money?" blurted Cornwall. "Wow, he had me convinced he was the consummate family man."

"Not exactly laundering, but he does have funding from sources that you will have no trouble pouring fire on. You asked about state actors? Well, Turner's in bed with the Chinese."

"What the...?" replied Cornwall. "David Turner is working with the Chinese government?"

"Make sure that's the story you run with. The outsourcing of American jobs and the trade deficit and all that crap. Keep the focus on the Chinese, and you'll make everyone happy... everyone."

Cornwall quickly searched his mind for a reason Parker would want to throw mud in the direction of the Chinese. A lot more was at stake than he could fathom. This was not about private citizens or control of the markets. Nation states were circling and posturing for their role in a new world order.

Cornwall was becoming anxious for the conversation to end, so he returned to what he needed to do and what he wanted out of Parker and the White House. "Any particular winners in the media on this one? To whom do you want me to give the story?"

"I don't really care who. You could even give the exclusive to your favorite news outlet," Parker said with a sarcastic chuckle. "Does it really matter? Don't you guys own all the stations anyway?"

"I can pour fire on the media storm around Turner, but no one can truly control how this eventually spins."

"Don't be naive," said Parker. "If they don't spin the direction we like, then we take them out of the picture too."

"You don't expect me to believe you can just snap your fingers and get the media to report a story exactly the way you want them to," replied Cornwall incredulously.

"I don't really care what you believe, Mr. Senator, but we have experience doing exactly that. So don't underestimate how far our reach can go. And don't forget that you serve at the pleasure of the president."

"Is that a threat?"

"It's whatever you want to believe it is," said Parker, wiping his mouth with his napkin. "You may still believe that you are elected by the voters of the great state of Illinois, but don't forget that it only takes one manufactured scandal for you to be out of a job. And voters don't usually have time to decide whether a scandal is even true."

"You are way out of line, Parker!" hissed Cornwall. "This is exactly the kind of attempted power grab that will bring down your father-in-law's administration."

"You see? There's the passion we knew was deep down inside you. That's why we knew we could use you on our side. Make sure that passion is unleashed on David Turner, and we will make sure you aren't on the receiving end yourself."

Parker left the table, and the Secret Service detail accompanied him out of the restaurant and into a waiting sedan. Cornwall was left alone at the table, rehashing the entire conversation. He was overwhelmed by all the information and was, for the first time in his life, at a loss for his next step.

When the waitress brought the dinners to the table, Cornwall waved her off. "We won't be staying for lunch today."

"Shall I pack these to go, sir?" asked the waitress.

"No, just throw them out," said Cornwall. "On second thought, pack mine up. And put it all on Parker's tab."

25

David woke when natural light filled the motel room. Neither Owen nor David had any reason to set an alarm. That day was a school day, but David had already decided Owen would call in sick. No sooner had he woken than his mobile phone started vibrating on the nightstand.

Owen was already up and glanced at the phone as he walked back from the bathroom. "It's the school calling. They must be wondering where I am."

David motioned for Owen to pass him the phone. "Hello, this is David Turner."

"Mr. Turner, this is Owen's school just checking on your son's whereabouts," said the voice on the other end of the line.

"Yes, I'm very sorry for not calling sooner. Owen is recovering from something and will not be in school today."

David winked at Owen, who was impressed that his father wasn't lying to the school, leaving the interpretation error up to them.

"Okay, no problem. Please be sure to call us tomorrow if

he will be out any additional days. And remember, if he has a fever or vomiting, he should stay home from school for twenty-four hours."

David checked his phone for emails and found one from Nicole asking him to come into the office for an urgent meeting. She'd left no details, so David tried calling her. When she didn't answer, he told Owen he might have to go in to work for an hour or so.

Owen did not want to leave the motel room, but he also did not want to be away from his father. This presented them with a dilemma. After much discussion, they concluded that if someone was looking for David, Owen would be safer remaining in the motel room. David would check in at work and let Nicole and Thomas know what had happened, then David would return for Owen and take him somewhere safe until the danger was contained.

After showering, David threw on some jeans and a sweatshirt and quietly left the motel parking lot, cautiously scanning the surrounding area for any suspicious activity.

By the time he got to the office, the time was almost ten, so he saw no traffic. He parked his car in the garage and made his way up to the office.

As soon as the elevator doors opened, he was surrounded by chaos. People were everywhere, and loud voices made it impossible to understand what was going on.

Many of the people had on jackets with large letters reading FBI. David froze, not knowing what to do. When the doors on the elevator started to close, one of the FBI agents slammed his hand against the button on the wall, causing the elevator doors to reopen.

"Let me see some ID," barked the agent.

David stepped from the elevator and reached for his

wallet. He produced his driver's license and continued scanning the room for a glimpse of someone he recognized.

The agent took one look at the ID and said, "David Turner, please come with me."

"Is there something wrong, sir? Did something happen?"

"Please keep your mouth shut until you are asked to open it," barked the agent.

"Sir, am I under arrest? Because if not, you have no right to speak to me that way," said David with irritation in his voice.

David was escorted into the NuKoin office and toward the large conference room, where the doors were closed. The agent whispered to another agent standing guard, and the conference room door was opened.

Inside, David could see most of the NuKoin employees seated in chairs with stunned looks on their faces. He mentally counted all the developers, as well as the two test engineers. He also saw Satish and Ramesh, but Thomas and Nicole were not in the room.

David's passive-aggressive side was firmly in control as he calmly spoke to the agent. "I am David Turner, the CEO of this company. I demand an explanation from the person in charge, which clearly isn't you."

"You better watch yourself," responded the agent. "Today can go two ways for you and your company. Neither is pleasant, but one will be more fun for me."

Ignoring the agent, David continued, "Do I need to start recording this conversation, or are you going to get the person in charge of this violation of civil rights?"

The agent moved closer to David, almost begging for an incident.

"Please, by all means, ignore the dozen witnesses

watching you and lose your career by making this violent," dared David.

The agent got in David's face but did not touch him. He then continued out of the room.

"Is anyone hurt?" asked David. "What's going on? Where are Thomas and Nicole?"

Most people silently indicated they were fine, and David realized everyone was shaken up. Finally, one of the developers spoke.

"They basically raided the office at exactly eight a.m. Most of us hadn't arrived yet and were basically pistol-whipped into this room when we did arrive. Thomas and Nicole are being questioned in one of the offices, I think. William got a little testy with the agents and was hand-cuffed and taken to a separate room."

"Is DeFrost here too? I would have paid money to see him handcuffed."

A few minutes later, another agent entered the room and introduced himself.

"David Turner? I'm Special Agent Holmes, and I'm in charge of this operation. I need you to come with me for some questions."

"Agent Holmes, I need some answers," David shot back. "What right do you have to invade a private corporation and disrupt our business like this?"

"Mr. Turner, I'd be glad to bring you up to speed in the room next door."

David glanced around the room and decided to play along for the time being. He followed Special Agent Holmes to the familiar location. The office belonged to David, but the agent didn't seem aware of that. David was given the guest chair while Special Agent Holmes sat in David's leather chair.

David decided to hold back, but he was keenly aware of the overt bullying tactic.

"Mr. Turner, we have orders from the Department of Justice to seize all your files and records in violation of the Anti–Money Laundering Act," said Holmes bluntly. "We have a signed warrant from a federal judge."

"Money laundering?" protested David. "What are you talking about? NuKoin has had a single Series A funding round from one VC firm based in the United States."

"Ah yes, Delphi Capital," replied Holmes, "a very nice shell-company move on your part. Did you honestly think that the DOJ wasn't actively investigating every crypto investor? Cryptocurrency is rife with dirty money, Mr. Turner, and you are responsible for making sure none of it flows your way."

"What dirty money? Every cent that NuKoin has raised has come from Delphi. How can we be guilty of money laundering?"

"We could take you down just on the suspicious-activity clauses alone, never mind the failure to disclose foreign bank transactions. But my personal favorite is the international transportation of currency, if you can call crypto a real currency. But either way, it is clearly a financial instrument, so you're hosed there too."

David was growing more confused by the minute. "Where is Nicole Mancini? She is the CFO. She should be answering these questions."

"Ah, yes, an excellent idea. Let's bring her in. Won't that be fun." Special Agent Holmes motioned to one of the other agents, who slipped out the door and returned, escorting Nicole.

"David Turner, I think you have met but have not been formally introduced," said Holmes, pointing at

Nicole. "I'd like you to meet Special Agent Nicole Rogers."

David's eyes bulged in disbelief. Turning to Nicole, he searched her eyes for verification of the truth. She nodded slowly, with a trace of shame on her face.

"Special Agent Rogers, would you care to bring Mr. Turner up to speed?"

Nicole calmly took the seat next to David and turned to him. She made a face that almost seemed to imply she was sorry, but it disappeared as quickly as it formed.

"I've been running an undercover FBI operation here at NuKoin for the past six months. I've been watching the financials and investigating the books. Delphi Capital is a shell company being used by the Chinese government to enter US markets in direct violation of the IMF and a host of trade agreements."

"Nicole... Damn it. Whatever the hell your name is..."

"My name is Nicole."

"Yeah, okay. Whatever... You know damn well that if Delphi is dirty, it has nothing to do with me or NuKoin, so why did you raid NuKoin and not Delphi?"

"David, this is a very large investigation, and my role is to provide the financial facts. DeFrost is in a room down the hall, singing like a songbird. He has implicated you, Thomas, and everyone else he can possibly name," said Nicole.

"Did he try and implicate you too?" asked David.

"That plan came to an end when he learned I worked for the FBI."

"So if he tried to implicate you, isn't that evidence that he's just making crap up to save his own ass?" David shot back.

"Yes, David, I believe you. I have worked with you for

these past months, and never once did you give me any reason to suspect your involvement, and that's exactly what I put in my report. Just let this take its course, and you'll be fine."

"Let it take its course? Just how long will it take for this to blow over?"

"Not more than two to three months," she answered.

"Two or three months?!" shouted David. "You know full well that in two months, we'll have no developers left, and our competitors will be at our heels."

"I feel terrible about that, David. I really do, and the raid today wasn't my idea. But the DOJ takes this very seriously, and when communist governments are covertly funding cryptocurrencies, it cannot be ignored. And David, you're not totally innocent here. When you, Thomas, and Mia went looking for funding, you should've been more careful with the source."

"Don't you dare bring up Mia!" growled David. "All those times you pretended to be a friend, you were just doing research. All that personal information I shared was just material for your official agency report, wasn't it?"

"David, no, it wasn't like that..."

Agent Holmes was clearly amused and wore a smirk that made David want to break his nose.

"So as you can see, David," Holmes chimed in, "we have all the facts to put NuKoin out of business forever." When Nicole tried to interject, he cut her off. "Thank you, Special Agent Rogers. That'll be all for now." He motioned toward the door.

Special Agent Nicole Rogers reluctantly obeyed her superior and left without even a glance in David's direction.

"Now, David, can we get down to business? I am a reasonable man, David, and I don't believe for one second that the rest of the employees had anything to do with this. It just wouldn't sit right with me to destroy their careers."

"Of course they had nothing to do with any of this," David shot back, "and neither did I! None of this will ever stick, and you know that. You have the real criminal in the other room. Lock DeFrost up, and let us get back to work."

"I don't think you get it, David. All of the Delphi money has to be returned. All of it. The money you have in the bank and even the money you have already spent has to be returned. How do you expect to get back to work if you cannot pay anyone to do the work?"

David was furious and overwhelmed at the same time. His company—indeed, his dream—seemed to be vaporizing before his eyes.

"Although that is a moot point since they will all be in jail," said Holmes.

"Give me a break," responded David. "You can't throw all the NuKoin employees in jail for any of this. Even I know that."

"Oh sure, they'll get off eventually, but in the short term, I can do a lot of things that will greatly impact their lives and the lives of their families," Holmes said. "All I need to do is throw in some suspicion of terrorism accusations, and everyone goes to the holding tank, just for safe measure. They'll each get a lawyer, who will get them out. But they will need to hit up relatives for money to pay the lawyers, blah, blah, blah. It's not something that I want to do, mind you, but I will if I have to."

David just shook his head. He had spent most of his adult life warning people that this type of government corruption was rampant, and now he had personal proof. But that would all be hearsay. He didn't have any way to prove any of it. Not that it mattered—this pissant FBI agent was just one in a thousand. David needed to focus on NuKoin and the people sacrificing their lives for the vision.

"David, I tell you what," said Holmes, "they're not the ones that need to pay the price for your sins, so why don't we make a deal? You confess, and I let them all go."

"Confess to what?"

"Confess, and everyone except William DeFrost goes free. It's a win-win. The innocent walk, and you get to see your friend DeFrost behind bars with you."

"DeFrost needs to go down for sure, but what exactly do you think I need to confess to?"

"David, what's your real vision at NuKoin? I don't buy the nonsense about anonymous transactions on the blockchain. What's your real endgame? Who are you really working for?"

"I work for myself, and NuKoin is all about people being free from the probing eyes of the government. Literally hundreds of my blog entries will confirm these facts."

"Free from the eyes of which governments, David?"

"All of them, to be honest. I'm not convinced, at the end of the day, there's a lot of difference between any of the people running the major governments of the world. It always boils down to power for the few. Sure, the communists might enforce their power differently than the capitalists, but at the end of the day, it's a thirst for power and control."

"Is that why you met with Vitalik Grune? Because you dislike your capitalist government?"

David could list off a hundred shortcomings of his own government, but finding information was not one of them. That only served to underscore the need for anonymity even more.

"I wouldn't characterize it as a meeting. I was basically kidnapped and forced into a room with him," said David.

"What did he want?"

"Ironically, he wanted the same thing as you, apparently. He wanted to control NuKoin."

"Control it in what way?"

"We need to pause for a minute," said David. "If I am going to tell you what I know, you have to give me something in writing that clears everyone else at NuKoin. And I'm not going to lie, so you won't get me incriminating myself either."

Agent Holmes had been anticipating this moment, and he produced a signed document holding all employees of NuKoin harmless. David scanned the document, signed it along with Holmes, then pulled out his phone and took a picture. He then tapped a few keys, sending the image off to every NuKoin employee and a few of his alternate email addresses for safe keeping.

Satisfied, David continued, "Grune wanted me to allow the Russian Federation to insert some code in our system that would allow them to know the identities of the parties transacting on the NuKoin network. He made reference to other blockchain networks already having made the wise decision to cooperate and stated emphatically that NuKoin needed to follow suit."

"And what did you tell him?"

"I was going to say anything I needed to say to get safely out of the room and back to the United States, but I had no intention of taking his offer."

"Is there any other reason why Grune would be contacting you?"

"None that I can think of," answered David. "We were

on a discussion panel at the conference, and that was the first time I'd ever heard of him."

"Apparently, he had heard of you."

"Well, he did say they had been watching NuKoin, which I took as a compliment, to be honest."

"About a week ago," Holmes said slowly, "a bitcoin wallet that had been dormant for quite some time suddenly appeared in the Bitcoin ledger. A small transaction of a couple hundred dollars."

He paused for dramatic effect, trying to read David's reaction.

"The bitcoin wallet was from early 2009 and has been associated in the past with the founder of Bitcoin, Satoshi Nakamoto," stated Holmes.

"I don't think I'm following you," said David. "Why is this germane to our discussion?"

"The transaction was made here in Boston, David. And we believe you have control of that bitcoin wallet. That means you are a person of interest in a lot more than just this one case."

David was stunned and unable to hide the expression that betrayed him. Owen had pulled two hundred dollars out of an ATM in exchange for bitcoin, which had to be why Holmes was bringing it up. But their bitcoin wallet had no connection to Satoshi Nakamoto. It was some small moment of forgetfulness by his late wife. Yes, it had enough bitcoin to be worth a good amount of money, but nothing on the scale of what Satoshi was known to possess.

"Agent Holmes..." David started.

"It's Special Agent Holmes."

"Ah, yes. Special Agent Holmes," said David, "are you telling me that you believe that I am in control of a bitcoin wallet that belongs to Satoshi Nakamoto?"

"David, don't play games," warned Holmes. "The ways I can make your life miserable are endless if you start denying things I already know are facts. We know your son pulled out the money from an ATM, and we know he spent it at the mall on a pair of sneakers. We have video evidence of both. Very clever of you to use a boy to avoid suspicion, but it does call into question your parental judgment."

"Special Agent Holmes, I do admit to owning some bitcoin, and my son did admit to me that he used some recently, but to suggest that we have a connection to Satoshi is ridiculous."

"David, why did you really meet with Vitalik Grune?"

"I told you why," answered David. "He forcibly pulled me into a room."

"Does Vitalik Grune know you are Satoshi Nakamoto?"

David laughed out loud. "Why would anyone think that? Thank you for lightening the mood with humor."

"Okay, David, I'll play along," said Holmes. "If you are not Satoshi, how is it that you both possess the bitcoin-wallet file and know Satoshi's password to unlock that wallet?"

"The wallet was not mine. It was my wife's bitcoin wallet," answered David. "We found it on an old computer, and we guessed the passphrase."

"You guessed the passphrase?" said Holmes incredulously.

"I know. I couldn't believe it either."

"And what exactly was the passphrase?" asked Holmes.

"It was p-a-s-s-w-o-r-d-1-2-3," David said with a straight face.

Holmes banged a fist on the table. "Turner, my patience grows thin, and your story is so full of holes it's all I can do to contain myself and not put you in an orange jumpsuit right now."

"If you think I'm telling you the bitcoin passphrase, you're crazy," answered David. "But I am telling you the truth. The bitcoin wallet was on an old computer that belonged to my late wife. How she got it I have no idea. But I can promise you that she was not Satoshi Nakamoto either. She was an accountant, not a computer scientist."

"David, where is Mia now?"

"Where is my late wife? Is that your question? Well, gosh, Special Agent Holmes, I didn't know we were going to switch our discussion to topics of religion and the afterlife."

Special Agent Holmes stopped talking and just stared at David for several minutes. David returned his gaze and let Holmes make the next move.

"Let me level with you," said Holmes. "There are people after that bitcoin wallet in your control who aren't interested in laws or even prisons. They will do everything in their power to get that wallet and all the other Satoshi wallets, and they will eliminate everyone in their wake."

David let a smirk pass across his face and even rolled his eyes so that Holmes could see it. "You've overplayed your hand, Special Agent Holmes," said David. "It simply makes no sense that the Russians would be after a single bitcoin wallet that, quite frankly, doesn't have that much bitcoin in it. The Russians mine billions in bitcoin every year. They have no need to get caught up in 'eliminations,' as you put it."

"Mr. Turner, even if it turns out that you are not Satoshi, if you possess the ability to unlock one of Satoshi's wallets, then they'll believe you possess the ability to open the others."

David's face recoiled as he realized the scale of what he

was caught up in. Satoshi Nakamoto was the creator of Bitcoin, and in the early years of 2009, he was one of the only people on the planet mining it. He accumulated thousands and thousands of bitcoin just to get the network up and running.

David worked with Satoshi back when they all were just anonymous usernames collaborating on the computer code. He knew Satoshi's bitcoin was not all in a single wallet file but spread out among dozens of wallets, most of which had never been touched.

As the popularity of bitcoin rose and fell over the next decade, Satoshi would have gone many times from being a paper billionaire to having it all worth pennies. But throughout the rising and falling, the bitcoin wallets remained untouched.

Many people believed that liquidating those wallets would cause a massive bitcoin price devaluation due to oversupply. Thus, Satoshi's billions could never be accessed. Other people wondered if Satoshi had another endgame in mind or if he was simply playing the long game.

Since the bitcoin ledger was public, it was very easy to identify the wallets that belonged to Satoshi and to track their transactions over time. Therefore, it was extremely simple to know that the wallets had remained inactive. If Satoshi ever did access the wallets, the world would know about it.

When they first gained access to Mia's bitcoin wallet, David told Owen to be cautious. If he'd known the wallet was linked to Satoshi Nakamoto, he would have treated it like the plague. But how could he possibly have known? Even more puzzling was how Mia had even come into its possession at all.

David now understood the gravity of the situation. If

people believed he possessed the passphrase for the Satoshi wallets, the passphrase would be worth billions of dollars, and David would be a marked man. Even worse, Owen was also caught up in the mess.

Satoshi Nakamoto had to have been an extremely intelligent computer scientist with an amazing aptitude for cryptography, the mathematical study of complex codes. No way would anyone would believe Mia was Satoshi Nakamoto, so perhaps they would leave his family alone.

But as David stared at Holmes, he realized Owen was in grave danger. Owen also knew the passphrase, so he was just as valuable as David. He had to find a way to get Owen to safety, and quickly.

"Special Agent Holmes, I have no idea how my late wife came into possession of that bitcoin wallet, and frankly, I don't need it nor the attention it will receive. So perhaps you and I can cut another deal."

The smug look of satisfaction that formed on Holmes's face made David sick to his stomach.

"Exactly what type of deal did you have in mind, Mr. Turner?"

"You agree to immediately call the feds off NuKoin, and I give you full control of the bitcoin wallet," offered David.

"How exactly does that help the US government?"

"I don't like politics, so I'll let you figure that out," replied David. "But I have a feeling that being given the passphrase to a Satoshi bitcoin wallet in addition to a few hundred million in bitcoin could go a long way toward satisfying whoever is really in control of this mockery of an investigation."

"And what do you get in return?"

"You give me my funding dollars back, and NuKoin releases our code on time," David answered. "And the feds leave NuKoin alone for good. Plus, you move the funds to a new wallet and publicly post the passphrase to the old wallet. That way, everyone in the shadow world knows that my son and I have nothing valuable."

Holmes nodded in apparent agreement. "I'll have the papers drafted immediately, but first, you need to prove you can access the wallet."

"No, first we go get Owen so the FBI can protect my family."

"Fair enough," replied Holmes. "We were looking for him anyway. You tell me where he is, and I will send a team to collect him."

"Not a chance. Trust is earned and not given," said David. "Until I see all the papers signed and in order, I'll trust no one. I'll guide the team to his location personally."

Special Agent Holmes signaled the other agents in the room to get ready to transport David so that Owen could be protected. He pulled out his mobile phone and informed his superiors as to the status of the investigation. David was given a bulletproof vest and was escorted to the parking garage. He was put into the backseat of a dark sedan with tinted windows and was joined by Holmes and two other agents. An additional sedan with three agents pulled along-side to accompany them. They quickly exited the garage and departed west on the interstate, per David's directions.

Across the street from the garage and directly outside of the NuKoin office building, just outside the FBI caution tape, a young woman was dressed in masculine clothing. Her hair was pulled up and fit neatly under a baseball cap.

Tina Wood even changed her gait to walk like a man, trying to blend into the milling crowds curious about the police action on an otherwise boring day at the office. She took a few discreet photos with her mobile phone, using a remote selfie device in her pocket.

She had returned to the NuKoin offices to question David Turner in the next step of her story. As she stared at the police presence, she realized that talking to David was her new number-one priority.

26

David considered taking the FBI convoy on a more circuitous route to make sure that no one could guess their destination in advance of their arrival. He still did not trust the FBI, especially Special Agent Holmes, but he wanted to get to Owen as quickly as possible.

He was careful to give the FBI driver each driving instruction only moments before he needed to make a turn. That ensured Owen's location could not be guessed by the FBI and provided David the additional pleasure of annoying Holmes.

Approximately fifteen minutes after they left the parking garage, David and his FBI escorts arrived at the Diamond Motel, just outside the downtown area. At David's instruction, the driver parked near Room 127, but David was prevented from exiting the vehicle.

"Let me go," cried David. "I need to get my son."

"Mr. Turner, please remain in the car while we check the area," said one of the agents gruffly.

Three of the agents in the other vehicle carefully

stepped forward and surveyed the situation. One of them went to the door marked 127 and knocked, while the other two took cover positions.

After a couple of minutes, one of the agents nodded, and the door was kicked in. The agents filed into the room with pistols drawn.

David watched in horror as his blood pressure soared with anxiety. Armed men were crashing into his motel room, and Owen could be in danger. David tried to break free from the grasp of the agent, but he was physically restrained and threatened with handcuffs.

Eventually, one of the agents returned to the open motel room door and motioned that it was clear. David was released and escorted into the motel room, but he saw no sign of Owen.

"Mr. Turner, you say your son was here in this motel room?" asked one of the agents.

"Yes, he was with me overnight, and we decided it would be best for him to stay here in case someone was looking for me. No one knew where we were, and I told him to stay inside with the shades drawn."

As the agents continued to search the room, David wasn't sure if they were looking for evidence of a struggle or evidence that David was lying. After several minutes, an agent found a mobile phone in the bed.

"That's Owen's mobile phone," David said. "There's no way he would go anywhere without it! Give it to me, and I'll unlock it."

The agent reluctantly passed the phone to David, who quickly entered a PIN, unlocking the device.

"One rule I always had for my son was to have a complicated PIN code, but he had to tell me what it was. There is too much crazy crap on the internet these days, so I demanded full access to his phone."

David searched the call log but found nothing. No calls, either inbound or outbound. But in the text message log, he found a partially composed message still in draft mode. He opened it.

men pnding on d

"Check out this text message he was trying to send," David told the agents. "Something happened to him. Where did you find this phone?"

"It was inside the pillowcase," an agent said.

"He must have been typing it and did not have time to send it," said David. "He must have hidden his phone so they wouldn't get it."

"Why would he not dial 911 if he thought he was in trouble?"

"We were attacked at the movie theater last night, and we didn't trust anyone. He was probably just nervous, not knowing who was really on his side."

"Nice job, Dad," mocked Special Agent Holmes. "You've managed to teach your son to disrespect authority, and now he may have been kidnapped because of it."

"With all due respect, your presence today has not exactly been all unicorns and rainbows."

"Mr. Turner, do you have any idea who would take your son?"

"You tell me. Up until an hour ago, I was oblivious to the fact that I was a marked international target."

Holmes ignored David and pulled out his mobile phone to contact the office. He strode outside, but David could hear his elevated tones. He couldn't make out what was being said and quickly grew distracted by thoughts of Owen. Dozens of memories seemed to fill his mind all at once. His eyes grew wet, and he closed them and used the side of one hand to remove his tears.

Holmes returned to the room moments later and commanded two of the agents to take David back to FBI headquarters in Chelsea, just northeast of downtown. The agents placed David in the car while Holmes and the other two agents remained to dust for fingerprints and check for additional evidence.

David was put in the back of the car and forced to lie down on the seat so he would be out of sight. They pulled onto the interstate and crossed the river, speeding toward the FBI building.

They exited the highway and merged into some slower-moving traffic, quite common for Boston.

A car in the left lane moved over without indicating and gently tapped the side of their sedan. The agent steering cursed at the driver, raising one hand in a gesture of frustration. The car then hit their sedan again, that time with more force and pushing them toward the edge of the road.

The agent driving switched into a different mental gear and immediately tried to accelerate through a small gap in the cars. David didn't need to be a genius to suspect something other than road rage. The gap in the cars closed when the driver in front of them slammed on the brakes, creating a rear-end collision that stopped the FBI sedan. They were pinned on three sides against the wall at the edge of the road, giving David's escort nowhere to flee.

The SUV had not even stopped moving when three Asian men jumped out of the vehicle in front of them and quickly descended upon the two agents with handguns raised. The agents weren't able to draw their weapons quickly enough to prevent the inevitable glass-shattering rounds that caught them in their chests.

David was frozen, not knowing what to do. One of the attackers yanked the back door open while another pointed a gun into David's face. Then he was pulled from the SUV with no instructions.

Seeing the murdered FBI agents in the front seat, David remained quiet as he was pushed into one of the vehicles. A hood was placed on his head while his hands were bound tightly on either side of his body. Then he was pushed to the floor of the vehicle, where he remained for the duration of a long, anxiety-filled drive.

When the vehicle came to a stop, David could hear many voices speaking in a language that wasn't English. He was pulled out, escorted into a room, and thrust into a chair.

Many voices echoed around him, and his head spun. He could feel the warmth of a bright light, even through the hood he was wearing. When his mask was removed, a blinding light shone in his eyes.

"Who are you working for, David Turner?"

David was not sure if he was supposed to respond or if the question was just meant to scare him. When it was repeated again with even more anger, he decided an answer was the best option.

"I work for NuKoin, a small—"

"Who do you really work for, Turner? Do you think this is a game?"

"Please, I don't know what you're talking about. I am a software developer, and I have no idea what you want from me."

Multiple voices around him started laughing—not friendly but cold and maniacal.

"You meet with the FSB, and you think no one takes notice?"

"I was kidnapped. I didn't exactly meet with him willingly."

"And what did he want, Mr. Turner?"

"He wanted to do business with my company... At least, that's what he told me."

"Oh yes, we bet he does have some business with you, and now you have that same business with us. Perhaps you just give us the wallets, and we'll let you go."

"What wallets? Who are you, and why did you bring me here?"

"Oh, you know exactly what wallets we want, and now we know you have the passwords to open them, don't you, Mr. Turner? Or should I say, Mr. Nakamoto?"

David felt a chill down his spine. His worst nightmare was unfolding. All the events of the last couple of months were spiraling in a web of misfortune. He was in the wrong place at the wrong time, and everyone was after him.

"Why the hell do you people think I have any connection with Satoshi? I am running a company that has the express goal of destroying Bitcoin! Why would Satoshi Nakamoto want to do that?" David tried to free his hands, but his restraints cut against his cold skin, causing him to recoil. He tried to open at least one of his eyes but had to squint against the bright light in his face.

"You double-crossed the Russians, so perhaps you are short on friends. Did you really not think they would go after your family?"

David was speechless as fears filled his mind. *Had Owen been taken by the Russians? Was Vitalik Grune really behind this whole mess?* After one careless business trip to Russia, his whole world was unwinding.

"Such a convenient and sudden silence. Perhaps you'd

rather start by explaining your connection to Senator Michael Cornwall?"

"Senator Cornwall? I have no connection to him," replied David.

More animated voices sounded, along with a commotion that was hard to identify, from farther away. David focused and thought he could hear the sound of metal on metal. The footsteps of the interrogator came closer, and David could make out his silhouette. He seemed to be a short Asian man, and he held two knives. The look on his face was haunting.

David's mind drifted to Owen then to Mia. He wasn't overly religious, but a sense of peace came over him at the thought of being united with his family in the afterlife.

The sound of breaking glass erupted into David's mind, along with loud voices and the popping of gunfire. The bright light was suddenly gone, and David was knocked to the floor, still bound and attached to the metal chair upon which he'd been sitting.

After several moments, David realized what had happened and broke out of his trance. A survival instinct kicked in as he tried to free his hands and feet. He craned his neck, searching the room and desperately trying to make sense of his new situation as his eyes readjusted to the darkness. A body loudly thumped on top of him, flooding his legs with pain. Squirming out from under the load, he wiggled and pushed the body away with his feet as best he could. Lying next to him were two metal knives and the dead body of his interrogator.

David rolled over, flipping the metal chair with him as he tried to get close to the knives. He wiggled his back and hips and managed to get one of the blades into his right hand. Then he turned onto his stomach and desperately sawed the blade at anything he could, rotating his wrists in every direction.

Gradually, he managed to free up additional mobility for his hands as the wires loosened. Against the background of the chaos surrounding him, his bonds gave way. He freed his feet then dropped the knife. Running along the far wall of the warehouse, he remained as low to the ground as he could.

The gunfire continued, intensifying at times as David managed to hide behind some metal barrels. Peering back into the room, he could clearly see heavily armed men in camouflage fighting his plainclothes captors.

The sound of police sirens grew steadily, creating a glimmer of hope. If he could only hang on until they arrived, he might make it out of the situation alive. But survival would require trusting the police. The FBI had proven they weren't on his side, but at least they hadn't shot at him or tried to torture him.

These new aggressors in the camouflage could be the Russians, or they could be some other paramilitary force. *Who else could it be? Everybody is already here except the North Koreans!* thought David.

Looking up, he saw the small table near the dead body. Crawling on the floor to the table, he found the two mobile phones that had been taken from his pockets. He glanced at the face of the dead man and decided he was Chinese. He put Owen's phone in his pocket next to his own and forced himself to slow his thinking.

Without Owen's phone, the Russians would have no access to the wallet. Even if Owen had given up the passphrase, they couldn't do anything until they had physical possession of the bitcoin wallet. The Russians had the passphrase, but the Chinese had the wallet—at least, they'd had his phone until David took it back. He couldn't risk either one of them getting both.

Stealing the contents of the bitcoin wallet would take only a few minutes, then David would lose his leverage with Special Agent Holmes and the FBI.

He quickly scanned the room and saw a ladder leading up to the second floor of the warehouse, about twenty feet away. The ground-floor exterior doors were too far away and were covered by either Chinese or Russian guns. He took a deep breath and bolted for the ladder then climbed to the upper level.

He ran across the deserted second-floor balcony, finding a window that opened onto a roof. Mustering his drive for survival, he broke the window with an elbow and jumped down onto the roof, which extended out from the second level. As he jumped through the window, he tried to tuck and roll, but his body complied only partially.

Attempting to stand and stretch out his legs, he mumbled, "Maybe that was more like a retired James Bond than Bourne..."

David moved more slowly, his limbs feeling the stress of his escape. He trotted along the roof line and onto an adjacent building. It was largely deserted, but he could hear some faint cries from the floor below. As David fled down a staircase, he found others running toward the exits and realized they were fleeing the gunfire next door.

He mustered his strength and ran toward the fleeing people, mixing in with them as they poured onto the streets. Police cars were already flooding the roads in pursuit of the fleeing gunmen.

First responders seemed to be everywhere, looking for people in need. Amazingly, no civilians seemed to be wounded, only some in need of treatment for shock and emotional distress. The paramedics were ushering people beyond a perimeter being solidified by a growing number of police in riot gear.

David let a paramedic examine him and was thankful to hear the report of no broken bones or open wounds. He was told to walk to an ambulance for transport to Massachusetts General Hospital, but he ignored that request and slipped down the adjacent street.

He pulled out his mobile phone and made sure the GPS was still off before quickly scanning his contacts list for someone he could trust. He needed help but not from anyone whom either the Russians or the Chinese would be watching—or the FBI, for that matter. He found a name in his contacts that might work. He memorized the number on the screen but, out of an abundance of caution, didn't use his own phone to dial the number.

As he passed farther from the crime scene, he came across a few curious onlookers that had descended upon the area. He quickly identified the most likely good Samaritan and asked to use their phone to call the last person on earth he'd ever imagined he would contact again. The person answered and recognized his voice right away.

"Um, hello? David Turner, is that you?" the person asked.

"I need help, and I didn't know who else to contact," David said into the borrowed phone. "There are all sorts of people after me, and someone has kidnapped my son."

"Dear God, David! Of course. Where are you?"

David asked his new friends for the nearest landmark and started walking.

Tina Wood hung up the phone and quickly arranged a short-term rental from ZipCar. Five minutes later, she was driving a blue Toyota Prius toward David's location.

27

David had never been so happy to get into a car in his life. He told Tina to drive as quickly as she could while not arousing suspicion. He took out his mobile phone and pulled the battery from the device.

"What are you doing?" asked Tina.

"Making sure no one can track me. I'm pretty sure that's how they found our motel room and were able to grab Owen."

"Who exactly is after you?"

He paused. "It's complicated."

"If I am going to help you run from something, I deserve to know what it is."

"Fair enough," said David as he nodded slowly. "I am fairly certain that the Russians have taken my son, Owen. Meanwhile, I was taken into custody by some jackass from the FBI, who said he could keep me safe. Turns out the Chinese disagreed with him, because they attacked my FBI escort and murdered two agents in front of me. The Chinese were about to torture me when the Russians—at least, I think it was the Russians—tried to kidnap me from the kidnappers who kidnapped me from the FBI. Still with me?"

"Um, barely."

"I managed to escape during a gunfight between the Russians and Chinese, then I called you," said David with a matter-of-fact tone in his voice, as if that sort of thing happened to him every day.

Tina made a few perplexed faces before turning toward him. "So that's it?"

They both laughed out loud, and David rubbed his head. The situation was so surreal that he didn't know how to process what was going on.

"I already knew the part about the FBI," said Tina after a few silent moments. "I was headed over to see you when I found your office cordoned off by the feds. It looked like they had the office pretty well locked down."

"Yeah, they did," agreed David. "The entire staff looked pretty scared. Oh, except Nicole, my CFO. Turns out she is an undercover FBI agent."

"Wow. That I definitely didn't see coming. She sure did play the part well. She even gave off the jealous office-fling vibe and everything."

"Office-fling vibe?"

"Give me a break, David. It didn't take a journalist to figure that one out."

"There was... is... was nothing between Nicole and me except a professional relationship."

Tina let David off the hook and didn't bring it up again.

"Wait, why were you coming to see me at my office?" asked David.

"Well, it seems you're not the only one they're after," she explained. "I was fired yesterday because someone sent my boss some photoshopped images that got some of the investors at the newspaper upset."

"What kind of photos?"

Tina shot David a glance with furrowed brows. "Use your imagination."

"Oh!" David exclaimed, feeling a mild blush coming to his face. "I see."

"Someone doesn't want me completing my story."

"No offense, Tina, but another story on cryptocurrency isn't exactly earth-shattering news."

"Okay, let me level with you. My story isn't really on crypto. I've been trying to track down Satoshi Nakamoto."

David gave Tina a look of his own. "You've been trying to track down Satoshi? Good grief. I wish you'd told me that weeks ago, and I would have spared you the effort."

"You know, every time someone finds out what I'm doing, they give me the same reaction, as if I'm some amateur. Why is someone upset and trying to silence me if my research hasn't been on target?"

David wasn't convinced and let his facial expressions show it. In an effort to prove she wasn't crazy, Tina filled David in on every detail of her encounters and various obstacles over the last several weeks. By the end, David was still not completely convinced, but he had to consider the possibility that their paths might have been crossing for more reasons than they'd both realized.

"Tina, you need to forgive me for not believing you are close to unmasking the true identity of Satoshi Nakamoto," said David with compassion in his voice. "Satoshi has been very good at remaining anonymous for many years, with lots of people trying to find him."

"What makes you think Satoshi is male?"

"Because I exchanged emails and notes with Satoshi

many years ago, back when Bitcoin was unknown and obscure. I feel like I have a pretty good idea he was male. After a few years, Satoshi went dark, and I respected that. You're not going to find him unless he wants to be found. I can promise you that."

"Then why is someone trying to take me off the story? Why now? Help me out, David. What am I not seeing here? You owe me a huge favor just by being in this car."

She was right, and David knew it. Tina was an accomplice, and some very powerful people were in pursuit of one or both of them. After a few minutes of silence, David decided to open up.

"A couple of months ago, my son, Owen, and I found a file on an old computer that belonged to my wife. It turned out to be a bitcoin wallet with a decent amount of bitcoin in it. It also turned out to be a file that people believe belongs to Satoshi Nakamoto. Unfortunately, people noticed and tracked us down. Boy, did they notice..."

"Wait, you're telling me that one of the bitcoin wallets belonging to Satoshi Nakamoto is suddenly active after a decade of dormancy, and you don't think that's a detail that I need to know about?"

"I agree with you. That's why I just told you."

"Was your wife Satoshi, then?"

David laughed out loud. "No, my wife did not have any computer training. She couldn't have been Satoshi."

"Then how did she get possession of one of his wallets?"

David shook his head. "I don't know. That's the part that doesn't make sense."

"Well, maybe it does explain why someone is suddenly trying to get me off this story. They must know that you and I have been in contact, and they think we're working together to try and draw him out."

"I wouldn't go quite that far..."

"David, think about it... Satoshi is used to people coming after him, and he has probably even been interviewed dozens of times and never been afraid of being unmasked. Like Clark Kent hiding in plain sight. He either ignores my story, or it means nothing to him. Then suddenly, someone activates one of his wallets, and it hits closer to home. He assumes I'm connected to the wallets and needs to derail me. He gets some photos and tries to blackmail me as a warning."

"I think you're reaching. I feel bad for you and the situation with the photos, but that could be any number of people getting revenge for some bad press you gave them in a previous article. It's quite a reach for Satoshi to suddenly think your story and the bitcoin wallet are connected."

Tina was suddenly flattered by even the hint of David respecting the quality of her investigative journalism.

"Sure, we've spent a grand total of a couple of hours in each other's presence, but anyone doing even the simplest amount of research would discover that we're not working together," said David.

"What about Russia, David? We met at the coffee shop in Russia. There's an excellent chance that Satoshi was at that conference. Don't you agree?"

"I have no idea if he was there. For all we know, Satoshi has moved on to other interests and left the world of crypto behind. There's no evidence to support that anyone thinks that you and I are connected in any way."

Tina was ready to respond but was distracted by her rear-view mirror. Seeing her reaction, David turned around to see for himself. Two or three sedans with lights and sirens pulled up behind and beside them.

"Damn it!" exclaimed David. "How did they find me?"

"What makes you think it's you they're after? Maybe it's me... or—"

"Or us," said David, finishing her sentence.

Tina and David knew their Toyota Prius was never going to outrun any other vehicle, so they pulled to the side of the road and into a deserted gas station parking lot. Two agents appeared on each side of the vehicle, instructing them both to exit the car.

They were placed in the backseat of one of the vehicles, wondering what was happening. The person in the passenger seat turned around and addressed them in a sing-songy voice.

"David and Tina, trying to break free, r-u-n-n-i-n-g," said Holmes in a poor attempt to change the words to the nursery rhyme. "We've been looking for you both."

"I guess we're going to skip the whole 'glad you're alive' routine?"

"David, once again, you have a choice to make. You can finally trust me, or you can lose the life of your son," remarked Holmes.

"Yeah, what about my son? Did you find him? Because last I checked, your agents were incapable of keeping people safe."

"Right after you fled the scene at the warehouse, we were contacted by the people that kidnapped your son. They want to make a trade: Owen for the bitcoin wallet and password."

"Thank God. He must be safe! Did you verify he was unharmed?"

"Your son is quite safe, David, as long as you play your cards right here. But you better be careful, because you're already facing charges of collusion with a foreign government."

"Collusion with what government?"

"It was a little coincidental that you suddenly break free from FBI custody with the help of the MSS, and now four FBI agents are dead."

"MSS? As in the Chinese Intelligence service? You think I'm colluding with the Chinese and I was set free? How about the inept FBI couldn't keep me safe, and I was nearly tortured? How about the fact that it's a little strange that you can suddenly find me and my exact location?"

"David, we're the FBI. Finding people is what we do. Very clever, though, to pull the battery out of your mobile phone. I must admit it was a little odd for an innocent person to do such a thing, but you probably should've asked your girlfriend to do the same."

"Damn it! You tracked my phone, didn't you!" asked Tina. "The FBI has been watching me for weeks, haven't they? And I bet you've been taking a lot of photographs of me," said Tina with a probing look at Special Agent Holmes.

Holmes just smirked at her then turned back to David. "We cannot guarantee your safety or the safety of your son unless you give me the bitcoin wallet and the password so we can make the trade. How much more has to happen to you before you are convinced to cooperate?"

"I thought the FBI wanted the wallet," asked David. "If I give the wallet and password to the Russians, then what happens to our deal?"

"If you help us bring down the Russians and the Chinese on this one, then our deal still stands," replied Holmes. "But this is getting too dangerous for you and your girlfriend. Give me the information, and I'll get your son back."

"No deal," replied David. "I will not hand over the

information until I personally get guarantees of Owen's safety."

Holmes swore out loud and told another agent to handcuff them and take them back to FBI headquarters. "I told you to be careful how you played your cards, Turner. Now we play it the hard way."

"Why are you handcuffing us?" asked Tina. "Are we being arrested for something?"

"No one is escaping on my watch again," said Holmes as they were being cuffed.

They remained quiet in the backseat, exchanging glances now and again as Holmes steamed in the front of the car.

When they got to the FBI Boston headquarters, they were uncuffed and led into a waiting area. David rubbed his wrists and paced the room, thinking. He decided to put the battery back in his phone since he no longer felt in any imminent danger—even the Russians and the Chinese wouldn't be crazy enough to attack an FBI building in broad daylight.

David's phone immediately started vibrating as the various missed notifications scrolled on his screen, and he took several minutes reading and listening to his messages.

28

When Special Agent Holmes returned to the waiting area a few hours later, he was in a very different mood, but David wasn't buying the good-cop routine.

"Mr. Turner, Ms. Wood, I want to apologize for my actions earlier," said Holmes. "It was unfair for me to accuse you of playing a role in this conspiracy when you were merely victims."

David was fairly certain that Tina did not buy the change in FBI strategy either, but she certainly played the part well.

"Thank you, Agent Holmes," replied Tina. "This whole day has been quite stressful for me."

"That's Special Agent Holmes, Tina," said David with a straight face.

"No, that's quite okay, David," insisted Holmes. "I want us to get a fresh start. We need to work together. We have the same goals from here on out."

David was still trying to figure out many things, but he knew he didn't have goals similar to Holmes's.

"Agent Holmes, where is my son?"

"Mr. Turner, over the past few hours, we have been in contact with the Russian FSB, who claim they can guarantee the safe return of your son. We have been negotiating and have secured a deal."

"Let me guess—they want the bitcoin wallet," said David. "Everyone seems to want the bitcoin wallet. It took you three hours to come to that agreement?"

"We all knew they wanted the wallet, but there's more."

"Why does everyone keep thinking there's more than one wallet?" asked David. "We have one wallet and one passphrase. I cannot give them more than one wallet because I only have one!"

"David, they want you and Ms. Wood to personally deliver the file and information," explained Holmes. "No agents."

"I don't understand," said Tina. "If they only want the wallet and password, who cares how they get it?"

"That's what we have spent the last few hours trying to figure out as well," replied Holmes. "We didn't want to ask you to do this until we could figure out their play."

"So then are you asking us? And have you figured out what they are up to?" responded David.

"Are we asking you to hand deliver the wallet file and passphrase? Yes, we believe this is our only move that can guarantee the safe return of your son. The Russians seem to have some personal attachment to this wallet file that goes beyond the value of the bitcoin within it," explained Holmes.

That got David thinking. Grune undoubtedly had the passphrase, since extracting it from Owen would have been extremely easy for the FSB. The thing they lacked was the physical wallet file. But all they needed was for David to email them the file, and within minutes, they could move the bitcoin to another wallet file. They didn't need to organize a physical meeting involving the FBI. David didn't trust Grune or Holmes, but his only move was to play along and see just how deep this rabbit hole went.

"Okay, I'll do it," said David. "I'll deliver the file and the passphrase to the Russians, but leave Tina out of this."

"I'm sorry, David," explained Holmes. "They were quite clear that this drop should be made by both of you."

David stood up in protest. "That's ridiculous! She has nothing to do with this. All she did was give me a ride away from that gunfight."

"David, it's okay," replied Tina. "I can do it. Saving a child from danger is more important than everything else."

"That's very kind of you, but you don't need to get involved in this," replied David.

"I'm already in the middle of it. Agent Holmes, I'll do it."

"David, we're going to protect both of you—trust me. We'll have eyes watching you the whole time. We have dozens of agents that'll be positioned in a wide perimeter, and we will place several different types of tracking devices on each of you."

"You think the FSB won't be able to detect tracking devices?" asked David incredulously.

"Oh, we know they will," answered Holmes. "That's why we are planting them on you. Once they find the decoy devices, they'll stop looking for the others."

"Okay, then what's the plan?" asked David.

"You and Tina take the T to Copley Square and await the next instruction from the Russians. They'll call your mobile phone at exactly seven p.m."

"That's in an hour," replied Tina.

"Yes, it is. We don't have a lot of time," said Holmes. "We'll have plainclothes agents swarming that subway station and additional agents on various rooftops. We're going to plant various devices on you that even you don't know about. Once you give them the thumb drive containing the wallet file, they'll want to verify the passphrase. During that time, we will close in. Once Owen is released, we'll capture as many of them as we can."

"What if they don't release Owen once they have what they want?" asked Tina.

"They will release him, Ms. Turner. These are not some third-world vigilantes. They back out of this deal, and they risk not being able to negotiate with the United States in the future. They won't do that over one child. Once they have what they want, they will release the boy."

"Okay, let's do it," replied David, satisfied with Holmes's response.

"Great," said Holmes. "Follow me."

David and Tina were ushered down the hall and into a preparation room, where they were fitted for bulletproof vests and given some other clothes to wear. David guessed that various tracking devices were already hidden in these accessories but didn't ask questions.

The agents that helped them get outfitted were all silent in a way that was contagious. Tina stood about ten feet away, focused on the female agents helping her. For the first time, David really looked at her. He hardly knew the woman, but she was willing to risk her life to help save his son. He'd never thought of Tina Wood as anything more than a journalist looking for a story, but now she was becoming part of his inner circle. As his admiration for her grew, he realized he was staring.

"Um, David," said Tina, "would you mind facing the other way for a minute?"

David felt blood rush to his face as he realized the female agents needed Tina to remove her blouse so that she could put on a bulletproof vest. David apologized and turned away, focusing on the plan to get his son back.

Holmes drove the car as they were escorted to the subway station, and he personally made sure they boarded the T successfully. Once the doors closed, David and Tina were alone. But they did not feel alone, for they knew agents were scattered throughout the whole mission.

"Are you scared?" asked David.

"Not really. I guess I'm just focused."

"You didn't have to do this, you know."

"Yes, I did, because it was the right thing to do."

"I'm sorry I got you involved in this mess," said David.

"You didn't get me involved in this. I got myself in this mess when I started my research."

"Well, I just wanted to say thank you," replied David reflectively.

"You're welcome. But you're making it sound like we're headed to our demise," Tina said with a chuckle. "We drop the thumb drive, Owen gets released, and we're on our way."

David started to say some other things, but Tina held an index finger to her lips to silence him. She pointed at her ears to remind David that people were listening—definitely the FBI but possibly also the Russians or even the Chinese.

The train slowed down as the conductor announced they were approaching the stop for Arlington Station. Without speaking, both knew that was the last stop before their destination. Just before the train stopped, David's mobile phone buzzed, causing him to pull it from his pocket to read the text message displayed on the screen.

Get off at Arlington and await instructions

The plan had apparently changed, and he quickly showed Tina the text message. They had no choice but to obey the instructions, so they both exited the subway car just before the doors closed.

They were fully committed now, focused on the goal of freeing Owen. David felt anxiety growing in his chest as he realized that his "guarantee" of FBI protection would erode if the Russian instructions continued to change.

They stood on the platform as the train left the station, waiting and wondering if the next instruction would come in person or via text message. David held his smartphone in his hand, staring anxiously at the blank screen. When he felt a buzzing in his coat pocket instead of his hand, he was confused. He reached into the pocket and pulled out a small flip phone from his jacket.

"This isn't my phone," said David out loud. "How did it get in my pocket?"

Somehow, David knew the answer. Somehow, they both knew the answer. Tina shook her head as the gravity of their game sank in. She scanned the waiting crowds for a face she might recognize from their subway ride while David read the text on the burner phone.

Board the approaching train back toward the city

David grabbed Tina's arm, and they swiftly took the stairs that allowed them to cross to the other side of the platform. Tina didn't say a word as they boarded the inbound train. David assumed Holmes would be aware of his movements and wondered how long the FBI would let this play out.

Their train passed through a couple of subway stops

without any further instructions on the burner phone, now in David's other hand. He grew nervous that he might have missed an instruction and checked his personal smartphone again. As they approached Park Street Station, the burner buzzed with another text message.

Get off now and walk up the stairs

David showed Tina the text message with a mix of relief and growing dread as the spy game continued to evolve.

They exited the train and joined the throngs of people going up the subway steps toward the main lobby. People were milling around in every direction, since that was the main junction point for the Red Line and the Green Line, Boston's two largest mass transit arteries.

Just as they reached the top of the steps, two men pushed them into a small nook to the side of the stairs, out of sight from the milling crowds. Both Tina and David remained silent, too surprised to call for help and too afraid of adversely affecting their mission.

The two men had nondescript faces, and each wore a simple wool hat that hid his hair from view. The men did not speak as they carefully moved small scanning devices over David's and Tina's bodies. They were thorough and quick, a bit too thorough for Tina's taste.

They found four items of interest, removing them quickly from their momentary captives' clothing with a small knife. Without expression, they placed the removed items into the trash bin next to them. Then the two strangers gave each of them a tiny metal box about the size of a golf ball.

"These devices will block all communication within a twenty-foot radius," said one of the men. "Just in case there are any more tracking devices on you that we didn't find. Don't remove them from your pockets if you want to see your son. Use the subway concourse to walk to the Downtown Crossing Station and board the Orange Line south."

Without another word, the two men abruptly disappeared into the crowded streets of Boston.

"What the hell is going on, David?" asked Tina.

"I guess this is all part of the play," answered David. "We should've expected this swap to be complicated. These guys are pros. They aren't going to let the FBI dictate how this goes down."

With a nod toward the signs on the wall, David guided Tina toward the pedestrian passage that led to the Orange Line.

They reached the Downtown Crossing station platform just as a train was arriving. The pair followed their next instruction, and as soon as the doors of the train closed, the burner phone buzzed again.

Follow the instructions on the note in your jacket pocket

David plunged both his hands into his pockets, letting go of the phone as he searched. Tina watched with growing curiosity as David produced a small white folded piece of paper. He read it quickly and handed it to Tina.

Get off at Chinatown and head east on Essex Street

David folded the paper and put it back into his pocket. A strange calm came over him. If the Russians were being that careful to disguise the meeting location, it seemed very likely that the meeting would go well and Owen would be safe. He tried to reassure himself with that thought. Owen's safety was the only thing that mattered.

They exited the train when the doors opened, making their way up the stairs. Both felt a growing sense of determination as their human scavenger hunt neared its end.

Back on the streets of Boston, they walked away from the subway as they had been instructed. David contemplated the meaning of going through Chinatown. The Chinese portion of the conspiracy returned to his mind. The Chinese, the Russians, the FBI—he just wanted his son back.

As they were walking, a soft whistle came from a parking garage they were passing, the kind of whistle used to call a dog. They both slowed their pace and glanced at one another. Shrugging toward Tina, David diverted his course and walked into the garage. Glancing around, they could see plenty of cars but no people. They stopped and stood in the middle of the ground level of the parking garage, wondering if they had misunderstood their last instruction.

Then they heard the sound of knocking against a steel door. David turned and caught a glimpse of a man standing near the pathway leading to the basement. He peered into the shadows surrounding the man, who beckoned them forward before disappearing into the stairwell.

"Does that guy think we're crazy?" asked David. "If they want to do this swap, why are they making it so difficult?"

"If they wanted to harm us, they would've done it already," Tina replied in a hushed tone. "Keep your focus on Owen."

They slowly made their way to the parking garage stairway door then paused. They glanced at each other once, then David opened it.

They stood motionless at the top of the stairwell, nervous to proceed but knowing they could not turn back. The whistle noise once again pierced the quiet, drawing their gaze downward. David peered over the railing and could just make out the silhouette of a figure two flights down.

They descended the stairs to the bottom level of the garage and opened the door. There, surrounded by a half dozen armed men, was Vitalik Grune.

Tina jumped back at the sight of the firepower, while David instinctively slid over to shield her in an act of chivalry.

"Oh, be assured, you have no reason to be afraid," said Grune in a gruff voice. "You are, in fact, much safer now than you were an hour ago."

"I'm pretty sure an hour ago, we didn't have a dozen automatic weapons aimed at us," Tina replied without thinking.

"We have to take precautions, Ms. Wood," said Grune. "Your government isn't easy to trust."

"Where is my son?" said David, cutting to the chase.

"He is safe, Mr. Turner, but I cannot tell you too much more than that."

"Why are you keeping him captive? Kidnapping and holding a boy for ransom," said David with disdain. "I expected more out of a man of your stature."

"Holding for ransom," answered Grune. "Is that what you think this is?"

"That's exactly what this is," replied David. "But we're here, aren't we? We're playing your little game. Now, what do you want?"

"I want my bitcoin wallets back."

"You already have the wallet and the passphrase. Don't insult my intelligence."

"If I had them, I wouldn't need you two. Besides, I want all the Satoshi wallets, not just one of them."

"That makes no sense," answered David. "You have Owen, and he knows the passphrase, and he knows where we backed up the wallet file."

"I never said that I had Owen in my possession. I told the FBI that I'd exchange him for the wallets."

David's face grew red and crumpled. His anger boiled over, and Tina could do nothing to calm him. He rushed at Grune with a yell but was tackled and taken down by two of his bodyguards.

Grune's voice came slowly and just above a whisper, but it had a paralyzing impact on both David and Tina. "Owen is in the custody of the Chinese."

David became placid. Grune signaled his men to allow David to sit and gather himself as Grune continued.

"It seems we're all after the same thing, David. The Chinese, the FBI... We all need something from Satoshi Nakamoto."

David shook his head, "Nice try, Grune. I have a very low opinion of the government, but even I'm not crazy enough to believe that the FBI would conspire to kidnap an American teenager and hold him for ransom just to get access to some cryptocurrency."

"Do you think I'd go through all of this just for a few million in crypto?" said Grune with a condescending smirk. "Were you followed?"

"The FBI planted bugs all over us, but we have no idea where," said Tina, "but you already know that."

"We took care of those," said Grune. "I'm asking if you saw anyone following you."

"Why would you ask such a dumb question?" remarked David. "Even if we did know someone was following us, we wouldn't tell you."

Grune studied their faces, trying to discern the truth from their expressions. After a few quiet moments, he walked toward the pair. Upon reaching David, he held out his hand. "You have what is mine?"

David looked at the armed men surrounding him and shook his head in disgust as he pulled a small thumb drive from his pocket and placed it in Grune's open palm.

Suddenly, the sound of gunshots erupted, sending two of Grune's men to the ground in a heap and causing the remaining bodyguards to raise their weapons and return fire. Grune dropped to one knee, clutching a shoulder.

Tina dove to the ground, and David grabbed her hand to pull her behind a nearby vehicle for cover. Gunfire came from all directions, sending everyone in Grune's gang scattering for cover.

"We can't stand still!" shouted David. "We have to keep moving."

Tina nodded as David, still holding her hand, led them low along the wall in front of a row of parked vehicles. Glancing backward, he saw Grune's men pull him down and into a nearby corridor.

David had no formal military training, but he grew strangely focused, digging into some innate protection mode. Scurrying along the wall, he found an alcove and thrust Tina inside.

Crouching down beside her, he whispered, "Let's wait here until the FBI arrives."

"What about Owen? If we lose Grune, then we lose our one shot at getting him back. We need to go after Grune."

"I can't let anyone else get hurt by this mess. I'm not letting you die. Besides, Grune is a liar. We can't trust a word from his mouth."

Just then, someone called out from nearby. "David... Tina..."

David slowly peeked his head around the corner. A smile crept onto his face as the familiar figure of Nicole

Mancini emerged with her gun drawn. David waved silently as Nicole crouch-walked her way toward the pair.

"Are you okay?" asked Nicole as she examined them visually.

"We're fine," replied Tina, "but we lost Grune in the gunfire."

"He won't get far. We have the building surrounded."

"I was hoping it was the FBI. How did you follow us?" asked David. "The Russians made us use this gadget that blocked all the electronic transmissions."

"We went old school. We have hundreds of agents deployed in the city right now," said Nicole with a look of pride. "We have every subway stop and corner in the city monitored visually by agents."

Tina cut her off. "Grune said he didn't have Owen."

"What do you mean? This whole stupid game was about a swap. If the Russians lie about their leverage now, then they'll never be able to negotiate on anything in the future." Nicole shook her head and mumbled, "This doesn't make sense. They wouldn't do that."

"Nicole, there's more. Grune also said it's the Chinese that actually have Owen and that the feds are in on it," said Tina.

Nicole stared at Tina in disbelief. She wanted to rebuke her, but something clicked in her mind that stopped the words from leaving her mouth—some thread of truth that connected the dots. Before she could process it further, she heard a noise.

"Shh," whispered Tina. "I hear someone."

They stared out into the darkness of the garage, straining their ears and eyes to discern the unknown.

"I'm going to go check it out," Nicole said. "You two stay out of view."

David wasn't going to argue with Nicole. She was a federal agent, and he trusted that she knew how to handle herself, but he was also losing trust in just about everyone.

As Nicole made her way through the parked cars, she passed out of view. She let the recent information about Grune filter through her mind, analyzing and processing the various scenarios. Doubts pervaded her thoughts as a bead of sweat formed on her brow. She thought she heard footsteps deeper within the maze of cars and cautiously followed, leaving David and Tina behind.

The darkness of the garage cast long shadows from the meager artificial light that could be found. Nicole dropped down to one knee as she took in the situation. Satisfied that no danger lay in front of her, she slowly turned her head just in time to see the muzzle of a handgun trained in her direction.

"What the hell, Holmes? You scared the crap out of me. Why are you sneaking up on me like that?" Nicole took a deep breath of relief and gave Holmes the update. "Grune got away, for now. David and Tina are okay, but they claim that Grune said he didn't have Owen."

"Where are David and Tina now?" asked Holmes.

"I left them back on the far side of this level of the garage. Grune seems to be on the run, and he has the wallet file but not the passphrase. We need to make sure David and Tina are safe in case Grune wants to clean up loose ends."

Holmes stared at Nicole, squinting slightly as if to peer into her mind. "What else did Grune say?"

"He has this crazy idea that the FBI knows that Owen is really being held by the Chinese. But why would Grune be playing along with this swap if he doesn't have Owen?"

Holmes nodded as he considered her words. Nicole gazed into the darkness as new doubts entered her mind.

She felt the sting of the bullet before she heard the sound. She managed to get her gun out of the holster but not before Holmes was able to put a round in her chest.

"Cleaning up loose ends," replied Holmes. "I think that sounds like a good idea."

Nicole gasped for air, but none came.

"Nicole Mancini murdered, such a shame. Shot by a Russian terrorist who was using crypto to finance his global network. Yes, that'll make a nice, believable story. But don't worry, Nicole. You'll get a spot on the Wall of Honor in the Hoover Building."

Nicole removed her blood-soaked hand from her chest and pointed at Holmes before letting her hand drop harmlessly to her side. Holmes held up the P-96 Glock for Nicole to see clearly in his gloved hand.

"I know what you're thinking, Nicole: perhaps the P-96 was a bit overkill—no pun intended—but I thought Grune might have a flare for the dramatic. Plus, it's Russian made, so it makes the story more convincing."

Holmes took hold of the weapon and pointed it at Nicole one last time. "Sorry, Nicole. It's nothing personal. It's just business."

Nicole closed her eyes as the muffled sound of a gunshot echoed through her body. Strangely, she didn't feel any pain. When she opened her eyes, she could see Holmes lying on the ground and Vitalik Grune standing over him, still clutching the pistol that had ended Holmes's life.

David and Tina came running around a corner.

"Dear God, Nicole!" David took in the scene, and his face fell upon seeing her condition.

"Nicole, you're going to make it," managed David, choking back tears.

Nicole smiled and took a deep breath, rallying with newfound energy.

"No, David, I'm not going to make it, and there are some things that I need to tell you."

"Nicole, don't talk like that. We can call an ambulance."

"David, listen to me. I want to apologize for deceiving you. At first, I justified it because we were trying to find Satoshi and it was for the greater good. But after I started working with you, I realized you were innocent, regardless of what Mia had done."

"Mia? What are you talking about, Nicole? What does Mia have to do with any of this?"

"The FBI has been tracking Satoshi for years, and we knew Mia was the key," explained Nicole. "We were closing in on Mia when she went missing, and the trail went cold. We were convinced that if we got close to you, something would pop up. And when you found the bitcoin wallet, we knew we were right."

"Nicole, I don't understand what you're talking about. Mia didn't go missing. She's dead. My wife, the mother of my son, had nothing to do with Bitcoin or Satoshi Nakamoto."

"Your wife was keeping a lot more secrets from you than a bitcoin wallet," muttered Nicole as her eyes sagged.

David's head swam. He'd already lost his wife, and his son was missing. If that wasn't enough, Nicole was digging up painful memories as she lay dying at his feet.

"Nicole," asked David as he gently shook her until she opened her eyes and focused on him. He cradled her in his arms, slowly lifting her upper body off the ground. "Is Mia still alive?"

Nicole's face moved to form a response, but no sound left her mouth except the nearly silent exhalation that proved to be her last breath.

David gently placed Nicole back on the ground, pushing himself back away from her body. Shaking his head, he looked up at Grune. "So help me God, I'm going to kill whoever is behind all this!"

Grune lowered his weapon and extended a hand toward the grieving man. "Give me the passphrases to all the Satoshi wallets, and we'll see if we can't get your son back. I'm not going to make a child pay for what your wife did to me."

David's rage returned. "What the hell do you know about my wife?"

"Oh, let me assure you, I know Mia quite well."

As Grune's men interrupted and escorted him toward the corner of the garage, he said, "David, if I wanted you killed, you'd be dead already. You have to decide whom to trust. Either way, I can't promise you that your son will be released unharmed, but if you come with me now, I will answer some of the questions that have plagued your mind regarding Mia."

David looked at Grune. His heart was conflicted and his mind confused. Everything seemed to swim in his brain as the image of Mia flickered deep in his memory. He contorted his face, trying to discern fact from fiction before slowly turning back toward Tina as he muttered, "I have to go. I need to know."

Tina nodded. "And I'm going with you."

David tried to dissuade her, but Grune cut him off. "David, there was a reason we wanted Tina to come with you. Let this play out."

The trio was escorted to a corner of the garage, where

one of Grune's men lifted a manhole cover, revealing a descending ladder. They took turns climbing down into the darkness, to a corridor illuminated by a pair of flashlights held by Grune's men. The manhole cover was replaced before the group walked silently for several minutes. When they came to another ladder, Grune took the lead, climbing upward through an already open hole leading to an alley, where a van waited. As they climbed into the back, David noticed diplomatic license plates on the vehicle—this was not going to be a covert escape. This was escalating quickly.

The driver pulled away before everyone could sit down. One of the men noticed the blood on Grune's shirt and began to bandage his wound. David could tell Grune's injury was not life-threatening, but the sight of more bloodshed made his stomach churn.

"I'm going to guess that this isn't the first time you've been shot," he said.

"Quite correct, I'm afraid," Grune replied without looking over at David. "But this hardly qualifies as being shot." Sensing David's next question, Grune answered before David could even get the words out: "Regardless of whether we manage to get your son back, you're going to give me what I want."

29

———

The van drove for several miles before pulling into an isolated warehouse garage. There, David and Tina were given some food and allowed to rest for a couple of hours. David Turner believed trust was earned not given. Vitalik Grune was a spy and therefore deserved none.

Special Agent Holmes, William DeFrost, and even his former co-worker Nicole Mancini had recently double crossed him, so David was not about to take any chances with Grune. David knew his only leverage for remaining alive was the Satoshi wallets, both for the immediate and the distant future. If he was to give up control of the wallets, he needed a way to ensure his family's long-term safety.

A frustrated Vitalik Grune finished an animated phone conversation and approached David and Tina.

"It seems that I've been declared persona non grata. I am to leave the country within twenty-four hours or face prosecution for the murder of two federal agents, Mancini and Holmes."

Tina looked confused. "We saw Holmes shoot Nicole, and they should be thanking you for taking out Holmes."

"Blaming their deaths on a Russian spy is more expedient than the truth of a traitor within their own government."

David and Tina remained silent as Grune continued to pour his frustration out to them.

"Let me assure you that I'm not leaving the country without the Satoshi wallets. Therefore, it appears you have run out of time."

"All I want is my son back alive, and you can have all the Satoshi wallets."

"Revenge on those Chinese agents from the warehouse is tempting, but your president has changed the timeline. It's time for you to be pragmatic about your own future."

David could feel his blood pressure rising, and he knew he had to take a bold step.

"What if you could have the Satoshi wallets *and* get the bogus murder charge erased?"

Grune was unmoved and kept his stone-cold stare on David.

"I think I have a way to get the Chinese to release Owen and give you the chance to blame them for the things that have happened. Besides, if you take the wallets, then you become Satoshi to the world. Won't you need a clean record?"

Grune nodded slowly as he considered the logic of David's words.

David continued. "Tell Parker that you have eyewitnesses that will testify to your innocence and that you have someone else to take the fall for those murders. I think I can get the Chinese to show up, but in return, I need your help to make sure that the Chinese deliver Owen unharmed."

Reluctantly, Grune agreed to play along with David's plan and suggested a location for the swap. David and Grune each made phone calls to put the plan in motion.

30

———

The docks on the south side of Boston were notorious for crime, and David knew no police would be present to bail him out if his plan went sideways. That thought plagued him over the next several hours as they waited to depart for the midnight meeting.

David and Tina were given the keys to an unmarked sedan along with simple directions to an empty parking lot by the water to wait for the kidnappers. They were assured that Russian agents were already in position and would reveal themselves at the appropriate time. A surveillance wire was placed under David's coat for his "protection," but David knew Grune just didn't trust him. The feeling was mutual.

Since the Russians were listening, David and Tina didn't speak to one another as they waited nervously outside their vehicle. They exchanged glances between searching the darkness of the parking lot perimeter for movement.

After almost an hour, they heard the slow roll of tires on the gravel road. Gradually, three vans approached without headlights. One van stopped at the entrance to the parking lot, while another drove to the opposite perimeter. After David and Tina were flanked, a third van approached rapidly and skidded to a stop. The rear door opened, and three heavily armed men took up positions around the van. After several moments, the rear door of the van opened, and a single man advanced toward them.

"I must admit I didn't think you would show up," said William DeFrost.

"Where is Owen?" asked David.

"These people tell me he's safe as long as they get the bitcoin you promised them."

"Quit the charade. You've been in bed with the Chinese since day one."

"A slanderous accusation from an exiled CEO. It seems you can't handle your business or your family."

"And yet, somehow, I make one phone call to you, and you are able to get the Chinese kidnappers to appear a few hours later. Circumstantial, I suppose?"

"I guess I was expecting a thank-you. You're playing a very dangerous game, David. The men in those vans are only keeping your son alive to make sure they get those bitcoin wallets."

"First, I need to know Owen is safe."

DeFrost pulled a mobile phone from his pocket and held it aloft. The phone rang, and he handed it to David, who cautiously answered the call and listened.

"Dad? Is that you?"

"Owen! Are you safe? Did they hurt you?"

"I'm fine. Starving, but fine."

"Are you nearby? Can you see me?"

The phone went dead before Owen could answer. DeFrost put the phone back in his pocket.

"These people mean business. They want their bitcoin.

Then you get Owen, and you agree to leave NuKoin forever."

David could feel his rage rising. "We had a deal! The bitcoin for Owen. You're still trying to take my company after all that's happened?"

"Just a business opportunity. We all get something we want."

David took a step closer to DeFrost with fists clenched, but he stopped when he heard sounds from all around the parking lot. The three Chinese men desperately fired in all directions but were quickly shot. Then the gunfire ceased, and a loud voice arose in the silence.

"You are surrounded. Put down your weapons and drop to your knees."

The command wasn't necessary for DeFrost, because he was already on his face. David and Tina were unarmed and instinctively raised their hands as they lowered themselves to the ground slowly. A tear formed in David's eyes as he contemplated the impact of his decisions and how they had affected the life of his only son.

David wasn't sure if he was relieved to hear it, but he recognized the voice of Vitalik Grune.

"Now is your chance to get your son."

After rising to his feet, David turned and walked over to DeFrost and delivered a quick kick to the man's stomach, causing DeFrost to double up in pain.

"Where is Owen, you son of a bitch?"

Two Russian agents quickly descended on David and pulled him away from DeFrost, who spat on the ground before raising his head.

"Owen is far away from here. Do you think I'd be that stupid to play all my cards at once?"

"I know you're that stupid," replied David. "And arrogant too."

Grune pulled a gun from his coat and placed it against DeFrost's head. "You Americans test my patience. I've already been declared a murderer by this country. One more won't change much."

"Okay, okay, calm down. You can have the boy. But the deal was the boy in exchange for the bitcoin."

"Release the boy, and I'll consider letting you live. That's the new deal," said Grune.

DeFrost didn't need any time to think it over and seemed motivated by the steel against his scalp. He waved his hand in the air, and a door of the van at the entrance to the parking lot opened. A lone figure walked toward the center of the lot.

When Owen saw his father, he began to run, no longer worrying about the drawn weapons all around him. Father and son were allowed a few moments to reunite before Grune got back to the business at hand.

"You have your son back. Now, give me the wallet passphrases!" Grune said to David.

David nodded and motioned for Grune to join him out of earshot of the rest of his men. After pulling a blank sheet of paper from his pocket, he wrote a few sentences and handed it to Grune.

As Grune was reading, David said, "The secret to the passphrases is in the original writings of Satoshi himself. Use the information on this piece of paper to extract the passphrases from the text of the whitepaper."

Grune was stunned. "Satoshi placed the passphrases in the text of the original description he wrote on Bitcoin?"

"Well, I suspect it was the other way around," said David. "He created the passphrases for the wallets from the text of his paper by using a simple cipher. That way, he never had to write the passphrases down. It's actually quite ingenious if you think about it."

David spent the next fifteen minutes showing Grune that, by applying the formula on the paper, the correct passphrase to one of the Satoshi wallets could be obtained—the same wallet that Owen had used to buy sneakers that had started this whole series of events.

"I have my doubts about your explanation, because this passphrase isn't random text as I would expect. It sounds like a poem or something," said Grune.

"That's the genius of it. Satoshi found an initial set of words in the white paper text that were simple to remember, then he reverse-engineered the cipher code that could be used to generate the other wallet passphrases. All you need to remember is that single sentence, then use it to get the cipher. Then you have access to all the Satoshi wallets. Nothing ever has to be written down. Hidden in plain sight. Just like Satoshi himself."

"But I don't intend to hide my identity now that I will be known as Satoshi Nakamoto."

"You are indeed the new steward, just like I was Satoshi for a time."

"I had plenty of bitcoin wallets," snarled Grune, "until you and your wife stole them from me!"

"You obviously never knew the Satoshi secret. You just happened to steal the passphrases from someone who was stupid enough to write them down. Mia had nothing to do with any of this."

Grune stared into David's eyes, trying to read his mind. He knew David was holding back information and decided to force his hand.

"Several years ago, there were two thieves that broke

into a home in Leningrad and murdered some of my friends," said Grune, referring to the former name of St. Petersburg. "They destroyed everything in the room and left no trace."

"Why would thieves destroy things that they could have stolen?" asked David.

"They were stealing bitcoin. They managed to transfer it to new wallets, ones whose owners were unknown."

David shrugged at Grune, failing to see the relevance in the conversation.

"They were trained assassins sent by your government. They were CIA agents," explained Grune. "The only way to track them was to wait for the bitcoin to be transferred again and follow the money trail. The bitcoin was moved a few times after that, and we finally were closing in on the killers. But right before we were able to close the net, your wife ended up dead in a car accident."

David could not hide his confusion. "You think Mia stole your bitcoin?"

"Don't insult my intelligence, David. We know your wife is CIA. And I must admit you had us fooled. We never suspected you because of your involvement with NuKoin. The CIA would be very foolish to try to hide you in—how did you say it?—in plain sight. But then several days ago, some of the bitcoin moves again. And what do you know, your son is the one using the wallet." As David shook his head and backed away slightly, Grune continued, "The part I can't figure out, though, is how long you have known that Mia was still alive. Were you a part of the plan to fake her death, or did she contact you after it was over?" Grune smirked and gave David a pat on the back. "The time for pretending is over. This doesn't have to end poorly for you and your son. All I want is Mia and my bitcoin."

As Grune interrogated David, no one seemed to notice that several boats had approached the docks. Silently, dozens of men in dark coats labeled "FBI" fanned out over the entire area. They waited until their equipment was in place before they simultaneously turned on portable floodlights, illuminating the parking lot from all directions.

Instinctively, the Russian agents turned to fire on the advancing FBI agents, but Grune ordered them to stand down. A small contingent of men escorted Brian Parker toward the group.

"I have enough agents with me to make sure this goes the way I want it to go, not to mention the drone surveillance overhead. So don't do anything stupid," said Parker.

It wasn't clear to whom Parker was speaking. He was, after all, the son-in-law of the president of the United States of America and a chief advisor to the White House. He sneered at all of them before approaching Grune alone, with his agents close enough to protect him but not close enough to listen to the conversation. David, Owen, Tina, and DeFrost heard his every word.

"Do you think you can bribe a federal agent and obstruct a federal investigation?" asked Parker.

Grune said, "I can't take credit for the idea. David Turner suggested that all you needed was a way to avoid the story of a spy inside the FBI. He turns over the bitcoin passphrases and gets his son's freedom. He was confident the charges against me would be dropped."

"What charges?"

"I told him I was being framed for the murder of two federal agents."

Parker laughed, which in turn made Grune laugh. The

two men exchanged a firm handshake and turned toward David, who sensed a ruse.

Parker said, "The only person being charged with a crime is you, Mr. Turner, for the murder of Special Agent Holmes and Agent Nicole Mancini. Tina Wood will be tried as an accomplice, and your son will be placed into the care of the foster care system of the Commonwealth of Massachusetts."

David's head was spinning. His plan had collapsed, and he was reeling at the double cross by Grune and Parker. He had been played all along, tricked into divulging the passphrases by a Russian banker who'd been conspiring with the White House all along.

"William DeFrost, we have no need for you and the remainder of your Chinese friends. I suggest you evacuate the area before I change my mind," said Parker.

DeFrost moved cautiously at first, eventually breaking into a jog toward his van. The other Chinese agents joined him, closing the doors behind themselves. FBI agents descended on David, Tina, and Owen, taking them into custody. As they were read their rights, they were escorted on foot across the parking lot toward the water.

The three barely had time to process the gravity of the moment before they heard the sound of helicopters. The echoes of rotor blades increased rapidly as multiple searchlights appeared out of the sky.

A voice descended from above. "This is the US Capitol Police. You are hereby ordered to stand down and surrender control of this operation."

The Chinese vans were blocked from leaving the area. All the FBI agents froze, unsure how to proceed. Parker considered ordering his men to open fire but decided to reassert his control once the birds landed.

Four military-style helicopters descended to the ground with multiple police officers swarming out of each one in full SWAT gear. The helicopter searchlights continued to focus on the center of the parking lot, severely limiting the vision of those waiting.

As David and Tina strained to see and understand what was unfolding, a tall and commanding presence appeared. He was the last person anyone expected to see.

Parker yelled to the approaching officers, "I am Brian Parker, chief counsel to the president of the United States! This is an FBI operation. By whose orders are you commanding us to stand down?"

"By my orders," thundered Senator Michael Cornwall.

"Congressman, you are way out of line. You have no jurisdiction here, and the US Capitol Police are far from DC."

"They have jurisdiction throughout the country to protect the interests of the United States Congress."

"That's a huge leap, one that would never stand up in court."

"Then go ahead—order the FBI to arrest a US senator and the US Capitol Police, and let's see where this goes. But I feel obliged to inform you of the fact that I have full audio and video surveillance of this entire evening that would make great sound bites for the evening news. You might want to consider your options before trying to make this worse than it is already."

"This is treasonous! Your career is over, Senator!"

"Careers are indeed ending tonight, my old friend, but not mine. And not Mr. Turner's either. Did you really think you could cover up that Special Agent Holmes was working for the White House? Not to mention that you fabricated a story to frame Mr. Turner. Extortion, blackmail, fraud, collusion with both the Russian and Chinese governments —how can this possibly end without impeachment of a sitting president and serious prison time?"

Parker was seething with anger, but he could not hide the fear in his eyes. Cornwall was clearly in control and was thoroughly enjoying his elevated position.

Cornwall continued, "Let's start with what I don't want. There is no need for an international incident. The Chinese nationals will face no prosecution for their activities as long as they leave the country immediately. Their actions of espionage with regard to NuKoin will be overlooked as long as they stay clear of Mr. Turner's company—and all US-based crypto companies—forever."

With a wave of a hand, Cornwall gave permission for the Chinese vans to leave, but not before William DeFrost was pulled from one of the vehicles. DeFrost tried to follow the vans on foot, but they pulled away before he could get anywhere near them. DeFrost cursed and gestured to the departing vehicles, but his cries went unheard. Capitol Police escorted him back to the center of the parking lot.

Cornwall laughed before continuing. Turning to Grune, he said, "You are indeed declared persona non grata, but not for the crime of murder. Your collusion with the White House cannot be overlooked, but it may be able to be kept from the public news cycle. That will depend on a lot of things, one of which is the continued safety of David Turner and his family. David deserves a medal for his role in this debacle, but for now, he will have to settle for a return to his position as CEO of NuKoin, which he will find is no longer under FBI investigation."

Parker interrupted, "Wait just a minute! You might have some shaky evidence against some members of the administration, but you don't control the Justice Department."

"No, but you do. And only for a short while longer. You will do exactly what I have said, and in return, I'll give you and your father-in-law a way to leave office without disgrace."

"How do you expect to sweep all this out of sight from the public? Someone has to take the fall!" cried Parker.

"A very good point! And that leads me to William DeFrost. Your actions have been treasonous, both your actions at NuKoin and those in your role in the violence of the Chinese. You're going to need a very good lawyer."

DeFrost was shocked. "You can bet I'll get a lawyer. You're going to get prison time for this extortion!"

"The only prison time will be yours, I'm afraid. And there are no lies. We have solid evidence of your financial misdeeds, the kidnapping of Owen Turner, and quite a few other crimes from your past we were able to dig up."

The US Capitol Police processed William DeFrost and placed him under arrest. Cornwall also called an ambulance to take Owen Turner to Mass General Hospital.

Parker turned to Cornwall in confusion and asked, "What do you get out of all this, Senator?"

"I was thinking Secretary of State. The president is in his second term anyway, and the party will be needing someone to run in a few years. There's really no need for any of this to go public, don't you think?"

Parker shook his head and rolled his eyes, clearly beaten. When he started to walk away toward one of the FBI vehicles, Cornwall yelled to him, "And be sure to destroy all those fake photos you circulated of Miss Wood!"

Parker paused, turned back toward the group, then continued walking.

Tina smiled and gave Senator Cornwall a hug. "Thank you."

"It's the least I could do. Especially since your story on finding Satoshi Nakamoto has reached a dead end."

Tina understood the inference. This was not a question—it was a command. Although she still thought the story had prize-winning potential, she also realized that some stories needed to lie dormant until the appropriate time.

"I've got some ideas for some new stories anyway," she said. "Maybe something on alternative cryptocurrencies, as long as I can spend some time with people that know the business."

David chuckled. "I think the identity of Satoshi Nakamoto is going to remain a secret for a long time."

Grune agreed, "I think Satoshi would be wise to remain anonymous. No need to upset the equilibrium."

Cornwall said, "Great. Then we all are on the same page. We each get to keep what we wanted. Mutually assured destruction will make sure it stays that way."

Vitalik Grune did not shake anyone's hands. He simply left with his men. Tina joined Owen in the ambulance, which left David and Senator Cornwall alone.

"I meant it when I said we are going to leave NuKoin alone. As long as you make sure you have clean investors, the government has no need to interfere in your business. I'm still not sure about cryptocurrency, but I have plenty of other companies to focus on."

David was escorted to the ambulance to join his family. The Capitol Police helicopters retreated low over the water, and the FBI cleaned up all traces of activity from the night.

31

In the evening on the following day, David, Owen, and Tina had finally been fully debriefed by Cornwall's officers. The FBI agreed to return them home, convinced that they were no longer in danger, since both the Chinese and Vitalik Grune were confirmed to have left the country and William DeFrost was in federal custody.

When Tina got out of the car in Cambridge, both David and Owen joined her.

After a moment of awkward silence that people get after going through a traumatic bonding experience, Owen was the one who broke the tension by giving Tina a hug. "Thank you for everything you did for my family."

Taking a cue from his son, David joined the embrace. "Maybe you could come down to the NuKoin offices next week, and we could talk about your ideas for that story you mentioned?"

"Sure. I think I'd like that," Tina replied with a smile.

The two Turner men got back in the car and rode home in silence. There, the agents informed David that they would be watching over them for a couple of weeks just to make sure they were safe.

"That won't be necessary, sir," responded David. But he knew they would do it anyway.

Owen forced his father to check in every closet and under every bed before settling into his room. David went back down to the kitchen to reflect on all the drama that had unfolded. He thought about his company and wondered if the lack of funding would affect their future. He thought about Nicole Mancini and wondered if she had family that would mourn her death. He thought about Holmes and Grune, about what role the president had played in this ordeal and the real scope of involvement of the president's son-in-law, Brian Parker. But most of all, he was just grateful to have his son back, safe from harm.

David walked upstairs and into the open doorway of his son's room. Owen was still awake, silently staring at the ceiling.

"Hey, buddy," said David, strolling inside. "Are you doing okay?"

"Yeah, Dad. I'm fine."

"What are you thinking about?"

"I wish we had kept some of that bitcoin. You could use it for your company."

"Who said I don't have some bitcoin of my own?"

Owen's eyes bulged in shock. "You have more bitcoin wallets?"

David let a smirk appear on his face. "Just because I stopped working on the bitcoin project doesn't mean that I got rid of all my bitcoin."

Owen and David both laughed and shared a lighter moment before Owen grew more serious. He hesitated then turned to look at his father. "Dad, do you think there is a chance that Mom is still alive?"

David hesitated as he recalled Grune's words. He did not trust him, but something about his story of Mia rang true. If Mia had been in the CIA, that would explain a lot of weird behavior on her part. But faking her own death and cutting off all ties to her family would've been pretty extreme. He had a lot to process before he could say anything to Owen.

"Buddy, there's a lot to process, especially about your mom. This whole adventure has shown me that both of us have never fully let go of her and moved on."

The two were silent for a few minutes before Owen nodded, got out of bed, and gave his father a hug. "You're right, Dad. Maybe we can help each other."

David paused before he responded, attempting to gain his composure. "Of course, buddy. I wouldn't have it any other way."

Owen crawled back into bed with a smile as David crossed the room toward the door.

As his father turned out the light, Owen said, "And if the road is too hard to cross..."

David smiled and replied, "We'll fly like ponies in the sky."

ABOUT THE AUTHOR

Jonathan W. Clark is an avid investor in cryptocurrency and a 25 year veteran in the Software Engineering industry who has designed multiple Blockchain systems. He has a bachelor's degree in Computer Science Engineering from The University of Connecticut and a masters degree in Computer Science from Rensselaer Polytechnic Institute. He is a communicator and storyteller who has spoken to a variety of audiences on four continents.

Visit his website and sign up for his newsletter at:
http://mrjonathanwclark.com/

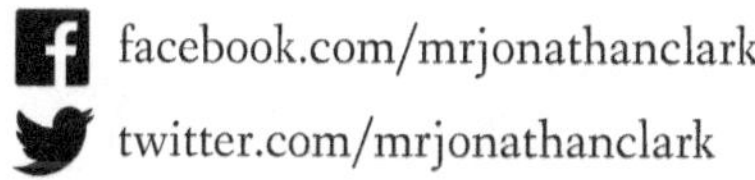

facebook.com/mrjonathanclark
twitter.com/mrjonathanclark